P. G. Wodehouse

'The ultimate in comfort reading because nothing bad ever happens in P.G. Wodehouse land. Or even if it does, it's always sorted out by the end of the book. For as long as I'm immersed in a P.G. Wodehouse book, it's possible to keep the real world at bay and live in a far, far nicer, funnier one where happy endings are the order of the day' *Marian Keyes*

'You should read Wodehouse when you're well and when you're poorly; when you're travelling, and when you're not; when you're feeling clever, and when you're feeling utterly dim. Wodehouse always lifts your spirits, no matter how high they happen to be already' *Lynne Truss*

'P.G. Wodehouse remains the greatest chronicler of a certain kind of Englishness, that no one else has ever captured quite so sharply, or with quite as much wit and affection' *Julian Fellowes*

'Not only the funniest English novelist who ever wrote but one of our finest stylists. His world is perfect, his stories are perfect, his writing is perfect. What more is there to be said?' *Susan Hill*

'One of my (few) proud boasts is that I once spent a day interviewing P.G. Wodehouse at his home in America. He was exactly as I'd expected: a lovely, modest man. He could have walked out of one of his own novels. It's dangerous to use the word genius to describe a writer, but I'll risk it with him' *John Humphrys*

'The ir ... readers of all ages, sl ...

'A genius . . . Elusive, delicate but lasting. He created such a credible world that, sadly, I suppose, never really existed but what a delight it always is to enter it and the temptation to linger there is sometimes almost overwhelming' *Alan Ayckbourn*

'Wodehouse was quite simply the Bee's Knees. And then some' *Joseph Connolly*

'Compulsory reading for anyone who has a pig, an aunt – or a sense of humour!' *Lindsey Davis*

'I constantly find myself drooling with admiration at the sublime way Wodehouse plays with the English language' *Simon Brett*

'I've recorded all the Jeeves books, and I can tell you this: it's like singing Mozart. The perfection of the phrasing is a physical pleasure. I doubt if any writer in the English language has more perfect music' *Simon Callow*

'Quite simply, the master of comic writing at work' *Jane Moore*

'To pick up a Wodehouse novel is to find oneself in the presence of genius – no writer has ever given me so much pure enjoyment' *John Julius Norwich*

'P.G. Wodehouse is the gold standard of English wit' *Christopher Hitchens*

'Wodehouse is so utterly, properly, simply funny' *Adele Parks*

'To dive into a Wodehouse novel is to swim in some of the most elegantly turned phrases in the English language' *Ben Schott*

'P.G. Wodehouse should be prescribed to treat depression. Cheaper, more effective than valium and far, far more addictive' *Olivia Williams*

'My only problem with Wodehouse is deciding which of his enchanting books to take to my desert island' *Ruth Dudley Edwards*

The author of almost a hundred books and the creator of
Jeeves, Blandings Castle, Psmith, Ukridge, Uncle Fred and
Mr Mulliner, P.G. Wodehouse was born in 1881 and educated
at Dulwich College. After two years with the Hong
Kong and Shanghai Bank he became a full-time writer,
contributing to a variety of periodicals including *Punch*
and the *Globe*. He married in 1914. As well as his novels
and short stories, he wrote lyrics for musical comedies
with Guy Bolton and Jerome Kern, and at one time had
five musicals running simultaneously on Broadway. His time in
Hollywood also provided much source material for fiction.

At the age of 93, in the New Year's Honours List of 1975,
he received a long-overdue knighthood, only to die
on St Valentine's Day some 45 days later.

P.G. Wodehouse titles available in Arrow Books

JEEVES

The Inimitable Jeeves
Carry On, Jeeves
Very Good, Jeeves
Thank You, Jeeves
Right Ho, Jeeves
The Code of the Woosters
Joy in the Morning
The Mating Season
Ring for Jeeves
Jeeves and the Feudal Spirit
Jeeves in the Offing
Stiff Upper Lip, Jeeves
Much Obliged, Jeeves
Aunts Aren't Gentlemen
The World of Jeeves

BLANDINGS

Something Fresh
Leave it to Psmith
Summer Lightning
Blandings Castle
Uncle Fred in the Springtime
Full Moon
Pigs Have Wings
Service with a Smile
A Pelican at Blandings
The World of Blandings

MULLINER

Meet Mr Mulliner
Mulliner Nights
Mr Mulliner Speaking

UNCLE FRED

Cocktail Time
Uncle Dynamite

GOLF

The Clicking of Cuthbert
The Heart of a Goof

OTHERS

Piccadilly Jim
Ukridge
The Luck of the Bodkins
Laughing Gas
A Damsel in Distress
The Small Bachelor
Hot Water
Summer Moonshine
The Adventures of Sally
Money for Nothing
The Girl in Blue
Big Money
Young Men in Spats

P. G. WODEHOUSE
Mulliner Nights

arrow books

Published by Arrow Books 2008

5 7 9 10 8 6 4

First published in the United Kingdom in 1933 by Herbert Jenkins Ltd

Arrow Books
The Random House Group Limited
20 Vauxhall Bridge Road, London, SW1V 2SA

www.rbooks.co.uk

www.wodehouse.co.uk

Addresses for companies within The Random House Group Limited can be
found at: www.randomhouse.co.uk/offices.htm

The Random House Group Limited Reg. No. 954009

A CIP catalogue record for this book
is available from the British Library

ISBN 9780099514053

The Random House Group Limited supports The Forest Stewardship
Council (FSC), the leading international forest certification organisation.
All our titles that are printed on Greenpeace approved FSC certified paper
carry the FSC logo. Our paper procurement policy can be found at
www.rbooks.co.uk/environment

Mixed Sources
Product group from well-managed
forests and other controlled sources
www.fsc.org Cert no. TT-COC-2139
© 1996 Forest Stewardship Council

Typeset by SX Composing DTP, Rayleigh, Essex
Printed in the UK by CPI Bookmarque, Croydon, CR0 4TD

Mulliner Nights

CONTENTS

The conversation in the bar-parlour of the Angler's Rest had turned to the subject of the regrettably low standard of morality prevalent among the nobility and landed gentry of Great Britain.

Miss Postlethwaite, our erudite barmaid, had brought the matter up by mentioning that in the novelette which she was reading a viscount had just thrown a family solicitor over a cliff.

'Because he had found out his guilty secret,' explained Miss Postlethwaite, polishing a glass a little severely, for she was a good woman. 'It was his guilty secret this solicitor had found out, so the viscount threw him over a cliff. I suppose, if one did but know, that sort of thing is going on all the time.'

Mr Mulliner nodded gravely.

'So much so,' he agreed, 'that I believe that whenever a family solicitor is found in two or more pieces at the bottom of a cliff, the first thing the Big Four at Scotland Yard do is make a round-up of all the viscounts in the neighbourhood.'

'Baronets are worse than viscounts,' said a Pint of Stout vehemently. 'I was done down by one only last month over the sale of a cow.'

'Earls are worse than baronets,' insisted a Whisky Sour. 'I could tell you something about earls.'

'How about O.B.E.s?' demanded a Mild and Bitter. 'If you ask me, O.B.E.s want watching, too.'

Mr Mulliner sighed.

'The fact is,' he said, 'reluctant though one may be to admit it, the entire British aristocracy is seamed and honeycombed with immorality. I venture to assert that, if you took a pin and jabbed it down anywhere in the pages of *Debrett's Peerage*, you would find it piercing the name of someone who was going about the place with a conscience as tender as a sunburned neck. If anything were needed to prove my assertion, the story of my nephew, Adrian Mulliner, the detective, would do it.'

'I didn't know you had a nephew who was a detective,' said the Whisky Sour.

Oh, yes. He has retired now, but at one time he was as keen an operator as anyone in the profession (said Mr Mulliner). After leaving Oxford and trying his hand at one or two uncongenial tasks, he had found his niche as a member of the firm of Widgery and Boon, Investigators, of Albemarle Street. And it was during his second year with this old-established house that he met and loved Lady Millicent Shipton-Bellinger, younger daughter of the fifth Earl of Brangbolton.

It was the Adventure of the Missing Sealyham that brought the young couple together. From the purely professional stand-point, my nephew has never ranked this among his greatest triumphs of ratiocination; but, considering what it led to, he might well, I think, be justified in regarding it as the most important case of his career. What happened was that he met the animal straying in the park, deduced from the name and address on its collar that it belonged to Lady Millicent

Shipton-Bellinger, of 18a, Upper Brook Street, and took it thither at the conclusion of his stroll and restored it.

'Child's-play' is the phrase with which, if you happen to allude to it, Adrian Mulliner will always airily dismiss this particular investigation; but Lady Millicent could not have displayed more admiration and enthusiasm had it been the supremest masterpiece of detective work. She fawned on my nephew. She invited him in to tea, consisting of buttered toast, anchovy sandwiches and two kinds of cake; and at the conclusion of the meal they parted on terms which, even at that early stage in their acquaintance, were something warmer than those of mere friendship.

Indeed, it is my belief that the girl fell in love with Adrian as instantaneously as he with her. On him, it was her radiant blonde beauty that exercised the spell. She, on her side, was fascinated, I fancy, not only by the regularity of his features, which, as is the case with all the Mulliners, was considerable, but also by the fact that he was dark and thin and wore an air of inscrutable melancholy.

This, as a matter of fact, was due to the troublesome attacks of dyspepsia from which he had suffered since boyhood; but to the girl it naturally seemed evidence of a great and romantic soul. Nobody, she felt, could look so grave and sad, had he not hidden deeps in him.

One can see the thing from her point of view. All her life she had been accustomed to brainless juveniles who eked out their meagre eyesight with monocles and, as far as conversation was concerned, were a spent force after they had asked her if she had seen the Academy or did she think she would prefer a glass of lemonade. The effect on her of a dark, keen-eyed man like Adrian Mulliner, who spoke well and easily of footprints, psychology and the underworld, must have been stupendous.

At any rate, their love ripened rapidly. It could not have been two weeks after their first meeting when Adrian, as he was giving her lunch one day at the Senior Bloodstain, the detectives' club in Rupert Street, proposed and was accepted. And for the next twenty-four hours, one is safe in saying, there was in the whole of London, including the outlying suburban districts, no happier private investigator than he.

Next day, however, when he again met Millicent for lunch, he was disturbed to perceive on her beautiful face an emotion which his trained eye immediately recognized as anguish.

'Oh, Adrian,' said the girl brokenly. 'The worst has happened. My father refuses to hear of our marrying. When I told him we were engaged, he said "Pooh!" quite a number of times, and added that he had never heard such dashed nonsense in his life. You see, ever since my Uncle Joe's trouble in nineteen-twenty-eight, father has had a horror of detectives.'

'I don't think I have met your Uncle Joe.'

'You will have the opportunity next year. With the usual allowance for good conduct he should be with us again about July. And there is another thing.'

'Not another?'

'Yes. Do you know Sir Jasper Addleton, O.B.E.?'

'The financier?'

'Father wants me to marry him. Isn't it awful!'

'I have certainly heard more enjoyable bits of news,' agreed Adrian. 'This wants a good deal of careful thinking over.'

The process of thinking over his unfortunate situation had the effect of rendering excessively acute the pangs of Adrian Mulliner's dyspepsia. During the past two weeks the ecstasy of being with Millicent and deducing that she loved him had caused a complete cessation of the attacks; but now they began again, worse than ever. At length, after a sleepless night during which he experienced all the emotions of one who has carelessly swallowed a family of scorpions, he sought a specialist.

The specialist was one of those keen, modern minds who disdain the outworn formulæ of the more conservative mass of the medical profession. He examined Adrian carefully, then sat back in his chair, with the tips of his fingers touching.

'Smile!' he said.

'Eh?' said Adrian.

'Smile, Mr Mulliner.'

'Did you say smile?'

'That's it. Smile.'

'But,' Adrian pointed out, 'I've just lost the only girl I ever loved.'

'Well, that's fine,' said the specialist, who was a bachelor. 'Come on, now, if you please. Start smiling.'

Adrian was a little bewildered.

'Listen,' he said. 'What *is* all this about smiling? We started, if I recollect, talking about my gastric juices. Now, in some mysterious way, we seem to have got on to the subject of smiles. How do you mean – smile? I never smile. I haven't smiled since the butler tripped over the spaniel and upset the melted butter on my Aunt Elizabeth, when I was a boy of twelve.'

The specialist nodded.

'Precisely. And that is why your digestive organs trouble you. Dyspepsia,' he proceeded, 'is now recognized by the progressive element of the profession as purely mental. We do not treat it with drugs and medicines. Happiness is the only cure. Be gay, Mr Mulliner. Be cheerful. And, if you can't do that, at any rate

smile. The mere exercise of the risible muscles is in itself bene-
ficial. Go out now and make a point, whenever you have a spare
moment, of smiling.'

'Like this?' said Adrian.

'Wider than that.'

'How about this?'

'Better,' said the specialist, 'but still not quite so elastic as one
could desire. Naturally, you need practice. We must expect the
muscles to work rustily for a while at their unaccustomed task.
No doubt things will brighten by and by.'

He regarded Adrian thoughtfully.

'Odd,' he said. 'A curious smile, yours, Mr Mulliner. It
reminds me a little of the Mona Lisa's. It has the same under-
lying note of the sardonic and the sinister. It virtually amounts to
a leer. Somehow it seems to convey the suggestion that you
know all. Fortunately, my own life is an open book, for all to
read, and so I was not discommoded. But I think it would be
better if, for the present, you endeavoured not to smile at
invalids or nervous persons. Good morning, Mr Mulliner.
That will be five guineas, precisely.'

On Adrian's face, as he went off that afternoon to perform the
duties assigned to him by his firm, there was no smile of any
description. He shrank from the ordeal before him. He had been
told off to guard the wedding-presents at a reception in Gros-
venor Square, and naturally anything to do with weddings was
like a sword through his heart. His face, as he patrolled the room
where the gifts were laid out, was drawn and forbidding. Hitherto, at these functions, it had always been his pride that nobody
could tell that he was a detective. To-day, a child could have
recognized his trade. He looked like Sherlock Holmes.

To the gay throng that surged about him he paid little attention. Usually tense and alert on occasions like this, he now found his mind wandering. He mused sadly on Millicent. And suddenly – the result, no doubt, of these gloomy meditations, though a glass of wedding champagne may have contributed its mite – there shot through him, starting at about the third button of his neat waistcoat, a pang of dyspepsia so keen that he felt the pressing necessity of doing something about it immediately.

With a violent effort he contorted his features into a smile. And, as he did so, a stout, bluff man of middle age, with a red face and a grey moustache, who had been hovering near one of the tables, turned and saw him.

'Egad!' he muttered, paling.

Sir Sutton Hartley-Wesping, Bart – for the red-faced man was he – had had a pretty good afternoon. Like all baronets who attend Society wedding-receptions, he had been going round the various tables since his arrival, pocketing here a fish-slice, there a jewelled egg-boiler, until now he had taken on about all the cargo his tonnage would warrant, and was thinking of strolling off to the pawnbroker's in the Euston Road, with whom he did most of his business. At the sight of Adrian's smile, he froze where he stood, appalled.

We have seen what the specialist thought of Adrian's smile. Even to him, a man of clear and limpid conscience, it had seemed sardonic and sinister. We can picture, then, the effect it must have had on Sir Sutton Hartley-Wesping.

At all costs, he felt, he must conciliate this leering man. Swiftly removing from his pockets a diamond necklace, five fish-slices, ten cigarette-lighters and a couple of egg-boilers, he placed them on the table and came over to Adrian with a nervous little laugh.

'How *are* you, my dear fellow?' he said.

Adrian said that he was quite well. And so, indeed, he was. The specialist's recipe had worked like magic. He was mildly surprised at finding himself so cordially addressed by a man whom he did not remember ever having seen before, but he attributed this to the magnetic charm of his personality.

'That's fine,' said the Baronet heartily. 'That's capital. That's splendid. Er – by the way – I fancied I saw you smile just now.'

'Yes,' said Adrian. 'I did smile. You see—'

'Of course I see. Of course, my dear fellow. You detected the joke I was playing on our good hostess, and you were amused because you understood that there is no animus, no *arrière-pensée*, behind these little practical pleasantries – nothing but good, clean fun, at which nobody would have laughed more heartily than herself. And now, what are you doing this week-end, my dear old chap? Would you care to run down to my place in Sussex?'

'Very kind of you,' began Adrian doubtfully. He was not quite sure that he was in the mood for strange week-ends.

'Here is my card, then. I shall expect you on Friday. Quite a small party. Lord Brangbolton, Sir Jasper Addleton, and a few more. Just loafing about, you know, and a spot of bridge at night. Splendid. Capital. See you, then, on Friday.'

And, carelessly dropping another egg-boiler on the table as he passed, Sir Sutton disappeared.

Any doubts which Adrian might have entertained as to accepting the Baronet's invitation had vanished as he heard the names of his fellow-guests. It always interests a fiancé to meet his fiancée's father and his fiancée's prospective fiancé. For the first time since Millicent had told him the bad news, Adrian became almost cheerful. If, he felt, this baronet had taken such a tremendous fancy to him at first sight, why might it not happen that Lord Brangbolton would be equally drawn to him – to the extent, in fact, of overlooking his profession and welcoming him as a son-in-law?

He packed, on the Friday, with what was to all intents and purposes a light heart.

A fortunate chance at the very outset of his expedition increased Adrian's optimism. It made him feel that Fate was fighting on his side. As he walked down the platform of Victoria Station, looking for an empty compartment in the train which was to take him to his destination, he perceived a tall, aristocratic old gentleman being assisted into a first-class carriage by a man of butlerine aspect. And in the latter he recognized the servitor who had admitted him to 18A, Upper Brook Street, when he visited the house after solving the riddle of the missing Sealyham. Obviously, then, the white-haired, dignified passenger could be none other than Lord Brangbolton. And Adrian felt that if on a long train journey he failed to ingratiate himself with the old buster, he had vastly mistaken his amiability and winning fascination of manner.

He leaped in, accordingly, as the train began to move, and the Earl, glancing up from his paper, jerked a thumb at the door.

'Get out, blast you!' he said. 'Full up.'

As the compartment was empty but for themselves, Adrian made no move to comply with the request. Indeed, to alight now, to such an extent had the train gathered speed, would have been impossible. Instead, he spoke cordially.

'Lord Brangbolton, I believe?'

'Go to hell,' said his lordship.

'I fancy we are to be fellow-guests at Wesping Hall this week-end.'

'What of it?'

'I just mentioned it.'

'Oh?' said Lord Brangbolton. 'Well, since you're here, how about a little flutter?'

As is customary with men of his social position, Millicent's father always travelled with a pack of cards. Being gifted by Nature with considerable manual dexterity, he usually managed to do well with these on race-trains.

'Ever played Persian Monarchs?' he asked, shuffling.

'I think not,' said Adrian.

'Quite simple,' said Lord Brangbolton. 'You just bet a quid or whatever it may be that you can cut a higher card than the other fellow, and, if you do, you win, and, if you don't, you don't.'

Adrian said it sounded a little like Blind Hooky.

'It is like Blind Hooky,' said Lord Brangbolton. 'Very like Blind Hooky. In fact, if you can play Blind Hooky, you can play Persian Monarchs.'

By the time they alighted at Wesping Parva Adrian was twenty pounds on the wrong side of the ledger. The fact, however, did not prey upon his mind. On the contrary, he was well satisfied with the progress of events. Elated with his winnings, the old Earl had become positively cordial, and Adrian resolved to press his advantage home at the earliest opportunity.

Arrived at Wesping Hall, accordingly, he did not delay. Shortly after the sounding of the dressing-gong he made his way to Lord Brangbolton's room and found him in his bath.

'Might I have a word with you, Lord Brangbolton?' he said.

'You can do more than that,' replied the other, with marked amiability. 'You can help me find the soap.'

'Have you lost the soap?'

'Yes. Had it a minute ago, and now it's gone.'

'Strange,' said Adrian.

'Very strange,' agreed Lord Brangbolton. 'Makes a fellow think a bit, that sort of thing happening. My own soap, too. Brought it with me.'

Adrian considered.

'Tell me exactly what occurred,' he said. 'In your own words. And tell me everything, please, for one never knows when the smallest detail may not be important.'

His companion marshalled his thoughts.

'My name,' he began, 'is Reginald Alexander Montacute James Bramfylde Tregennis Shipton-Bellinger, fifth Earl of Brangbolton. On the sixteenth of the present month – to-day, in fact – I journeyed to the house of my friend Sir Sutton Hartley-Wesping, Bart – here, in short – with the purpose of spending the week-end there. Knowing that Sir Sutton likes to have his guests sweet and fresh about the place, I decided to take a bath before dinner. I unpacked my soap and in a short space of time had lathered myself thoroughly from the neck upwards. And then, just as I was about to get at my right leg, what should I find but that the soap had disappeared. Nasty shock it gave me, I can tell you.'

Adrian had listened to this narrative with the closest attention. Certainly the problem appeared to present several points of interest.

'It looks like an inside job,' he said thoughtfully. 'It could scarcely be the work of a gang. You would have noticed a gang. Just give me the facts briefly once again, if you please.'

'Well, I was here, in the bath, as it might be, and the soap was here – between my hands, as it were. Next moment it was gone.'

'Are you sure you have omitted nothing?'

Lord Brangbolton reflected.

'Well, I was singing, of course.'

A tense look came into Adrian's face.

'Singing what?'

' "Sonny boy". '

Adrian's face cleared.

'As I suspected,' he said, with satisfaction. 'Precisely as I had supposed. I wonder if you are aware, Lord Brangbolton, that in the singing of that particular song the muscles unconsciously contract as you come to the final "boy"? Thus – "I still have you, sonny BOY." You observe? It would be impossible for anyone, rendering the number with the proper gusto, not to force his hands together at this point, assuming that they were in anything like close juxtaposition. And if there were any slippery object between them, such as a piece of soap, it would inevitably shoot sharply upwards and fall' – he scanned the room keenly – 'outside the bath on the mat. As, indeed,' he concluded, picking up the missing object and restoring it to its proprietor, 'it did.'

Lord Brangbolton gaped.

'Well, dash my buttons,' he cried, 'if that isn't the smartest bit of work I've seen in a month of Sundays!'

'Elementary,' said Adrian with a shrug.

'You ought to be a detective.'

Adrian took the cue.

'I am a detective,' he said. 'My name is Mulliner. Adrian Mulliner, Investigator.'

For an instant the words did not appear to have made any impression. The aged peer continued to beam through the soap-suds. Then suddenly his geniality vanished with an ominous swiftness.

'Mulliner? Did you say Mulliner?'

'I did.'

'You aren't by any chance the feller—'

'...who loves your daughter Millicent with a fervour he cannot begin to express? Yes, Lord Brangbolton, I am. And I am hoping that I may receive your consent to the match.'

A hideous scowl had darkened the Earl's brow. His fingers, which were grasping a loofah, tightened convulsively.

'Oh?' he said. 'You are, are you? You imagine, do you, that I propose to welcome a blighted footprint-and-cigar-ash inspector into my family? It is your idea, is it, that I shall acquiesce in the union of my daughter to a dashed feller who goes about the place on his hands and knees with a magnifying-glass, picking up small objects and putting them carefully away in his pocket-book? I seem to see myself! Why, rather than permit Millicent to marry a bally detective...'

'What is your objection to detectives?'

'Never you mind what's my objection to detectives. Marry my daughter, indeed! I like your infernal check. Why, you couldn't keep her in lipsticks.'

Adrian preserved his dignity.

'I admit that my services are not so amply remunerated as I could wish, but the firm hint at a rise next Christmas....'

'Tchah!' said Lord Brangbolton. 'Pshaw! If you are interested in my daughter's matrimonial arrangements, she is going, as soon as he gets through with this Bramah-Yamah Gold Mines flotation of his, to marry my old friend Jasper Addleton. As for you, Mr Mulliner, I have only two words to say to you. One is POP, the other is OFF. And do it now.'

Adrian sighed. He saw that it would be hopeless to endeavour to argue with the haughty old man in his present mood.

'So be it, Lord Brangbolton,' he said quietly.

And, affecting not to notice the nail-brush which struck him smartly on the back of the head, he left the room.

The food and drink provided for his guests by Sir Sutton Hartley-Wesping at the dinner which began some half-hour later were all that the veriest gourmet could have desired; but Adrian gulped them down, scarcely tasting them. His whole attention was riveted on Sir Jasper Addleton, who sat immediately opposite him.

And the more he examined Sir Jasper, the more revolting seemed the idea of his marrying the girl he loved.

Of course, an ardent young fellow inspecting a man who is going to marry the girl he loves is always a stern critic. In the peculiar circumstances Adrian would, no doubt, have looked askance at a John Barrymore or a Ronald Colman. But, in the case of Sir Jasper, it must be admitted that he had quite reasonable grounds for his disapproval.

In the first place, there was enough of the financier to make two financiers. It was as if Nature, planning a financier, had said to itself: 'We will do this thing well. We will not skimp,' with the result that, becoming too enthusiastic, it had overdone it. And then, in addition to being fat, he was also bald and goggle-eyed. And, if you overlooked his baldness and the goggly protuberance of his eyes, you could not get away from the fact that he was well advanced in years. Such a man, felt Adrian, would have been better employed in pricing burial-lots in Kensal Green Cemetery than in forcing his unwelcome attentions on a sweet young girl like Millicent: and as soon as the meal was concluded he approached him with cold abhorrence.

'A word with you,' he said, and led him out on to the terrace.

The O.B.E., as he followed him into the cool night air, seemed surprised and a little uneasy. He had noticed Adrian scrutinizing him closely across the dinner table, and if there is one thing a financier who has just put out a prospectus of a gold mine dislikes, it is to be scrutinized closely.

'What do you want?' he asked nervously.

Adrian gave him a cold glance.

'Do you ever look in a mirror, Sir Jasper?' he asked curtly.

'Frequently,' replied the financier, puzzled.

'Do you ever weigh yourself?'

'Often.'

'Do you ever listen while your tailor is toiling round you with the tape-measure and calling out the score to his assistant?'

'I do.'

'Then,' said Adrian, 'and I speak in the kindest spirit of disinterested friendship, you must have realized that you are an overfed old bohunkus. And how you ever got the idea that you were a fit mate for Lady Millicent Shipton-Bellinger frankly beats me. Surely it must have occurred to you what a priceless ass you will look, walking up the aisle with that young and lovely girl at your side? People will mistake you for an elderly uncle taking his niece to the Zoo.'

The O.B.E. bridled.

'Ho!' he said.

'It is no use saying "Ho!"' said Adrian. 'You can't get out of it with any "Ho's". When all the talk and argument have died away, the fact remains that, millionaire though you be, you are a nasty-looking, fat, senile millionaire. If I were you, I should give the whole thing a miss. What do you want to get married for, anyway? You are much happier as you are. Besides, think of the risks of a financier's life. Nice it would be for that sweet girl suddenly to get a wire from you telling her not to wait dinner for you as you had just started a seven-year stretch at Dartmoor!'

An angry retort had been trembling on Sir Jasper's lips during the early portion of this speech, but at these concluding words it died unspoken. He blenched visibly, and stared at the speaker with undisguised apprehension.

'What do you mean?' he faltered.

'Never mind,' said Adrian.

He had spoken, of course, purely at a venture, basing his remarks on the fact that nearly all O.B.E.s who dabble in High Finance go to prison sooner or later. Of Sir Jasper's actual affairs he knew nothing.

'Hey, listen!' said the financier.

But Adrian did not hear him. I have mentioned that during dinner, preoccupied with his thoughts, he had bolted his food. Nature now took its toll. An acute spasm suddenly ran through him, and with a brief 'Ouch!' of pain he doubled up and began to walk round in circles.

Sir Jasper clicked his tongue impatiently.

'This is no time for doing the Astaire pom-pom dance,' he said sharply. 'Tell me what you meant by that stuff you were talking about prison.'

Adrian had straightened himself. In the light of the moon which flooded the terrace with its silver beams, his clean-cut face was plainly visible. And with a shiver of apprehension Sir Jasper saw that it wore a sardonic, sinister smile – a smile which, it struck him, was virtually tantamount to a leer.

I have spoken of the dislike financiers have for being scrutinized closely. Still more vehemently do they object to being leered at. Sir Jasper reeled, and was about to press his question when Adrian, still smiling, tottered off into the shadows and was lost to sight.

The financier hurried into the smoking-room, where he knew there would be the materials for a stiff drink. A stiff drink was what he felt an imperious need of at the moment. He tried to tell himself that that smile could not really have had the inner meaning which he had read into it; but he was still quivering nervously as he entered the smoking-room.

As he opened the door, the sound of an angry voice smote his ears. He recognized it as Lord Brangbolton's.

'I call it dashed low,' his lordship was saying in his high-pitched tenor.

Sir Jasper gazed in bewilderment. His host, Sir Sutton Hartley-Wesping, was standing backed against the wall, and Lord Brangbolton, tapping him on the shirt-front with a piston-like forefinger, was plainly in the process of giving him a thorough ticking off.

'What's the matter?' asked the financier.

'I'll tell you what's the matter,' cried Lord Brangbolton. 'This hound here has got down a detective to watch his guests. A dashed fellow named Mulliner. So much,' he said bitterly, 'for our boasted English hospitality. Egad!' he went on, still tapping the baronet round and about the diamond solitaire. 'I call it thoroughly low. If I have a few of my society chums down to my little place for a visit, naturally I chain up the hair-brushes and tell the butler to count the spoons every night, but I'd never dream of going so far as to employ beastly detectives. One has one's code. *Noblesse*, I mean to say, *oblige*, what, what?'

'But, listen,' pleaded the Baronet. 'I keep telling you. I had to invite the fellow here. I thought that if he had eaten my bread and salt, he would not expose me.'

'How do you mean, expose you?'

Sir Sutton coughed.

'Oh, it was nothing. The merest trifle. Still, the man undoubtedly could have made things unpleasant for me, if he had wished. So, when I looked up and saw him smiling at me in that frightful sardonic, knowing way—'

Sir Jasper Addleton uttered a sharp cry.

'Smiling!' He gulped. 'Did you say smiling?'

'Smiling,' said the Baronet, 'is right. It was one of those smiles that seem to go clean through you and light up all your inner being as if with a searchlight.'

Sir Jasper gulped again.

'Is this fellow – this smiler fellow – is he a tall, dark, thin chap?'

'That's right. He sat opposite you at dinner.'

'And he's a detective?'

'He is,' said Lord Brangbolton. 'As shrewd and smart a detective,' he added grudgingly, 'as I ever met in my life. The way he found that soap. . . . Feller struck me as having some sort of a sixth sense, if you know what I mean, dash and curse him. I hate detectives,' he said with a shiver. 'They give me the creeps. This one wants to marry my daughter, Millicent, of all the dashed nerve!'

'See you later,' said Sir Jasper. And with a single bound he was out of the room and on his way to the terrace. There was, he felt, no time to waste. His florid face, as he galloped along, was twisted and ashen. With one hand he drew from his inside pocket a cheque-book, with the other from his trouser-pocket a fountain-pen.

Adrian, when the financier found him, was feeling a good deal better. He blessed the day when he had sought the specialist's advice. There was no doubt about it, he felt, the man knew his business. Smiling might make the cheek-muscles ache, but it undoubtedly did the trick as regarded the pangs of dyspepsia.

For a brief while before Sir Jasper burst onto the terrace, waving fountain-pen and cheque-book, Adrian had been giving his face a rest. But now, the pain in his cheeks having abated, he deemed it prudent to resume the treatment. And so it came about that the financier, hurrying towards him, was met with a smile so meaning, so suggestive, that he stopped in his tracks and for a moment could not speak.

'Oh, there you are!' he said, recovering at length. 'Might I have a word with you in private, Mr Mulliner?'

Adrian nodded, beaming. The financier took him by the coat-sleeve and led him across the terrace. He was breathing a little stertorously.

'I've been thinking things over,' he said, 'and I've come to the conclusion that you were right.'

'Right?' said Adrian.

'About me marrying. It wouldn't do.'

'No?'

'Positively not. Absurd. I can see it now. I'm too old for the girl.'

'Yes.'

'Too bald.'

'Exactly.'

'And too fat.'

'Much too fat,' agreed Adrian. This sudden change of heart puzzled him, but none the less the other's words were as music to his ears. Every syllable the O.B.E. had spoken had caused his heart to leap within him like a young lamb in springtime, and his mouth curved in a smile.

Sir Jasper, seeing it, shied like a frightened horse. He patted Adrian's arm feverishly.

'So I have decided,' he said, 'to take your advice and – if I recall your expression – give the thing a miss.'

'You couldn't do better,' said Adrian heartily.

'Now, if I were to remain in England in these circumstances,' proceeded Sir Jasper, 'there might be unpleasantness. So I propose to go quietly away at once to some remote spot – say, South America. Don't you think I am right?' he asked, giving the cheque-book a twitch.

'Quite right,' said Adrian.

'You won't mention this little plan of mine to anyone? You will keep it as just a secret between ourselves? If, for instance, any of your cronies at Scotland Yard should express curiosity as to my whereabouts, you will plead ignorance?'

'Certainly.'

'Capital!' said Sir Jasper, relieved. 'And there is one other thing. I gather from Brangbolton that you are anxious to marry Lady Millicent yourself. And, as by the time of the wedding I shall doubtless be in – well, Callao is a spot that suggests itself off-hand, I would like to give you my little wedding-present now.'

He scribbled hastily in his cheque-book, tore out a page and handed it to Adrian.

'Remember!' he said. 'Not a word to anyone!'

'Quite,' said Adrian.

He watched the financier disappear in the direction of the garage, regretting that he could have misjudged a man who so evidently had much good in him. Presently the sound of a motor engine announced that the other was on his way. Feeling that one obstacle, at least, between himself and his happiness had been removed, Adrian strolled indoors to see what the rest of the party were doing.

It was a quiet, peaceful scene that met his eyes as he wandered into the library. Overruling the request of some of the members of the company for a rubber of bridge, Lord Brangbolton had gathered them together at a small table and was initiating them into his favourite game of Persian Monarchs.

'It's perfectly simple, dash it,' he was saying. 'You just take the pack and cut. You bet – let us say ten pounds – that you will cut a higher card than the feller you're cutting against. And, if you do, you win, dash it. And, if you don't, the other dashed feller wins. Quite clear, what?'

Somebody said that it sounded a little like Blind Hooky.

'It is like Blind Hooky,' said Lord Brangbolton. 'Very like Blind Hooky. In fact, if you can play Blind Hooky, you can play Persian Monarchs.'

They settled down to their game, and Adrian wandered about the room, endeavouring to still the riot of emotion which his recent interview with Sir Jasper Addleton had aroused in his bosom. All that remained for him to do now, he reflected, was by some means or other to remove the existing prejudice against him from Lord Brangbolton's mind.

It would not be easy, of course. To begin with, there was the matter of his straitened means.

He suddenly remembered that he had not yet looked at the cheque which the financier had handed him. He pulled it out of his pocket.

And, having glanced at it, Adrian Mulliner swayed like a poplar in a storm.

Just what he had expected, he could not have said. A fiver, possibly. At the most, a tenner. Just a trifling gift, he had imagined, with which to buy himself a cigarette-lighter, a fish-slice, or an egg-boiler.

The cheque was for a hundred thousand pounds.

So great was the shock that, as Adrian caught sight of himself in the mirror opposite to which he was standing, he scarcely recognized the face in the glass. He seemed to be seeing it through a mist. Then the mist cleared, and he saw not only his own face clearly, but also that of Lord Brangbolton, who was in the act of cutting against his left-hand neighbour, Lord Knubble of Knopp.

And, as he thought of the effect this sudden accession of wealth must surely have on the father of the girl he loved, there came into Adrian's face a sudden, swift smile.

And simultaneously from behind him he heard a gasping exclamation, and, looking in the mirror, he met Lord Brangbolton's eyes. Always a little prominent, they were now almost prawn-like in their convexity.

Lord Knubble of Knopp had produced a bank-note from his pocket and was pushing it along the table.

'Another ace!' he exclaimed. 'Well I'm dashed!'

Lord Brangbolton had risen from his chair.

'Excuse me,' he said in a strange, croaking voice. 'I just want to have a little chat with my friend, my dear old friend, Mulliner here. Might I have a word in private with you, Mr Mulliner?'

There was silence between the two men until they had reached a corner of the terrace out of earshot of the library window. Then Lord Brangbolton cleared his throat.

'Mulliner,' he began, 'or, rather – what is your Christian name?'

'Adrian.'

'Adrian, my dear fellow,' said Lord Brangbolton, 'my memory is not what it should be, but I seem to have a distinct recollection that, when I was in my bath before dinner, you said something about wanting to marry my daughter Millicent.'

'I did,' replied Adrian. 'And, if your objections to me as a suitor were mainly financial, let me assure you that, since we last spoke, I have become a wealthy man.'

'I never had any objections to you, Adrian, financial or otherwise,' said Lord Brangbolton, patting his arm affectionately. 'I have always felt that the man my daughter married ought to be a fine, warm-hearted young fellow like you. For you, Adrian,' he proceeded, 'are essentially warm-hearted. You would never dream of distressing a father-in-law by mentioning any... any little ... well, in short, I saw from your smile in there that you had noticed that I was introducing into that game of Blind Hooky – or, rather, Persian Monarchs – certain little – shall I say variations, designed to give it additional interest and excitement, and I feel sure that you would scorn to embarrass a father-in-law by... Well, to cut a long story short, my boy, take Millicent and with her a father's blessing.'

He extended his hand. Adrian clasped it warmly.

'I am the happiest man in the world,' he said, smiling.

Lord Brangbolton winced.

'Do you mind not doing that?' he said.

'I only smiled,' said Adrian.

'I know,' said Lord Brangbolton.

Little remains to be told. Adrian and Millicent were married three months later at a fashionable West End church. All Society was there. The presents were both numerous and costly, and the bride looked charming. The service was conducted by the Very Reverend the Dean of Bittlesham.

It was in the vestry afterwards, as Adrian looked at Millicent and seemed to realize for the first time that all his troubles were over and that this lovely girl was indeed his, for better or worse, that a full sense of his happiness swept over the young man.

All through the ceremony he had been grave, as befitted a man at the most serious point of his career. But now, fizzing as if with some spiritual yeast, he clasped her in his arms and over her shoulder his face broke into a quick smile.

He found himself looking into the eyes of the Dean of Bittlesham. A moment later he felt a tap on his arm.

'Might I have a word with you in private, Mr Mulliner?' said the Dean in a low voice.

'Cats are not dogs!'

There is only one place where you can hear good things like that thrown off quite casually in the general run of conversation, and that is the bar-parlour of the Angler's Rest. It was there, as we sat grouped about the fire, that a thoughtful Pint of Bitter had made the statement just recorded.

Although the talk up to this point had been dealing with Einstein's Theory of Relativity, we readily adjusted our minds to cope with the new topic. Regular attendance at the nightly sessions over which Mr Mulliner presides with such unfailing dignity and geniality tends to produce mental nimbleness. In our little circle I have known an argument on the Final Destination of the Soul to change inside forty seconds into one concerning the best method of preserving the juiciness of bacon fat.

'Cats,' proceeded the Pint of Bitter, 'are selfish. A man waits on a cat hand and foot for weeks, humouring its lightest whim, and then it goes and leaves him flat because it has found a place down the road where the fish is more frequent.'

'What I've got against cats,' said a Lemon Sour, speaking feelingly, as one brooding on a private grievance, 'is their unreliability. They lack candour and are not square shooters. You get your cat and you call him Thomas or George, as the case may be.

So far, so good. Then one morning you wake up and find six kittens in the hat-box and you have to reopen the whole matter, approaching it from an entirely different angle.'

'If you want to know what's the trouble with cats,' said a red-faced man with glassy eyes, who had been rapping on the table for his fourth whisky, 'they've got no tact. That's what's the trouble with them. I remember a friend of mine had a cat. Made quite a pet of that cat, he did. And what occurred? What was the outcome? One night he came home rather late and was feeling for the keyhole with his corkscrew; and, believe me or not, his cat selected that precise moment to jump on the back of his neck out of a tree. No tact.'

Mr Mulliner shook his head.

'I grant you all this,' he said, 'but still, in my opinion, you have not got quite to the root of the matter. The real objection to the great majority of cats is their insufferable air of superiority. Cats, as a class, have never completely got over the snootiness caused by the fact that in Ancient Egypt they were worshipped as gods. This makes them too prone to set themselves up as critics and censors of the frail and erring human beings whose lot they share. They stare rebukingly. They view with concern. And on a sensitive man this often has the worst effects, inducing an inferiority complex of the gravest kind. It is odd that the conversation should have taken this turn,' said Mr Mulliner, sipping his hot Scotch and lemon, 'for I was thinking only this afternoon of the rather strange case of my cousin Edward's son, Lancelot.'

'I knew a cat—' began a Small Bass.

My cousin Edward's son, Lancelot (said Mr Mulliner) was, at the time of which I speak, a comely youth of some twenty-five summers. Orphaned at an early age, he had been brought up in the home of his Uncle Theodore, the saintly Dean of Bolsover; and it was a great shock to that good man when Lancelot, on attaining his majority, wrote from London to inform him that he had taken a studio in Bott Street, Chelsea, and proposed to remain in the metropolis and become an artist.

The Dean's opinion of artists was low. As a prominent member of the Bolsover Watch Committee, it had recently been his distasteful duty to be present at a private showing of the super-super-film, 'Palettes of Passion'; and he replied to his nephew's communication with a vibrant letter in which he emphasized the grievous pain it gave him to think that one of his flesh and blood should deliberately be embarking on a career which must inevitably lead sooner or later to the painting of Russian princesses lying on divans in the semi-nude with their arms round tame jaguars. He urged Lancelot to return and become a curate while there was yet time.

But Lancelot was firm. He deplored the rift between himself and a relative whom he had always respected; but he was dashed if he meant to go back to an environment where his individuality had been stifled and his soul confined in chains. And for four years there was silence between uncle and nephew.

During these years Lancelot had made progress in his chosen profession. At the time at which this story opens, his prospects seemed bright. He was painting the portrait of Brenda, only daughter of Mr and Mrs B. B. Carberry-Pirbright, of 11, Maxton Square, South Kensington, which meant thirty pounds in his sock on delivery. He had learned to cook eggs and bacon. He had practically mastered the ukulele. And, in addition, he was engaged to be married to a fearless young *vers libre* poetess of the name of Gladys Bingley, better known as The Sweet Singer of

Garbidge Mews, Fulham – a charming girl who looked like a pen-wiper.

It seemed to Lancelot that life was very full and beautiful. He lived joyously in the present, giving no thought to the past.

But how true it is that the past is inextricably mixed up with the present and that we can never tell when it may not spring some delayed bomb beneath our feet. One afternoon, as he sat making a few small alterations in the portrait of Brenda Carberry-Pirbright, his fiancée entered.

He had been expecting her to call, for to-day she was going off for a three weeks' holiday to the South of France, and she had promised to look in on her way to the station. He laid down his brush and gazed at her with a yearning affection, thinking for the thousandth time how he worshipped every spot of ink on her nose. Standing there in the doorway with her bobbed hair sticking out in every direction like a golliwog's she made a picture that seemed to speak to his very depths.

'Hullo, Reptile!' he said lovingly.

'What ho, Worm!' said Gladys, maidenly devotion shining through the monocle which she wore in her left eye. 'I can stay just half an hour.'

'Oh, well, half an hour soon passes,' said Lancelot. 'What's that you've got there?'

'A letter, ass. What did you think it was?'

'Where did you get it?'

'I found the postman outside.'

Lancelot took the envelope from her and examined it.

'Gosh!' he said.

'What's the matter?'

'It's from my Uncle Theodore.'

'I didn't know you had an Uncle Theodore.'

'Of course I have. I've had him for years.'

'What's he writing to you about?'

'If you'll kindly keep quiet for two seconds, if you know how,' said Lancelot, 'I'll tell you.'

And in a clear voice which, like that of all the Mulliners, however distant from the main branch, was beautifully modulated, he read as follows:

> 'The Deanery,
> 'Bolsover,
> 'Wilts.

'MY DEAR LANCELOT,

'As you have, no doubt, already learned from your *Church Times*, I have been offered and have accepted the vacant Bishopric of Bongo-Bongo in West Africa. I sail immediately to take up my new duties, which I trust will be blessed.

'In these circumstances, it becomes necessary for me to find a good home for my cat Webster. It is, alas, out of the question that he should accompany me, as the rigours of the climate and the lack of essential comforts might well sap a constitution which has never been robust.

'I am dispatching him, therefore, to your address, my dear boy, in a straw-lined hamper, in the full confidence that you will prove a kindly and conscientious host.

> 'With cordial good wishes,
> 'Your affectionate uncle,
> 'THEODORE BONGO-BONGO.'

For some moments after he had finished reading this communication, a thoughtful silence prevailed in the studio. Finally Gladys spoke.

'Of all the nerve!' she said. 'I wouldn't do it.'

'Why not?'

'What do you want with a cat?'

Lancelot reflected.

'It is true,' he said, 'that, given a free hand, I would prefer not to have my studio turned into a cattery or cat-bin. But consider the special circumstances. Relations between Uncle Theodore and self have for the last few years been a bit strained. In fact, you might say we had definitely parted brass-rags. It looks to me as if he were coming round. I should describe this letter as more or less what you might call an olive-branch. If I lush this cat up satisfactorily, shall I not be in a position later on to make a swift touch?'

'He is rich, this bean?' said Gladys, interested.

'Extremely.'

'Then,' said Gladys, 'consider my objections withdrawn. A good stout cheque from a grateful cat-fancier would undoubtedly come in very handy. We might be able to get married this year.'

'Exactly,' said Lancelot. 'A pretty loathsome prospect, of course, but still, as we've arranged to do it, the sooner we get it over, the better, what?'

'Absolutely.'

'Then that's settled. I accept custody of cat.'

'It's the only thing to do,' said Gladys. 'Meanwhile, can you lend me a comb? Have you such a thing in your bedroom?'

'What do you want with a comb?'

'I got some soup in my hair at lunch. I won't be a minute.'

She hurried out, and Lancelot, taking up the letter again, found that he had omitted to read a continuation of it on the back page.

It was to the following effect:

'P.S. In establishing Webster in your home, I am actuated by another motive than the simple desire to see to it that my faithful friend and companion is adequately provided for.

'From both a moral and an educative standpoint, I am convinced that Webster's society will prove of inestimable value to you. His advent, indeed, I venture to hope, will be a turning-point in your life. Thrown, as you must be, incessantly among loose and immoral Bohemians, you will find in this cat an example of upright conduct which cannot but act as an antidote to the poison cup of temptation which is, no doubt, hourly pressed to your lips.

'P.P.S. Cream only at midday, and fish not more than three times a week.'

He was reading these words for the second time, when the front door-bell rang and he found a man on the steps with a hamper. A discreet mew from within revealed its contents, and Lancelot, carrying it into the studio, cut the strings.

'Hi!' he bellowed, going to the door.

'What's up?' shrieked his betrothed from above.

'The cat's come.'

'All right. I'll be down in a jiffy.'

Lancelot returned to the studio.

'What ho, Webster!' he said cheerily. 'How's the boy?'

The cat did not reply. It was sitting with bent head, performing that wash and brush up which a journey by rail renders so necessary.

In order to facilitate these toilet operations, it had raised its left leg and was holding it rigidly in the air. And there flashed into Lancelot's mind an old superstition handed on to him, for what it was worth, by one of the nurses of his infancy. If, this woman had said, you creep up to a cat when its leg is in the air and give it a pull, then you make a wish and your wish comes true in thirty days.

It was a pretty fancy, and it seemed to Lancelot that the theory might as well be put to the test. He advanced warily, therefore, and was in the act of extending his fingers for the pull, when Webster, lowering the leg, turned and raised his eyes.

He looked at Lancelot. And suddenly with sickening force, there came to Lancelot the realization of the unpardonable liberty he had been about to take.

Until this moment, though the postscript to his uncle's letter should have warned him, Lancelot Mulliner had had no suspicion of what manner of cat this was that he had taken into his home. Now, for the first time, he saw him steadily and saw him whole.

Webster was very large and very black and very composed. He conveyed the impression of being a cat of deep reserves. Descendant of a long line of ecclesiastical ancestors who had conducted their decorous courtships beneath the shadow of cathedrals and on the back walls of bishops' palaces, he had that exquisite poise which one sees in high dignitaries of the church. His eyes were clear and steady, and seemed to pierce to the very roots of the young man's soul, filling him with a sense of guilt.

Once, long ago, in his hot childhood, Lancelot, spending his summer holidays at the deanery, had been so far carried away by ginger-beer and original sin as to plug a senior canon in the leg with his air-gun – only to discover, on turning, that a visiting archdeacon had been a spectator of the entire incident from his immediate rear. As he had felt then, when meeting the archdeacon's eye, so did he feel now as Webster's gaze played silently upon him.

Webster, it is true, had not actually raised his eyebrows. But this, Lancelot felt, was simply because he hadn't any.

He backed, blushing.

'Sorry!' he muttered.

There was a pause. Webster continued his steady scrutiny. Lancelot edged towards the door.

'Er – excuse me – just a moment...' he mumbled. And, sidling from the room, he ran distractedly upstairs.

'I say,' said Lancelot.

'Now what?' asked Gladys.

'Have you finished with the mirror?'

'Why?'

'Well, I – er – I thought,' said Lancelot, 'that I might as well have a shave.'

The girl looked at him, astonished.

'Shave? Why, you shaved only the day before yesterday.'

'I know. But, all the same...I mean to say, it seems only respectful. That cat, I mean.'

'What about him?'

'Well, he seems to expect it, somehow. Nothing actually said, don't you know, but you could tell by his manner. I thought a quick shave and perhaps change into my blue serge suit—'

'He's probably thirsty. Why don't you give him some milk?'

'Could one, do you think?' said Lancelot doubtfully. 'I mean, I hardly seem to know him well enough.' He paused. 'I say, old girl,' he went on, with a touch of hesitation.

'Hullo?'

'I know you won't mind my mentioning it, but you've got a few spots of ink on your nose.'

'Of course I have. I always have spots of ink on my nose.'

'Well...you don't think...a quick scrub with a bit of pumice-stone...I mean to say, you know how important first impressions are....'

The girl stared.

'Lancelot Mulliner,' she said, 'if you think I'm going to skin my nose to the bone just to please a mangy cat—'

'Sh!' cried Lancelot, in agony.

'Here, let me go down and look at him,' said Gladys petulantly.

As they re-entered the studio, Webster was gazing with an air of quiet distaste at an illustration from *La Vie Parisienne* which adorned one of the walls. Lancelot tore it down hastily.

Gladys looked at Webster in an unfriendly way.

'So that's the blighter!'

'Sh!'

'If you want to know what I think,' said Gladys, 'that cat's been living too high. Doing himself a dashed sight too well. You'd better cut his rations down a bit.'

In substance, her criticism was not unjustified. Certainly, there was about Webster more than a suspicion of *embonpoint*. He had that air of portly well-being which we associate with those who dwell in cathedral closes. But Lancelot winced uncomfortably. He had so hoped that Gladys would make a good impression, and here she was, starting right off by saying the tactless thing.

He longed to explain to Webster that it was only her way; that in the Bohemian circles of which she was such an ornament genial chaff of a personal order was accepted and, indeed, relished. But it was too late. The mischief had been done. Webster turned in a pointed manner and withdrew silently behind the chesterfield.

Gladys, all unconscious, was making preparations for departure.

'Well, bung-oh,' she said lightly. 'See you in three weeks. I suppose you and that cat'll both be out on the tiles the moment my back's turned.'

'Please! Please!' moaned Lancelot. 'Please!'

He had caught sight of the tip of a black tail protruding from behind the chesterfield. It was twitching slightly, and Lancelot could read it like a book. With a sickening sense of dismay, he knew that Webster had formed a snap judgment of his fiancée and condemned her as frivolous and unworthy.

It was some ten days later that Bernard Worple, the neo-Vorticist sculptor, lunching at the Puce Ptarmigan, ran into Rodney Scollop, the powerful young surrealist. And after talking for a while of their art—

'What's all this I hear about Lancelot Mulliner?' asked Worple. 'There's a wild story going about that he was seen shaved in the middle of the week. Nothing in it, I suppose?'

Scollop looked grave. He had been on the point of mentioning Lancelot himself, for he loved the lad and was deeply exercised about him.

'It is perfectly true,' he said.

'It sounds incredible.'

Scollop leaned forward. His fine face was troubled.

'Shall I tell you something, Worple?'

'What?'

'I know for an absolute fact,' said Scollop, 'that Lancelot Mulliner now shaves every morning.'

Worple pushed aside the spaghetti which he was wreathing about him and through the gap stared at his companion.

'Every morning?'

'Every single morning. I looked in on him myself the other day, and there he was, neatly dressed in blue serge and shaved to the core. And, what is more, I got the distinct impression that he had used talcum powder afterwards.'

'You don't mean that!'

'I do. And shall I tell you something else? There was a book lying open on the table. He tried to hide it, but he wasn't quick enough. It was one of those etiquette books!'

'An etiquette book!'

' "Polite Behaviour", by Constance, Lady Bodbank.'

Worple unwound a stray tendril of spaghetti from about his left ear. He was deeply agitated. Like Scollop, he loved Lancelot.

'He'll be dressing for dinner next!' he exclaimed.

'I have every reason to believe,' said Scollop gravely, 'that he does dress for dinner. At any rate, a man closely resembling him was seen furtively buying three stiff collars and a black tie at Hope Brothers in the King's Road last Tuesday.'

Worple pushed his chair back, and rose. His manner was determined.

'Scollop,' he said, 'we are friends of Mulliner's, you and I. It is evident from what you tell me that subversive influences are at work and that never has he needed our friendship more. Shall we not go round and see him immediately?'

'It was what I was about to suggest myself,' said Rodney Scollop.

Twenty minutes later they were in Lancelot's studio, and with a significant glance Scollop drew his companion's notice to their host's appearance. Lancelot Mulliner was neatly, even foppishly, dressed in blue serge with creases down the trouser-legs, and his chin, Worple saw with a pang, gleamed smoothly in the afternoon light.

At the sight of his friends' cigars, Lancelot exhibited unmistakable concern.

'You don't mind throwing those away, I'm sure,' he said pleadingly.

Rodney Scollop drew himself up a little haughtily.

'And since when,' he asked, 'have the best fourpenny cigars in Chelsea not been good enough for you?'

Lancelot hastened to soothe him.

'It isn't me,' he exclaimed. 'It's Webster. My cat. I happen to know he objects to tobacco smoke. I had to give up my pipe in deference to his views.'

Bernard Worple snorted.

'Are you trying to tell us,' he sneered, 'that Lancelot Mulliner allows himself to be dictated to by a blasted cat?'

'Hush!' cried Lancelot, trembling. 'If you knew how he disapproves of strong language!'

'Where is this cat?' asked Rodney Scollop. 'Is that the animal?' he said, pointing out of the window to where, in the yard, a tough-looking Tom with tattered ears stood mewing in a hard-boiled way out of the corner of its mouth.

'Good heavens, no!' said Lancelot. 'That is an alley cat which comes round here from time to time to lunch at the dust-bin. Webster is quite different. Webster has a natural dignity and repose of manner. Webster is a cat who prides himself on always being well turned out and whose high principles and lofty ideals shine from his eyes like beacon-fires. . . .' And then suddenly, with an abrupt change of manner, Lancelot broke down and in a low voice added: 'Curse him! Curse him! Curse him! Curse him!'

Worple looked at Scollop. Scollop looked at Worple.

'Come, old man,' said Scollop, laying a gentle hand on Lancelot's bowed shoulder. 'We are your friends. Confide in us.'

'Tell us all,' said Worple. 'What's the matter?'

Lancelot uttered a bitter, mirthless laugh.

'You want to know what's the matter? Listen, then. I'm cat-pecked!'

'Cat-pecked?'

'You've heard of men being hen-pecked, haven't you?' said Lancelot with a touch of irritation. 'Well, I'm cat-pecked.'

And in broken accents he told his story. He sketched the history of his association with Webster from the letter's first entry into the studio. Confident now that the animal was not within earshot, he unbosomed himself without reserve.

'It's something in the beast's eye,' he said in a shaking voice. 'Something hypnotic. He casts a spell upon me. He gazes at me and disapproves. Little by little, bit by bit, I am degenerating under his influence from a wholesome, self-respecting artist into ... well, I don't know what you would call it. Suffice it to say that I have given up smoking, that I have ceased to wear carpet slippers and go about without a collar, that I never dream of sitting down to my frugal evening meal without dressing, and' – he choked – 'I have sold my ukulele.'

'Not that!' said Worple, paling.

'Yes,' said Lancelot. 'I felt he considered it frivolous.'

There was a long silence.

'Mulliner,' said Scollop, 'this is more serious than I had supposed. We must brood upon your case.'

'It may be possible,' said Worple, 'to find a way out.'

Lancelot shook his head hopelessly.

'There is no way out. I have explored every avenue. The only thing that could possibly free me from this intolerable bondage would be if once – just once – I could catch that cat unbending. If once – merely once – it would lapse in my presence from its austere dignity for but a single instant, I feel that the spell would be broken. But what hope is there of that?' cried Lancelot passionately. 'You were pointing just now to that alley cat in the yard. There stands one who has strained every nerve and spared no effort to break down Webster's inhuman self-control. I have heard that animal say things to him which you would think no cat with red blood in its veins would suffer for an instant. And Webster merely looks at him like a Suffragan Bishop eyeing an erring choir-boy and turns his head and falls into a refreshing sleep.'

He broke off with a dry sob. Worple, always an optimist, attempted in his kindly way to minimize the tragedy.

'Ah, well,' he said. 'It's bad, of course, but still, I suppose there is no actual harm in shaving and dressing for dinner and so on. Many great artists ... Whistler, for example—'

'Wait!' cried Lancelot. 'You have not heard the worst.'

He rose feverishly, and, going to the easel, disclosed the portrait of Brenda Carberry-Pirbright.

'Take a look at that,' he said, 'and tell me what you think of her.'

His two friends surveyed the face before them in silence. Miss Carberry-Pirbright was a young woman of prim and glacial aspect. One sought in vain for her reasons for wanting to have her portrait painted. It would be a most unpleasant thing to have about any house.

Scollop broke the silence.

'Friend of yours?'

'I can't stand the sight of her,' said Lancelot vehemently.

'Then,' said Scollop, 'I may speak frankly. I think she's a pill.'

'A blister,' said Worple.

'A boil and a disease,' said Scollop, summing up.

Lancelot laughed hackingly.

'You have described her to a nicety. She stands for everything most alien to my artist soul. She gives me a pain in the neck. I'm going to marry her.'

'What!' cried Scollop.

'But you're going to marry Gladys Bingley,' said Worple.

'Webster thinks not,' said Lancelot bitterly. 'At their first meeting he weighed Gladys in the balance and found her wanting. And the moment he saw Brenda Carberry-Pirbright he stuck his tail up at right angles, uttered a cordial gargle, and rubbed his head against her leg. Then, turning, he looked at me. I could read that glance. I knew what was in his mind. From that moment he has been doing everything in his power to arrange the match.'

'But, Mulliner,' said Worple, always eager to point out the bright side, 'why should this girl want to marry a wretched, scrubby, hard-up footler like you? Have courage, Mulliner. It is simply a question of time before you repel and sicken her.'

Lancelot shook his head.

'No,' he said. 'You speak like a true friend, Worple, but you do not understand. Old Ma Carberry-Pirbright, this exhibit's mother, who chaperons her at the sittings, discovered at an early date my relationship to my Uncle Theodore, who, as you know, has got it in gobs. She knows well enough that some day I shall be a rich man. She used to know my Uncle Theodore when he was Vicar of St Botolph's in Knightsbridge, and from the very first she assumed towards me the repellent chumminess of an old family friend. She was always trying to lure me to her At Homes, her Sunday luncheons, her little dinners. Once she actually suggested that I should escort her and her beastly daughter to the Royal Academy.'

He laughed bitterly. The mordant witticisms of Lancelot Mulliner at the expense of the Royal Academy were quoted from Tite Street in the south to Holland Park in the north and eastward as far as Bloomsbury.

'To all these overtures,' resumed Lancelot, 'I remained firmly unresponsive. My attitude was from the start one of frigid aloofness. I did not actually say in so many words that I would rather be dead in a ditch than at one of her At Homes, but my manner indicated it. And I was just beginning to think I had choked her off when in crashed Webster and upset everything. Do you know how many times I have been to that infernal house in the last week? Five. Webster seemed to wish it. I tell you, I am a lost man.'

He buried his face in his hands. Scollop touched Worple on the arm, and together the two men stole silently out.

'Bad!' said Worple.

'Very bad,' said Scollop.

'It seems incredible.'

'Oh, no. Cases of this kind are, alas, by no means uncommon among those who, like Mulliner, possess to a marked degree the highly-strung, ultra-sensitive artistic temperament. A friend of mine, a rhythmical interior decorator, once rashly consented to put his aunt's parrot up at his studio while she was away visiting friends in the north of England. She was a woman of strong evangelical views, which the bird had imbibed from her. It had a way of putting its head on one side, making a noise like some one drawing a cork from a bottle, and asking my friend if he was saved. To cut a long story short, I happened to call on him a month later and he had installed a harmonium in his studio and was singing hymns, ancient and modern, in a rich tenor, while the parrot, standing on one leg on its perch, took the bass. A very sad affair. We were all much upset about it.'

Worple shuddered.

'You appal me, Scollop! Is there nothing we can do?'

Rodney Scollop considered for a moment.

'We might wire Gladys Bingley to come home at once. She might possibly reason with the unhappy man. A woman's gentle influence . . . Yes, we could do that. Look in at the post office on your way home and send Gladys a telegram. I'll owe you for my half of it.'

In the studio they had left, Lancelot Mulliner was staring dumbly at a black shape which had just entered the room. He had the appearance of a man with his back to the wall.

'No!' he was crying. 'No! I'm dashed if I do!'

Webster continued to look at him.

'Why should I?' demanded Lancelot weakly.

Webster's gaze did not flicker.

'Oh, all right,' said Lancelot sullenly.

He passed from the room with leaden feet, and, proceeding upstairs, changed into morning clothes and a top hat. Then, with a gardenia in his buttonhole, he made his way to 11, Maxton Square, where Mrs Carberry-Pirbright was giving one of her intimate little teas ('just a few friends') to meet Clara Throckmorton Stooge, authoress of 'A Strong Man's Kiss'.

Gladys Bingley was lunching at her hotel in Antibes when Worple's telegram arrived. It occasioned her the gravest concern.

Exactly what it was all about, she was unable to gather, for emotion had made Bernard Worple rather incoherent. There were moments, reading it, when she fancied that Lancelot had met with a serious accident; others when the solution seemed to be that he had sprained his brain to such an extent that rival lunatic asylums were competing eagerly for his custom; others, again, when Worple appeared to be suggesting that he had gone into partnership with his cat to start a harem. But one fact emerged clearly. Her loved one was in serious trouble of some kind, and his best friends were agreed that only her immediate return could save him.

Gladys did not hesitate. Within half an hour of the receipt of the telegram she had packed her trunk, removed a piece of asparagus from her right eyebrow, and was negotiating for accommodation on the first train going north.

Arriving in London, her first impulse was to go straight to Lancelot. But a natural feminine curiosity urged her, before doing so, to call upon Bernard Worple and have light thrown on some of the more abstruse passages in the telegram.

Worple, in his capacity of author, may have tended towards obscurity, but, when confining himself to the spoken word, he told a plain story well and clearly. Five minutes of his society enabled Gladys to obtain a firm grasp on the salient facts, and there appeared on her face that grim, tight-lipped expression which is seen only on the faces of fiancées who have come back from a short holiday to discover that their dear one has been straying in their absence from the straight and narrow path.

'Brenda Carberry-Pirbright, eh?' said Gladys, with ominous calm. 'I'll give him Brenda Carberry-Pirbright! My gosh, if one can't go off to Antibes for the merest breather without having one's betrothed getting it up his nose and starting to act like a Mormon Elder, it begins to look a pretty tough world for a girl.'

Kind-hearted Bernard Worple did his best.

'I blame the cat,' he said. 'Lancelot, to my mind, is more sinned against than sinning. I consider him to be acting under undue influence or duress.'

'How like a man!' said Gladys. 'Shoving it all off on to an innocent cat!'

'Lancelot says it has a sort of something in its eye.'

'Well, when I meet Lancelot,' said Gladys, 'he'll find that I have a sort of something in my eye.'

She went out, breathing flame quietly through her nostrils. Worple, saddened, heaved a sigh and resumed his neo-Vorticist sculpting.

It was some five minutes later that Gladys, passing through Maxton Square on her way to Bott Street, stopped suddenly in her tracks. The sight she had seen was enough to make any fiancée do so.

Along the pavement leading to Number Eleven two figures were advancing. Or three, if you counted a morose-looking dog of a semi-Dachshund nature which preceded them, attached to a leash. One of the figures was that of Lancelot Mulliner, natty in grey herring-bone tweed and a new Homburg hat. It was he who held the leash. The other Gladys recognized from the portrait which she had seen on Lancelot's easel as that modern Du Barry, that notorious wrecker of homes and breaker-up of love-nests, Brenda Carberry-Pirbright.

The next moment they had mounted the steps of Number Eleven, and had gone in to tea, possibly with a little music.

It was perhaps an hour and a half later that Lancelot, having wrenched himself with difficulty from the lair of the Philistines, sped homeward in a swift taxi. As always after an extended *tête-à-tête* with Miss Carberry-Pirbright, he felt dazed and bewildered, as if he had been swimming in a sea of glue and had swallowed a good deal of it. All he could think of clearly was that he wanted a drink and that the materials for that drink were in the cupboard behind the chesterfield in his studio.

He paid the cab and charged in with his tongue rattling dryly against his front teeth. And there before him was Gladys Bingley, whom he had supposed far, far away.

'You!' exclaimed Lancelot.

'Yes, me!' said Gladys.

Her long vigil had not helped to restore the girl's equanimity. Since arriving at the studio she had had leisure to tap her foot three thousand, one hundred and forty-two times on the carpet, and the number of bitter smiles which had flitted across her face was nine hundred and eleven. She was about ready for the battle of the century.

She rose and faced him, all the woman in her flashing from her eyes.

'Well, you Casanova!' she said.

'You who?' said Lancelot.

'Don't say "Yoo-hoo!" to me!' cried Gladys. 'Keep that for your Brenda Carberry-Pirbrights. Yes, I know all about it, Lancelot Don Juan Henry the Eighth Mulliner! I saw you with her just now. I hear that you and she are inseparable. Bernard Worple says you said you were going to marry her.'

'You mustn't believe everything a neo-Vorticist sculptor tells you,' quavered Lancelot.

'I'll bet you're going back to dinner there to-night,' said Gladys.

She had spoken at a venture, basing the charge purely on a possessive cock of the head which she had noticed in Brenda Carberry-Pirbright at their recent encounter. There, she had said to herself at the time, had gone a girl who was about to invite – or had just invited – Lancelot Mulliner to dine quietly and take her to the pictures afterwards. But the shot went home. Lancelot hung his head.

'There was some talk of it,' he admitted.

'Ah!' exclaimed Gladys.

Lancelot's eyes were haggard.

'I don't want to go,' he pleaded. 'Honestly I don't. But Webster insists.'

'Webster!'

'Yes, Webster. If I attempt to evade the appointment, he will sit in front of me and look at me.'

'Tchah!'

'Well, he will. Ask him for yourself.'

Gladys tapped her foot six times in rapid succession on the carpet, bringing the total to three thousand, one hundred and forty-eight. Her manner had changed and was now dangerously calm.

'Lancelot Mulliner,' she said, 'you have your choice. Me, on the one hand, Brenda Carberry-Pirbright on the other. I offer you a home where you will be able to smoke in bed, spill the ashes on the floor, wear pyjamas and carpet-slippers all day and shave only on Sunday mornings. From her, what have you to hope? A house in South Kensington – possibly the Brompton Road – probably with her mother living with you. A life that will be one long round of stiff collars and tight shoes, of morning-coats and top hats.'

Lancelot quivered, but she went on remorselessly.

'You will be at home on alternate Thursdays, and will be expected to hand the cucumber sandwiches. Every day you will air the dog, till you become a confirmed dog-airer. You will dine out in Bayswater and go for the summer to Bournemouth or Dinard. Choose well, Lancelot Mulliner! I will leave you to think it over. But one last word. If by seven-thirty on the dot you have not presented yourself at 6A, Garbidge Mews ready to take me out to dinner at the Ham and Beef, I shall know what to think and shall act accordingly.'

And brushing the cigarette ashes from her chin, the girl strode haughtily from the room.

'Gladys!' cried Lancelot.

But she had gone.

For some minutes Lancelot Mulliner remained where he was, stunned. Then, insistently, there came to him the recollection that he had not had that drink. He rushed to the cupboard and produced the bottle. He uncorked it, and was pouring out a lavish stream, when a movement on the floor below him attracted his attention.

Webster was standing there, looking up at him. And in his eyes was that familiar expression of quiet rebuke.

'Scarcely what I have been accustomed to at the Deanery,' he seemed to be saying.

Lancelot stood paralysed. The feeling of being bound hand and foot, of being caught in a snare from which there was no escape, had become more poignant than ever. The bottle fell from his nerveless fingers and rolled across the floor, spilling its contents in an amber river, but he was too heavy in spirit to notice it. With a gesture such as Job might have made on discovering a new boil, he crossed to the window and stood looking moodily out.

Then, turning with a sigh, he looked at Webster again – and, looking, stood spellbound.

The spectacle which he beheld was of a kind to stun a stronger man than Lancelot Mulliner. At first, he shrank from believing his eyes. Then, slowly, came the realization that what he saw was no mere figment of a disordered imagination. This unbelievable thing was actually happening.

Webster sat crouched upon the floor beside the widening pool of whisky. But it was not horror and disgust that had caused him to crouch. He was crouched because, crouching, he could get nearer to the stuff and obtain crisper action. His tongue was moving in and out like a piston.

And then abruptly, for one fleeting instant, he stopped lapping and glanced up at Lancelot, and across his face there flitted a quick smile – so genial, so intimate, so full of jovial camaraderie, that the young man found himself automatically smiling back, and not only smiling but winking. And in answer to that wink Webster winked, too – a wholehearted, roguish wink that said as plainly as if he had spoken the words:

'How long has this been going on?'

Then with a slight hiccough he turned back to the task of getting his quick before it soaked into the floor.

Into the murky soul of Lancelot Mulliner there poured a sudden flood of sunshine. It was as if a great burden had been lifted from his shoulders. The intolerable obsession of the last two weeks had ceased to oppress him, and he felt a free man. At the eleventh hour the reprieve had come. Webster, that seeming pillar of austere virtue, was one of the boys, after all. Never again would Lancelot quail beneath his eye. He had the goods on him.

Webster, like the stag at eve, had now drunk his fill. He had left the pool of alcohol and was walking round in slow, meditative circles. From time to time he mewed tentatively, as if he were trying to say 'British Constitution'. His failure to articulate the syllables appeared to tickle him, for at the end of each attempt he would utter a slow, amused chuckle. It was at about this moment that he suddenly broke into a rhythmic dance, not unlike the old Saraband.

It was an interesting spectacle, and at any other time Lancelot would have watched it raptly. But now he was busy at his desk, writing a brief note to Mrs Carberry-Pirbright, the burden of which was that if she thought he was coming within a mile of her foul house that night or any other night she had vastly underrated the dodging powers of Lancelot Mulliner.

And what of Webster? The Demon Rum now had him in an iron grip. A lifetime of abstinence had rendered him a ready victim to the fatal fluid. He had now reached the stage when geniality gives way to belligerence. The rather foolish smile had gone from his face, and in its stead there lowered a fighting frown. For a few moments he stood on his hind legs, looking about him for a suitable adversary: then, losing all vestiges of self-control, he ran five times round the room at a high rate of speed and, falling foul of a small footstool, attacked it with the utmost ferocity, sparing neither tooth nor claw.

But Lancelot did not see him. Lancelot was not there. Lancelot was out in Bott Street, hailing a cab.

'6 A, Garbidge Mews, Fulham,' said Lancelot to the driver.

There had fallen upon the bar-parlour of the Angler's Rest one of those soothing silences which from time to time punctuate the nightly feasts of Reason and flows of Soul in that cosy resort. It was broken by a Whisky and Splash.

'I've been thinking a lot,' said the Whisky and Splash, addressing Mr Mulliner, 'about that cat of yours, that Webster.'

'Has Mr Mulliner got a cat named Webster?' asked a Small Port who had just rejoined our little circle after an absence of some days.

The Sage of the bar-parlour shook his head smilingly.

'Webster,' he said, 'did not belong to me. He was the property of the Dean of Bolsover who, on being raised to a bishopric and sailing from England to take up his episcopal duties at his See of Bongo-Bongo in West Africa, left the animal in the care of his nephew, my cousin Edward's son Lancelot, the artist. I was telling these gentlemen the other evening how Webster for a time completely revolutionized Lancelot's life. His early upbringing at the Deanery had made him austere and censorious, and he exerted on my cousin's son the full force of a powerful and bigoted personality. It was as if Savonarola or some minor prophet had suddenly been introduced into the carefree, Bohemian atmosphere of the studio.'

'He stared at Lancelot and unnerved him,' explained a Pint of Bitter.

'He made him shave daily and knock off smoking,' added a Lemon Sour.

'He thought Lancelot's fiancée, Gladys Bingley, worldly,' said a Rum and Milk, 'and tried to arrange a match between him and a girl called Brenda Carberry-Pirbright.'

'But one day,' concluded Mr Mulliner, 'Lancelot discovered that the animal, for all its apparently rigid principles, had feet of clay and was no better than the rest of us. He happened to drop a bottle of alcoholic liquor and the cat drank deeply of its contents and made a sorry exhibition of itself, with the result that the spell was, of course, instantly broken. What aspect of the story of Webster,' he asked the Whisky and Splash, 'has been engaging your thoughts?'

'The psychological aspect,' said the Whisky and Splash. 'As I see it, there is a great psychological drama in this cat. I visualize his higher and lower selves warring. He has taken the first false step, and what will be the issue? Is this new, demoralizing atmosphere into which he has been plunged to neutralize the pious teachings of early kittenhood at the Deanery? Or will sound churchmanship prevail and keep him the cat he used to be?'

'If,' said Mr Mulliner, 'I am right in supposing that you want to know what happened to Webster at the conclusion of the story I related the other evening, I can tell you. There was nothing that you could really call a war between his higher and lower selves. The lower self won hands down. From the moment when he went on that first majestic toot this once saintly cat became a Bohemian of Bohemians. His days started early and finished late, and were a mere welter of brawling and loose gallantry. As early as the end of the second week his left ear had been reduced through incessant gang-warfare to a mere tattered scenario and his battle-cry had become as familiar to the denizens of Bott Street, Chelsea, as the yodel of the morning milkman.'

The Whisky and Splash said it reminded him of some great Greek tragedy. Mr Mulliner said yes, there were points of resemblance.

'And what,' enquired the Rum and Milk, 'did Lancelot think of all this?'

'Lancelot,' said Mr Mulliner, 'had the easy live-and-let-live creed of the artist. He was indulgent towards the animal's excesses. As he said to Gladys Bingley one evening, when she was bathing Webster's right eye in a boric solution, cats will be cats. In fact, he would scarcely have given a thought to the matter had there not arrived one morning from his uncle a wireless message, dispatched in mid-ocean, announcing that he had resigned his bishopric for reasons of health and would shortly be back in England once more. The communication ended with the words: "All my best to Webster."'

If you recall the position of affairs between Lancelot and the Bishop of Bongo-Bongo, as I described them the other night (said Mr Mulliner), you will not need to be told how deeply this news affected the young man. It was a bomb-shell. Lancelot, though earning enough by his brush to support himself, had been relying on touching his uncle for that extra bit which would enable him to marry Gladys Bingley. And when he had been placed *in loco parentis* to Webster, he had considered this touch a certainty. Surely, he told himself, the most ordinary gratitude would be sufficient to cause his uncle to unbelt.

But now what?

'You saw that wireless,' said Lancelot, agitatedly discussing the matter with Gladys. 'You remember the closing words: "All my best to Webster." Uncle Theodore's first act on landing in England will undoubtedly be to hurry here for a sacred reunion with this cat. And what will he find? A feline plug-ugly. A gangster. The Big Shot of Bott Street. Look at the animal now,' said Lancelot, waving a distracted hand at the cushion where it lay. 'Run your eye over him. I ask you!'

Certainly Webster was not a natty spectacle. Some tough cats from the public-house on the corner had recently been trying to muscle in on his personal dust-bin, and, though he had fought them off, the affair had left its mark upon him. A further section had been removed from his already abbreviated ear, and his once sleek flanks were short of several patches of hair. He looked like the late Legs Diamond after a social evening with a few old friends.

'What,' proceeded Lancelot, writhing visibly, 'will Uncle Theodore say on beholding that wreck? He will put the entire blame on me. He will insist that it was I who dragged that fine spirit down into the mire. And phut will go any chance I ever had of getting into his ribs for a few hundred quid for honeymoon expenses.'

Gladys Bingley struggled with a growing hopelessness.

'You don't think a good wig-maker could do something?'

'A wig-maker might patch on a little extra fur,' admitted Lancelot, 'but how about that ear?'

'A facial surgeon?' suggested Gladys.

Lancelot shook his head.

'It isn't merely his appearance,' he said. 'It's his entire personality. The poorest reader of character, meeting Webster now, would recognize him for what he is – a hard egg and a bad citizen.'

'When do you expect your uncle?' asked Gladys, after a pause.

'At any moment. He must have landed by this time. I can't understand why he has not turned up.'

At this moment there sounded from the passage outside the *plop* of a letter falling into the box attached to the front door. Lancelot went listlessly out. A few moments later Gladys heard him utter a surprised exclamation, and he came hurrying back, a sheet of note-paper in his hand.

'Listen to this,' he said. 'From Uncle Theodore.'

'Is he in London?'

'No. Down in Hampshire, at a place called Widdrington Manor. And the great point is that he does not want to see Webster yet.'

'Why not?'

'I'll read you what he says.'

And Lancelot proceeded to do so, as follows:

> 'Widdrington Manor,
> 'Bottleby-in-the-Vale,
> 'Hants.

'MY DEAR LANCELOT,

'You will doubtless be surprised that I have not hastened to greet you immediately upon my return to these shores. The explanation is that I am being entertained at the above address by Lady Widdrington, widow of the late Sir George Widdrington, C.B.E., and her mother, Mrs Pulteney-Banks, whose acquaintance I made on shipboard during my voyage home.

'I find our English countryside charming after the somewhat desolate environment of Bongo-Bongo, and am enjoying a pleasant and restful visit. Both Lady Widdrington and her mother are kindness itself, especially the former, who is my constant companion on every country ramble. We have a strong bond in our mutual love of cats.

'And this, my dear boy, brings me to the subject of Webster. As you can readily imagine, I am keenly desirous of seeing him once more and noting all the evidences of the loving care which, I have no doubt, you have lavished upon him in my absence, but I do not wish you to forward him to me here. The fact is, Lady Widdrington, though a charming woman, seems entirely lacking in discrimination in the matter of cats. She owns and is devoted to a quite impossible orange-coloured animal of the name of Percy, whose society could not but prove distasteful to one of Webster's high principles. When I tell you that only last night this Percy was engaging in personal combat – quite obviously from the worst motives – with a large tortoiseshell beneath my very window, you will understand what I mean.

'My refusal to allow Webster to join me here is, I fear, puzzling my kind hostess, who knows how greatly I miss him, but I must be firm.

'Keep him, therefore, my dear Lancelot, until I call in person, when I shall remove him to the quiet rural retreat where I plan to spend the evening of my life.

'With every good wish to you both,

'Your affectionate uncle,

'THEODORE.'

Gladys Bingley had listened intently to this letter, and as Lancelot came to the end of it she breathed a sigh of relief.

'Well, that gives us a bit of time,' she said.

'Yes,' agreed Lancelot. 'Time to see if we can't awake in this animal some faint echo of its old self-respect. From to-day Webster goes into monastic seclusion. I shall take him round to the vet.'s, with instructions that he be forced to lead the simple life. In those pure surroundings, with no temptations, no late nights, plain food and a strict milk diet, he may become himself again.'

'"The Man Who Came Back",' said Gladys.

'Exactly,' said Lancelot.

And so for perhaps two weeks something approaching tranquillity reigned once more in my cousin Edward's son's studio in Bott Street, Chelsea. The veterinary surgeon issued encouraging reports. He claimed a distinct improvement in Webster's character and appearance, though he added that he would still not care to meet him at night in a lonely alley. And then one morning there arrived from his Uncle Theodore a telegram which caused the young man to knit his brows in bewilderment.

It ran thus:

'On receipt of this come immediately Widdrington Manor prepared for indefinite visit period Circumstances comma I regret to say comma necessitate innocent deception semi-colon so will you state on arrival that you are my legal representative and have come to discuss important family matters with me period Will explain fully when see you comma but rest assured comma my dear boy comma that would not ask this were it not absolutely essential period Do not fail me period Regards to Webster.'

Lancelot finished reading this mysterious communication, and looked at Gladys with raised eyebrows. There is unfortunately in most artists a material streak which leads them to place an unpleasant interpretation on telegrams like this. Lancelot was no exception to the rule.

'The old boy's been having a couple,' was his verdict.

Gladys, a woman and therefore more spiritual, demurred.

'It sounds to me,' she said, 'more as if he had gone off his onion. Why should he want you to pretend to be a lawyer?'

'He says he will explain fully.'

'And how *do* you pretend to be a lawyer?'

Lancelot considered.

'Lawyers cough dryly, I know that,' he said. 'And then I suppose one would put the tips of the fingers together a good deal and talk about Rex *v.* Biggs Ltd and torts and malfeasances and so forth. I think I could give a reasonably realistic impersonation.'

'Well, if you're going, you'd better start practising.'

'Oh, I'm going all right,' said Lancelot. 'Uncle Theodore is evidently in trouble of some kind, and my place is by his side. If all goes well, I might be able to bite his ear before he sees Webster. About how much ought we to have in order to get married comfortably?'

'At least five hundred.'

'I will bear it in mind,' said Lancelot, coughing dryly and putting the tips of his fingers together.

Lancelot had hoped, on arriving at Widdrington Manor, that the first person he met would be his Uncle Theodore, explaining fully. But when the butler ushered him into the drawing-room only Lady Widdrington, her mother Mrs Pulteney-Banks, and her cat Percy were present. Lady Widdrington shook hands,

Mrs Pulteney-Banks bowed from the arm-chair in which she sat swathed in shawls, but when Lancelot advanced with the friendly intention of tickling the cat Percy under the right ear, he gave the young man a cold, evil look out of the corner of his eye and, backing a pace, took an inch of skin off his hand with one well-judged swipe of a steel-pronged paw.

Lady Widdrington stiffened.

'I'm afraid Percy does not like you,' she said in a distant voice.

'They know, they know!' said Mrs Pulteney-Banks darkly. She knitted and purled a moment, musing. 'Cats are cleverer than we think,' she added.

Lancelot's agony was too keen to permit him even to cough dryly. He sank into a chair and surveyed the little company with watering eyes.

They looked to him a hard bunch. Of Mrs Pulteney-Banks he could see little but a cocoon of shawls, but Lady Widdrington was right out in the open, and Lancelot did not like her appearance. The chatelaine of Widdrington Manor was one of those agate-eyed, purposeful, tweed-clad women of whom rural England seems to have a monopoly. She was not unlike what he imagined Queen Elizabeth must have been in her day. A determined and vicious specimen. He marvelled that even a mutual affection for cats could have drawn his gentle uncle to such a one.

As for Percy, he was pure poison. Orange of body and inky-black of soul, he lay stretched out on the rug, exuding arrogance and hate. Lancelot, as I have said, was tolerant of toughness in cats, but there was about this animal none of Webster's jolly, whole-hearted, swashbuckling rowdiness. Webster was the sort of cat who would charge, roaring and ranting, to dispute with some rival the possession of a decaying sardine, but there was no more vice in him than in the late John L. Sullivan. Percy, on the other hand, for all his sleek exterior, was mean and bitter. He had no music in his soul, and was fit for treasons, stratagems and spoils. One could picture him stealing milk from a sick tabby.

Gradually the pain of Lancelot's wound began to abate, but it was succeeded by a more spiritual discomfort. It was plain to him that the recent episode had made a bad impression on the two women. They obviously regarded him with suspicion and dislike. The atmosphere was frigid, and conversation proceeded jerkily. Lancelot was glad when the dressing-gong sounded and he could escape to his room.

He was completing the tying of his tie when the door opened and the Bishop of Bongo-Bongo entered.

'Lancelot, my boy!' said the Bishop.

'Uncle!' cried Lancelot.

They clasped hands. More than four years had passed since these two had met, and Lancelot was shocked at the other's appearance. When last he had seen him, at the dear old deanery, his Uncle Theodore had been a genial, robust man who wore his gaiters with an air. Now, in some subtle way, he seemed to have shrunk. He looked haggard and hunted. He reminded Lancelot of a rabbit with a good deal on its mind.

The Bishop had moved to the door. He opened it and glanced along the passage. Then he closed it and tip-toeing back, spoke in a cautious undertone.

'It was good of you to come, my dear boy,' he said.

'Why, of course I came,' replied Lancelot heartily. 'Are you in trouble of some kind, Uncle Theodore?'

'In the gravest trouble,' said the Bishop, his voice a mere whisper. He paused for a moment. 'You have met Lady Widdrington?'

'Yes.'

'Then when I tell you that, unless ceaseless vigilance is exercised, I shall undoubtedly propose marriage to her, you will appreciate my concern.'

Lancelot gaped.

'But why do you want to do a potty thing like that?'

The Bishop shivered.

'I do not want to do it, my boy,' he said. 'Nothing is further from my wishes. The salient point, however, is that Lady Widdrington and her mother want me to do it, and you must have seen for yourself that they are strong, determined women. I fear the worst.'

He tottered to a chair and dropped into it, shaking. Lancelot regarded him with affectionate pity.

'When did this start?' he asked.

'On board ship,' said the Bishop. 'Have you ever made an ocean voyage, Lancelot?'

'I've been to America a couple of times.'

'That can scarcely be the same thing,' said the Bishop, musingly. 'The transatlantic trip is so brief, and you do not get those nights of tropic moon. But even on your voyages to America you must have noticed the peculiar attitude towards the opposite sex induced by the salt air.'

'They all look good to you at sea,' agreed Lancelot.

'Precisely,' said the Bishop. 'And during a voyage, especially at night, one finds oneself expressing oneself with a certain warmth which even at the time one tells oneself is injudicious. I fear that on board the liner with Lady Widdrington, my dear boy, I rather let myself go.'

Lancelot began to understand.

'You shouldn't have come to her house,' he said.

'When I accepted the invitation, I was, if I may use a figure of speech, still under the influence. It was only after I had been here some ten days that I awoke to the realization of my peril.'

'Why didn't you leave?'

The Bishop groaned softly.

'They would not permit me to leave. They countered every excuse. I am virtually a prisoner in this house, Lancelot. The other day I said that I had urgent business with my legal adviser and that this made it imperative that I should proceed instantly to the metropolis.'

'That should have worked,' said Lancelot.

'It did not. It failed completely. They insisted that I invite my legal adviser down here where my business could be discussed in the calm atmosphere of the Hampshire countryside. I endeavoured to reason with them, but they were firm. You do not know how firm women can be,' said the Bishop, shivering, 'till you have placed yourself in my unhappy position. How well I appreciate now that powerful image of Shakespeare's – the one about grappling with hoops of steel. Every time I meet Lady Widdrington, I can feel those hoops drawing me ever closer to her. And the woman repels me even as that cat of hers repels me. Tell me, my boy, to turn for an instant to a pleasanter subject, how is my dear Webster?'

Lancelot hesitated.

'Full of beans,' he said.

'He is on a diet?' asked the Bishop anxiously. 'The doctor has ordered vegetarianism?'

'Just an expression,' explained Lancelot, 'to indicate robustness.'

'Ah!' said the Bishop, relieved. 'And what disposition have you made of him in your absence? He is in good hands, I trust?'

'The best,' said Lancelot. 'His host is the ablest veterinary in London – Doctor J. G. Robinson of 9 Bott Street, Chelsea, a man not only skilled in his profession but of the highest moral tone.'

'I knew I could rely on you to see that all was well with him,' said the Bishop emotionally. 'Otherwise, I should have shrunk from asking you to leave London and come here – strong shield of defence though you will be to me in my peril.'

'But what use can I be to you?' said Lancelot, puzzled.

'The greatest,' the Bishop assured him. 'Your presence will be invaluable. You must keep the closest eye upon Lady Widdrington and myself, and whenever you observe us wandering off together – she is assiduous in her efforts to induce me to visit the rose-garden in her company, for example – you must come hurrying up and detach me with the ostensible purpose of discussing legal matters. By these means we may avert what I had come to regard as the inevitable.'

'I understand thoroughly,' said Lancelot. 'A jolly good scheme. Rely on me.'

'The ruse I have outlined,' said the Bishop regretfully, 'involves, as I hinted in my telegram, a certain innocent deception, but at times like this one cannot afford to be too nice in one's methods. By the way, under what name did you make your appearance here?'

'I used my own.'

'I would have preferred Polkinghorne or Gooch or Withers,' said the Bishop pensively. 'They sound more legal. However, that is a small matter. The essential thing is that I may rely on you to – er – to—?'

'To stick around?'

'Exactly. To adhere. From now on, my boy, you must be my constant shadow. And if, as I trust, our efforts are rewarded, you will not find me ungrateful. In the course of a lifetime I have contrived to accumulate no small supply of this world's goods, and if there is any little venture or enterprise for which you require a certain amount of capital—'

'I am glad,' said Lancelot, 'that you brought this up, Uncle Theodore. As it so happens, I am badly in need of five hundred pounds – and could, indeed, do with a thousand.'

The Bishop grasped his hand.

'See me through this ordeal, my dear boy,' he said, 'and you shall have it. For what purpose do you require this money?'

'I want to get married.'

'Ugh!' said the Bishop, shuddering strongly. 'Well, well,' he went on, recovering himself, 'it is no affair of mine. No doubt you know your own mind best. I must confess, however, that the mere mention of the holy state occasions in me an indefinable sinking feeling. But then, of course, you are not proposing to marry Lady Widdrington.'

'And nor,' cried Lancelot heartily, 'are you, uncle – not while I'm around. Tails up, Uncle Theodore, tails up!'

'Tails up!' repeated the Bishop dutifully, but he spoke the words without any real ring of conviction in his voice.

It was fortunate that, in the days which followed, my cousin Edward's son Lancelot was buoyed up not only by the prospect of collecting a thousand pounds, but also by a genuine sympathy and pity for a well-loved uncle. Otherwise, he must have faltered and weakened.

To a sensitive man – and all artists are sensitive – there are few things more painful than the realization that he is an unwelcome guest. And not even if he had had the vanity of a Narcissus could Lancelot have persuaded himself that he was *persona grata* at Widdrington Manor.

The march of civilization has done much to curb the natural ebullience of woman. It has brought to her the power of self-restraint. In emotional crises nowadays women seldom give physical expression to their feelings; and neither Lady Widdrington nor her mother, the aged Mrs Pulteney-Banks, actually struck Lancelot or spiked him with a knitting-needle. But there were moments when they seemed only by a miracle of strong will to check themselves from such manifestations of dislike.

As the days went by, and each day the young man skilfully broke up a promising *tête-à-tête*, the atmosphere grew more tense and electric. Lady Widdrington spoke dreamily of the excellence of the train service between Bottleby-in-the-Vale and London, paying a particularly marked tribute to the 8.45 a.m. express. Mrs Pulteney-Banks mumbled from among her shawls of great gowks – she did not specify more exactly, courteously refraining from naming names – who spent their time idling in the country (where they were not wanted) when their true duty and interest lay in the metropolis. The cat Percy, by word and look, continued to affirm his low opinion of Lancelot.

And, to make matters worse, the young man could see that his principal's *morale* was becoming steadily lowered. Despite the uniform success of their manœuvres, it was evident that the strain was proving too severe for the Bishop. He was plainly cracking. A settled hopelessness had crept into his demeanour. More and more had he come to resemble a rabbit who, fleeing from a stoat, draws no cheer from the reflection that he is all right so far, but flings up his front paws in a gesture of despair, as if to ask what profit there can be in attempting to evade the inevitable.

And, at length, one night when Lancelot had switched off his light and composed himself for sleep, it was switched on again and he perceived his uncle standing by the bedside, with a haggard expression on his fine features.

At a glance Lancelot saw that the good old man had reached breaking-point.

'Something the matter, uncle?' he asked.

'My boy,' said the Bishop, 'we are undone.'

'Oh, surely not?' said Lancelot, as cheerily as his sinking heart would permit.

'Undone,' repeated the Bishop hollowly. 'To-night Lady Widdrington specifically informed me that she wishes you to leave the house.'

Lancelot drew in his breath sharply. Natural optimist though he was, he could not minimize the importance of this news.

'She has consented to allow you to remain for another two days, and then the butler has instructions to pack your belongings in time for the eight-forty-five express.'

'H'm!' said Lancelot.

'H'm, indeed,' said the Bishop. 'This means that I shall be left alone and defenceless. And even with you sedulously watching over me it has been a very near thing once or twice. That afternoon in the summer-house!'

'And that day in the shrubbery,' said Lancelot. There was a heavy silence for a moment.

'What are you going to do?' asked Lancelot.

'I must think...think,' said the Bishop. 'Well, good night, my boy.'

He left the room with bowed head, and Lancelot, after a long period of wakeful meditation, fell into a fitful slumber.

From this he was aroused some two hours later by an extraordinary commotion somewhere outside his room. The noise appeared to proceed from the hall, and, donning a dressing-gown, he hurried out.

A strange spectacle met his eyes. The entire numerical strength of Widdrington Manor seemed to have assembled in the hall. There was Lady Widdrington in a mauve *négligé*, Mrs Pulteney-Banks in a system of shawls, the butler in pyjamas, a footman or two, several maids, the odd-job man, and the boy who cleaned the shoes. They were gazing in manifest astonishment at the Bishop of Bongo-Bongo, who stood, fully clothed, near the front door, holding in one hand an umbrella, in the other a bulging suit-case.

In a corner sat the cat, Percy, swearing in a quiet undertone.

As Lancelot arrived the Bishop blinked and looked dazedly about him.

'Where am I?' he said.

Willing voices informed him that he was at Widdrington Manor, Bottleby-in-the-Vale, Hants, the butler going so far as to add the telephone number.

'I think,' said the Bishop, 'I must have been walking in my sleep.'

'Indeed?' said Mrs Pulteney-Banks, and Lancelot could detect the dryness in her tone.

'I am sorry to have been the cause of robbing the household of its well-earned slumber,' said the Bishop nervously. 'Perhaps it would be best if I now retired to my room.'

'Quite,' said Mrs Pulteney-Banks, and once again her voice crackled dryly.

'I'll come and tuck you up,' said Lancelot.

'Thank you, my boy,' said the Bishop.

Safe from observation in his bedroom, the Bishop sank wearily on the bed, and allowed the umbrella to fall hopelessly to the floor.

'It is Fate,' he said. 'Why struggle further?'

'What happened?' asked Lancelot.

'I thought matters over,' said the Bishop, 'and decided that my best plan would be to escape quietly under cover of the night. I had intended to wire to Lady Widdrington on the morrow that urgent matters of personal importance had necessitated a sudden visit to London. And just as I was getting the front door open I trod on that cat.'

'Percy?'

'Percy,' said the Bishop bitterly. 'He was prowling about in the hall, on who knows what dark errand. It is some small satisfaction to me in my distress to recall that I must have flattened out his tail properly. I came down on it with my full weight, and I am not a slender man. Well,' he said, sighing drearily, 'this is the end. I give up. I yield.'

'Oh, don't say that, uncle.'

'I do say that,' replied the Bishop, with some asperity. 'What else is there to say?'

It was a question which Lancelot found himself unable to answer. Silently he pressed the other's hand, and walked out.

In Mrs Pulteney-Banks's room, meanwhile, an earnest conference was taking place.

'Walking in his sleep, indeed!' said Mrs Pulteney-Banks.

Lady Widdrington seemed to take exception to the older woman's tone.

'Why shouldn't he walk in his sleep?' she retorted.

'Why should he?'

'Because he was worrying.'

'Worrying!' sniffed Mrs Pulteney-Banks.

'Yes, worrying,' said Lady Widdrington, with spirit. 'And I know why. You don't understand Theodore as I do.'

'As slippery as an eel,' grumbled Mrs Pulteney-Banks. 'He was trying to sneak off to London.'

'Exactly,' said Lady Widdrington. 'To his cat. You don't understand what it means to Theodore to be separated from his cat. I have noticed for a long time that he was restless and ill at ease. The reason is obvious. He is pining for Webster. I know what it is myself. That time when Percy was lost for two days I nearly went off my head. Directly after breakfast to-morrow I shall wire to Doctor Robinson of Bott Street, Chelsea, in whose charge Webster now is, to send him down here by the first train. Apart from anything else, he will be nice company for Percy.'

'Tchah!' said Mrs Pulteney-Banks.

'What do you mean, Tchah?' demanded Lady Widdrington.

'I mean Tchah,' said Mrs Pulteney-Banks.

An atmosphere of constraint hung over Widdrington Manor throughout the following day. The natural embarrassment of the Bishop was increased by the attitude of Mrs Pulteney-Banks, who had contracted a habit of looking at him over her zareba of shawls and sniffing meaningly. It was with relief that towards the middle of the afternoon he accepted Lancelot's suggestion that they should repair to the study and finish up what remained of their legal business.

The study was on the ground floor, looking out on pleasant lawns and shrubberies. Through the open window came the scent of summer flowers. It was a scene which should have soothed the most bruised soul, but the Bishop was plainly unable to draw refreshment from it. He sat with his head in his hands, refusing all Lancelot's well-meant attempts at consolation.

'Those sniffs!' he said, shuddering, as if they still rang in his ears. 'What meaning they held! What a sinister significance!'

'She may just have got a cold in the head,' urged Lancelot.

'No. The matter went deeper than that. They meant that that terrible old woman saw through my subterfuge last night. She read me like a book. From now on there will be added vigilance. I shall not be permitted out of their sight, and the end can be only a question of time. Lancelot, my boy,' said the Bishop, extending a trembling hand pathetically towards his nephew, 'you are a young man on the threshold of life. If you wish that life to be a happy one, always remember this: when on an ocean voyage, never visit the boat-deck after dinner. You will be tempted. You will say to yourself that the lounge is stuffy and that the cool breezes will correct that replete feeling which so many of us experience after the evening meal . . . you will think how pleasant it must be up there, with the rays of the moon turning the waves to molten silver . . . but don't go, my boy, don't go!'

'Right-ho, uncle,' said Lancelot soothingly.

The Bishop fell into a moody silence.

'It is not merely,' he resumed, evidently having followed some train of thought, 'that, as one of Nature's bachelors, I regard the married state with alarm and concern. It is the peculiar conditions of my tragedy that render me distraught. My lot once linked to that of Lady Widdrington, I shall never see Webster again.'

'Oh, come, uncle. This is morbid.'

The Bishop shook his head.

'No,' he said. 'If this marriage takes place, my path and Webster's must divide. I could not subject that pure cat to life at Widdrington Manor, a life involving, as it would, the constant society of the animal Percy. He would be contaminated. You know Webster, Lancelot. He has been your companion – may I not almost say your mentor? – for months. You know the loftiness of his ideals.'

For an instant, a picture shot through Lancelot's mind – the picture of Webster, as he had seen him only a brief while since – standing in the yard with the backbone of a herring in his mouth, crooning a war-song at the alley cat from whom he had stolen the *bonne-bouche*. But he replied without hesitation.

'Oh, rather.'

'They are very high.'

'Extremely high.'

'And his dignity,' said the Bishop. 'I deprecate a spirit of pride and self-esteem, but Webster's dignity was not tainted with those qualities. It rested on a clear conscience and the knowledge that, even as a kitten, he had never permitted his feet to stray. I wish you could have seen Webster as a kitten, Lancelot.'

'I wish I could, uncle.'

'He never played with balls of wool, preferring to sit in the shadow of the cathedral wall, listening to the clear singing of the choir as it melted on the sweet stillness of the summer day. Even then you could see that deep thoughts exercised his mind. I remember once...'

But the reminiscence, unless some day it made its appearance in the good old man's memoirs, was destined to be lost to the world. For at this moment the door opened and the butler entered. In his arms he bore a hamper, and from this hamper there proceeded the wrathful ejaculations of a cat who has had a long train-journey under constricted conditions and is beginning to ask what it is all about.

'Bless my soul!' cried the Bishop, startled.

A sickening sensation of doom darkened Lancelot's soul. He had recognized that voice. He knew what was in that hamper.

'Stop!' he exclaimed. 'Uncle Theodore, don't open that hamper!'

But it was too late. Already the Bishop was cutting the strings with a hand that trembled with eagerness. Chirruping noises proceeded from him. In his eyes was the wild gleam seen only in the eyes of cat-lovers restored to their loved one.

'Webster!' he called in a shaking voice.

And out of the hamper shot Webster, full of strange oaths. For a moment he raced about the room, apparently searching for the man who had shut him up in the thing, for there was flame in his eye. Becoming calmer, he sat down and began to lick himself, and it was then for the first time that the Bishop was enabled to get a steady look at him.

Two weeks' residence at the vet.'s had done something for Webster, but not enough. Not, Lancelot felt agitatedly, nearly enough. A mere fortnight's seclusion cannot bring back fur to lacerated skin; it cannot restore to a chewed ear that extra inch which makes all the difference. Webster had gone to Doctor Robinson looking as if he had just been caught in machinery of some kind, and that was how, though in a very slightly modified degree, he looked now. And at the sight of him the Bishop uttered a sharp, anguished cry. Then, turning on Lancelot, he spoke in a voice of thunder.

'So this, Lancelot Mulliner, is how you have fulfilled your sacred trust!'

Lancelot was shaken, but he contrived to reply.

'It wasn't my fault, uncle. There was no stopping him.'

'Pshaw!'

'Well, there wasn't,' said Lancelot. 'Besides, what harm is there in an occasional healthy scrap with one of the neighbours? Cats will be cats.'

'A sorry piece of reasoning,' said the Bishop, breathing heavily.

'Personally,' Lancelot went on, though speaking dully, for he realized how hopeless it all was, 'if I owned Webster, I should be proud of him. Consider his record,' said Lancelot, warming a little as he proceeded. 'He comes to Bott Street without so much as a single fight under his belt, and, despite this inexperience, shows himself possessed of such genuine natural talent that in two weeks he has every cat for streets around jumping walls and climbing lamp-posts at the mere sight of him. I wish,' said Lancelot, now carried away by his theme, 'that you could have seen him clean up a puce-coloured Tom from Number Eleven. It was the finest sight I have ever witnessed. He was conceding pounds to this animal, who, in addition, had a reputation extending as far afield as the Fulham Road. The first round was even, with the exchanges perhaps a shade in favour of his opponent. But when the gong went for Round Two . . .'

The Bishop raised his hand. His face was drawn.

'Enough!' he cried. 'I am inexpressibly grieved. I . . .'

He stopped. Something had leaped upon the window-sill at his side, causing him to start violently. It was the cat Percy who, hearing a strange feline voice, had come to investigate.

There were days when Percy, mellowed by the influence of cream and the sunshine, could become, if not agreeable, at least free from active venom. Lancelot had once seen him actually playing with a ball of paper. But it was evident immediately that this was not one of those days. Percy was plainly in evil mood. His dark soul gleamed from his narrow eyes. He twitched his tail to and fro, and for a moment stood regarding Webster with a hard sneer.

Then, wiggling his whiskers, he said something in a low voice.

Until he spoke, Webster had apparently not observed his arrival. He was still cleaning himself after the journey. But, hearing this remark, he started and looked up. And, as he saw Percy, his ears flattened and the battle-light came into his eye.

There was a moment's pause. Cat stared at cat. Then, swishing his tail to and fro, Percy repeated his statement in a louder tone. And from this point, Lancelot tells me, he could follow the conversation word for word as easily as if he had studied cat-language for years.

This, he says, is how the dialogue ran:

WEBSTER: Who, me?

PERCY: Yes, you.

WEBSTER: A what?

PERCY: You heard.

WEBSTER: Is that so?

PERCY: Yeah.

WEBSTER: Yeah?

PERCY: Yeah. Come on up here and I'll bite the rest of your ear off.

WEBSTER: Yeah? You and who else?

PERCY: Come on up here. I dare you.

WEBSTER (*flushing hotly*): You do, do you? Of all the nerve! Of all the crust! Why, I've eaten better cats than you before breakfast.

(*to Lancelot*)

Here, hold my coat and stand to one side. Now, then!

And, with this, there was a whizzing sound and Webster had advanced in full battle-order. A moment later, a tangled mass that looked like seventeen cats in close communion fell from the window-sill into the room.

A cat-fight of major importance is always a spectacle worth watching, but Lancelot tells me that, vivid and stimulating though this one promised to be, his attention was riveted not upon it, but upon the Bishop of Bongo-Bongo.

In the first few instants of the encounter the prelate's features had betrayed no emotion beyond a grievous alarm and pain. 'How art thou fallen from Heaven, oh Lucifer, Son of Morning,' he seemed to be saying as he watched his once blameless pet countering Percy's onslaught with what had the appearance of being about sixteen simultaneous legs. And then, almost abruptly, there seemed to awake in him at the same instant a passionate pride in Webster's prowess and that sporting spirit which lies so near the surface in all of us. Crimson in the face, his eyes gleaming with partisan enthusiasm, he danced round the combatants, encouraging his nominee with word and gesture.

'Capital! Excellent! Ah, stoutly struck, Webster!'

'Hook him with your left, Webster!' cried Lancelot.

'Precisely!' boomed the Bishop.

'Soak him, Webster!'

'Indubitably!' agreed the Bishop. 'The expression is new to me, but I appreciate its pith and vigour. By all means, soak him, my dear Webster.'

And it was at this moment that Lady Widdrington, attracted by the noise of battle, came hurrying into the room. She was just in time to see Percy run into a right swing and bound for the window-sill, closely pursued by his adversary. Long since Percy had begun to realize that, in inviting this encounter, he had gone out of his class and come up against something hot. All he wished for now was flight. But Webster's hat was still in the ring, and cries from without told that the battle had been joined once more on the lawn.

Lady Widdrington stood appalled. In the agony of beholding her pet so manifestly getting the loser's end she had forgotten her matrimonial plans. She was no longer the calm, purposeful woman who intended to lead the Bishop to the altar if she had to use chloroform; she was an outraged cat-lover, and she faced him with blazing eyes.

'What,' she demanded, 'is the meaning of this?'

The Bishop was still labouring under obvious excitement.

'That beastly animal of yours asked for it, and did Webster give it to him!'

'Did he!' said Lancelot. 'That corkscrew punch with the left!'

'That sort of quick upper-cut with the right!' cried the Bishop,

'There isn't a cat in London that could beat him.'

'In London?' said the Bishop warmly. 'In the whole of England. O admirable Webster!'

Lady Widdrington stamped a furious foot.

'I insist that you destroy that cat!'

'Which cat?'

'That cat,' said Lady Widdrington, pointing.

Webster was standing on the window-sill. He was panting slightly, and his ear was in worse repair than ever, but on his face was the satisfied smile of a victor. He moved his head from side to side, as if looking for the microphone through which his public expected him to speak a modest word or two.

'I demand that that savage animal be destroyed,' said Lady Widdrington.

The Bishop met her eye steadily.

'Madam,' he replied, 'I shall sponsor no such scheme.'

'You refuse?'

'Most certainly I refuse. Never have I esteemed Webster so highly as at this moment. I consider him a public benefactor, a selfless altruist. For years every right-thinking person must have yearned to handle that inexpressibly abominable cat of yours as Webster has just handled him, and I have no feelings towards him but those of gratitude and admiration. I intend, indeed, personally and with my own hands to give him a good plate of fish.'

Lady Widdrington drew in her breath sharply.

'You will not do it here,' she said.

She pressed the bell.

'Fotheringay,' she said in a tense, cold voice, as the butler appeared, 'the Bishop is leaving us to-night. Please see that his bags are packed for the six-forty-one.'

She swept from the room. The Bishop turned to Lancelot with a benevolent smile.

'It will just give me nice time,' he said, 'to write you that cheque, my boy.'

He stooped and gathered Webster into his arms, and Lancelot, after one quick look at them, stole silently out. This sacred moment was not for his eyes.

Some sort of smoking-concert seemed to be in progress in the large room across the passage from the bar-parlour of the Angler's Rest, and a music-loving Stout and Mild had left the door open, the better to enjoy the entertainment. By this means we had been privileged to hear Kipling's 'Mandalay', 'I'll Sing Thee Songs of Araby', 'The Midshipmite', and 'Ho, Jolly Jenkin!': and now the piano began to tinkle again and a voice broke into a less familiar number.

The words came to us faintly, but clearly:

'The days of Chivalry are dead,
Of which in stories I have read,
When knights were bold and acted kind of scrappy;
They used to take a lot of pains
And fight all day to please the Janes,
And if their dame was tickled they was happy.
But now the men are mild and meek:
They seem to have a yellow streak:
They never lay for other guys, to flatten 'em:
They think they've done a darned fine thing
If they just buy the girl a ring
Of imitation diamonds and platinum.

'Oh, it makes me sort of sad
To think about Sir Galahad
And all the knights of that romantic day:
To amuse a girl and charm her
They would climb into their armour
And jump into the fray:
They called her "Lady love",
They used to wear her little glove,
And everything that she said went:
For those were the days when a lady was a lady
And a gent was a perfect gent.'

A Ninepennyworth of Sherry sighed.
'True,' he murmured. 'Very true.'
The singer continued:

'Some night when they sat down to dine,
Sir Claude would say: "That girl of mine
Makes every woman jealous when she sees her."
Then someone else would shout: "Behave,
Thou malapert and scurvy knave,
Or I will smite thee one upon the beezer!"
And then next morning in the lists
They'd take their lances in their fists
And mount a pair of chargers, highly mettled:
And when Sir Claude, so fair and young,
Got punctured in the leg or lung,
They looked upon the argument as settled.'

The Ninepennyworth of Sherry sighed again.

'He's right,' he said. 'We live in degenerate days, gentlemen. Where now is the fine old tradition of derring-do? Where,' demanded the Ninepennyworth of Sherry with modest fervour, 'shall we find in these prosaic modern times the spirit that made the knights of old go through perilous adventures and brave dreadful dangers to do their lady's behest?'

'In the Mulliner family,' said Mr Mulliner, pausing for a moment from the sipping of his hot Scotch and lemon, 'in the clan to which I have the honour to belong, the spirit to which you allude still flourishes in all its pristine vigour. I can scarcely exemplify this better than by relating the story of my cousin's son, Mervyn, and the strawberries.'

'But I want to listen to the concert,' pleaded a Rum and Milk. 'I just heard the curate clear his throat. That always means "Dangerous Dan McGrew".'

'The story,' repeated Mr Mulliner with quiet firmness, as he closed the door, 'of my cousin's son, Mervyn, and the strawberries.'

In the circles in which the two moved (said Mr Mulliner) it had often been debated whether my cousin's son, Mervyn, was a bigger chump than my nephew Archibald – the one who, if you recall, was so good at imitating a hen laying an egg. Some took one side, some the other; but, though the point still lies open, there is no doubt that young Mervyn was quite a big enough chump for everyday use. And it was this quality in him that deterred Clarice Mallaby from consenting to become his bride.

He discovered this one night when, as they were dancing at the Restless Cheese, he put the thing squarely up to her, not mincing his words.

'Tell me, Clarice,' he said, 'why is it that you spurn a fellow's suit? I can't for the life of me see why you won't consent to marry a chap. It isn't as if I hadn't asked you often enough. Playing fast and loose with a good man's love is the way I look at it.'

And he gazed at her in a way that was partly melting and partly suggestive of the dominant male. And Clarice Mallaby gave one of those light, tinkling laughs and replied:

'Well, if you really want to know, you're such an ass.'

Mervyn could make nothing of this.

'An ass? How do you mean an ass? Do you mean a silly ass?'

'I mean a goof,' said the girl. 'A gump. A poop. A nitwit and a returned empty. Your name came up the other day in the course of conversation at home, and mother said you were a vapid and irreflective guffin, totally lacking in character and purpose.'

'Oh?' said Mervyn. 'She did, did she?'

'She did. And while it isn't often that I think along the same lines as mother, there – for once – I consider her to have hit the bull's-eye, rung the bell, and to be entitled to a cigar or coco-nut, according to choice. It seemed to me what they call the *mot juste*.'

'Indeed?' said Mervyn, nettled. 'Well, let me tell you something. When it comes to discussing brains, your mother, in my opinion, would do better to recede modestly into the background and not try to set herself up as an authority. I strongly suspect her of being the woman who was seen in Charing Cross Station the other day, asking a porter if he could direct her to Charing Cross Station. And, in the second place,' said Mervyn, 'I'll show you if I haven't got character and purpose. Set me some quest, like the knights of old, and see how quick I'll deliver the goods as per esteemed order.'

'How do you mean – a quest?'

'Why, bid me do something for you, or get something for you, or biff somebody in the eye for you. You know the procedure.'

Clarice thought for a moment. Then she said:

'All my life I've wanted to eat strawberries in the middle of winter. Get me a basket of strawberries before the end of the month and we'll take up this matrimonial proposition of yours in a spirit of serious research.'

'Strawberries?' said Mervyn.

'Strawberries.'

Mervyn gulped a little.

'Strawberries?'

'But, I say, dash it! *Strawberries?*'

'Strawberries,' said Clarice.

And then at last Mervyn, reading between the lines, saw that what she wanted was strawberries. And how he was to get any in December was more than he could have told you.

'I could do you oranges,' he said.

'Strawberries.'

'Or nuts. You wouldn't prefer a nice nut?'

'Strawberries,' said the girl firmly. 'And you're jolly lucky, my lad, not to be sent off after the Holy Grail or something, or told to pluck me a sprig of edelweiss from the top of the Alps. Mind you, I'm not saying yes and I'm not saying no, but this I will say – that if you bring me that basket of strawberries in the stated time, I shall know that there's more in you than sawdust – which the casual observer wouldn't believe – and I will reopen your case and examine it thoroughly in the light of the fresh evidence. Whereas, if you fail to deliver the fruit, I shall know that mother was right, and you can jolly well make up your mind to doing without my society from now on.'

Here she stopped to take in breath, and Mervyn, after a lengthy pause, braced himself up and managed to utter a brave laugh. It was a little roopy, if not actually hacking, but he did it.

'Right-ho,' he said. 'Right-ho. If that's the way you feel, well, to put it in a nutshell, right-ho.'

My cousin's son Mervyn passed a restless night that night, tossing on the pillow not a little, and feverishly at that. If this girl had been a shade less attractive, he told himself, he would have sent her a telegram telling her to go to the dickens. But, as it so happened, she was not; so the only thing that remained for him to do was to pull up the old socks and take a stab at the programme, as outlined. And he was sipping his morning cup of tea, when something more or less resembling an idea came to him.

He reasoned thus. The wise man, finding himself in a dilemma, consults an expert. If, for example, some knotty point of the law has arisen, he will proceed immediately in search of a legal expert, bring out his eight-and-six, and put the problem up to him. If it is a cross-word puzzle and he is stuck for the word in three letters, beginning with E and ending with U and meaning 'large Australian bird', he places the matter in the hands of the editor of the *Encyclopædia Britannica*.

And, similarly, when the question confronting him is how to collect strawberries in December, the best plan is obviously to seek out that one of his acquaintances who has the most established reputation for giving expensive parties.

This, Mervyn considered, was beyond a doubt Oofy Prosser. Thinking back, he could recall a dozen occasions when he had met chorus-girls groping their way along the street with a dazed look in their eyes, and when he had asked them what the matter was they had explained that they were merely living over again the exotic delights of the party Oofy Prosser had given last night. If anybody knew how to get strawberries in December, it would be Oofy.

He called, accordingly, at the latter's apartment, and found him in bed, staring at the ceiling and moaning in an undertone.

'Hullo!' said Mervyn. 'You look a bit red-eyed, old corpse.'

'I feel red-eyed,' said Oofy. 'And I wish, if it isn't absolutely necessary, that you wouldn't come charging in here early in the morning like this. By about ten o'clock to-night, I imagine, if I take great care of myself and keep quite quiet, I shall once more be in a position to look at gargoyles without wincing; but at the moment the mere sight of your horrible face gives me an indefinable shuddering feeling.'

'Did you have a party last night?'

'I did.'

'I wonder if by any chance you had strawberries?'

Oofy Prosser gave a sort of quiver and shut his eyes. He seemed to be wrestling with some powerful emotion. Then the spasm passed, and he spoke.

'Don't talk about the beastly things,' he said. 'I never want to see strawberries again in my life. Nor lobster, caviare, pâté de fois gras, prawns in aspic, or anything remotely resembling Bronx cocktails, Martinis, Side-Cars, Lizard's Breaths, All Quiet on the Western Fronts, and any variety of champagne, whisky, brandy, chartreuse, benedictine, and curaçoa.'

Mervyn nodded sympathetically.

'I know just how you feel, old man,' he said. 'And I hate to have to press the point. But I happen – for purposes which I will not reveal – to require about a dozen strawberries.'

'Then go and buy them, blast you,' said Oofy, turning his face to the wall.

'*Can* you buy strawberries in December?'

'Certainly. Bellamy's in Piccadilly have them.'

'Are they frightfully expensive?' asked Mervyn, feeling in his pocket and fingering the one pound, two shillings and three-pence which had got to last him to the end of the quarter when his allowance came in. 'Do they cost a fearful lot?'

'Of course not. They're dirt cheap.'

Mervyn heaved a relieved sigh.

'I don't suppose I pay more than a pound apiece – or at most, thirty shillings – for mine,' said Oofy. 'You can get quite a lot for fifty quid.'

Mervyn uttered a hollow groan.

'Don't gargle,' said Oofy. 'Or, if you must gargle, gargle outside.'

'Fifty quid?' said Mervyn.

'Fifty or a hundred, I forget which. My man attends to these things.'

Mervyn looked at him in silence. He was trying to decide whether the moment had arrived to put Oofy into circulation.

In the matter of borrowing money, my cousin's son, Mervyn, was shrewd and level-headed. He had vision. At an early date he had come to the conclusion that it would be foolish to fritter away a fellow like Oofy in a series of ten bobs and quids. The prudent man, he felt, when he has an Oofy Prosser on his list, nurses him along till he feels the time is ripe for one of those quick Send-me-two-hundred-by-messenger-old-man-or-my-head-goes-in-the-gas-oven touches. For years accordingly, he had been saving Oofy up for some really big emergency.

And the point he had to decide was: Would there ever be a bigger emergency than this? That was what he asked himself.

Then it came home to him that Oofy was not in the mood. The way it seemed to Mervyn was that, if Oofy's mother had crept to Oofy's bedside at this moment and tried to mace him for as much as five bob, Oofy would have risen and struck her with the bromo-seltzer bottle.

With a soft sigh, therefore, he gave up the idea and oozed out of the room and downstairs into Piccadilly.

Piccadilly looked pretty mouldy to Mervyn. It was full, he tells me, of people and other foul things. He wandered along for a while in a distrait way, and then suddenly out of the corner of his eye he became aware that he was in the presence of fruit. A shop on the starboard side was full of it, and he discovered that he was standing outside Bellamy's.

And what is more, there, nestling in a basket in the middle of a lot of cotton-wool and blue paper, was a platoon of strawberries.

And, as he gazed at them, Mervyn began to see how this thing could be worked with the minimum of discomfort and the maximum of profit to all concerned. He had just remembered that his maternal uncle Joseph had an account at Bellamy's.

The next moment he had bounded through the door and was in conference with one of the reduced duchesses who do the fruit-selling at this particular emporium. This one, Mervyn tells me, was about six feet high and looked down at him with large, haughty eyes in a derogatory manner – being, among other things, dressed from stem to stern in black satin. He was conscious of a slight chill, but he carried on according to plan.

'Good morning,' he said, switching on a smile and then switching it off again as he caught her eye. 'Do you sell fruit?'

If she had answered 'No,' he would, of course, have been nonplussed. But she did not. She inclined her head proudly.

'Quate,' she said.

'That's fine,' said Mervyn heartily. 'Because fruit happens to be just what I'm after.'

'Quate.'

'I want that basket of strawberries in the window.'

'Quate.'

She reached for them and started to wrap them up. She did not seem to enjoy doing it. As she tied the string, her brooding look deepened. Mervyn thinks she may have had some great love tragedy in her life.

'Send them to the Earl of Blotsam, 66A, Berkeley Square,' said Mervyn, alluding to his maternal uncle Joseph.

'Quate.'

'On second thoughts,' said Mervyn, 'no. I'll take them with me. Save trouble. Hand them over, and send the bill to Lord Blotsam.'

This, naturally, was the crux or nub of the whole enterprise. And to Mervyn's concern, his suggestion did not seem to have met with the ready acceptance for which he had hoped. He had looked for the bright smile, the courteous inclination of the head. Instead of which, the girl looked doubtful.

'You desi-ah to remove them in person?'

'Quate,' said Mervyn.

'Podden me,' said the girl, suddenly disappearing.

She was not away long. In fact, Mervyn, roaming hither and thither about the shop, had barely had time to eat three or four dates and a custard apple, when she was with him once more.

And now she was wearing a look of definite disapproval, like a duchess who has found half a caterpillar in the castle salad.

'His lordship informs me that he desi-ahs no strawberries.'

'Eh?'

'I have been in telephonic communication with his lordship and he states explicitly that he does not desi-ah strawberries.'

Mervyn gave a little at the knees, but he came back stoutly.

'Don't you listen to what he says,' he urged. 'He's always kidding. That's the sort of fellow he is. Just a great big happy schoolboy. Of course he desi-ahs strawberries. He told me so himself. I'm his nephew.'

Good stuff, he felt, but it did not seem to be getting over. He caught a glimpse of the girl's face, and it was definitely cold and hard and proud. However, he gave a careless laugh, just to show that his heart was in the right place, and seized the basket.

'Ha, ha!' he tittered lightly, and started for the street at something midway between a saunter and a gallop.

And he had not more than reached the open spaces when he heard the girl give tongue behind him.

'EEEE – EEEE – EEEE – EEEE – EEEEEE-EEEEE!' she said, in substance.

Now, you must remember that all this took place round about the hour of noon, when every young fellow is at his lowest and weakest and the need for the twelve o'clock bracer has begun to sap his morale pretty considerably. With a couple of quick cold ones under his vest, Mervyn would, no doubt, have faced the situation and carried it off with an air. He would have raised his eyebrows. He would have been nonchalant and lit a Murad. But, coming on him in his reduced condition, this fearful screech unnerved him completely.

The duchess had now begun to cry 'Stop thief!' and Mervyn, most injudiciously, instead of keeping his head and leaping carelessly into a passing taxi, made the grave strategic error of picking up his feet with a jerk and starting to run along Piccadilly.

Well, naturally, that did him no good at all. Eight hundred people appeared from nowhere, willing hands gripped his collar and the seat of his trousers, and the next thing he knew he was cooling off in Vine Street Police Station.

After that, everything was more or less of a blur. The scene seemed suddenly to change to a police-court, in which he was confronted by a magistrate who looked like an owl with a dash of weasel blood in him.

A dialogue then took place, of which all he recalls is this:

POLICEMAN: 'Earing cries of 'Stop thief!' your worship, and observing the accused running very 'earty, I apprehended 'im.

MAGISTRATE: How did he appear, when apprehended?

POLICEMAN: Very apprehensive, your worship.

MAGISTRATE: You mean he had a sort of pinched look?

(*Laughter in court.*)

POLICEMAN: It then transpired that 'e 'ad been attempting to purloin strawberries.

MAGISTRATE: He seems to have got the raspberry.

(*Laughter in court.*)

Well, what have you to say, young man?

MERVYN: Oh, ah!

MAGISTRATE: More 'owe' than 'ah', I fear.

(*Laughter in court, in which his worship joined.*)

Ten pounds or fourteen days.

Well, you can see how extremely unpleasant this must have been for my cousin's son. Considered purely from the dramatic angle, the magistrate had played him right off the stage, hogging all the comedy and getting the sympathy of the audience from the start; and, apart from that, here he was, nearing the end of the quarter, with all his allowance spent except one pound, two and threepence, suddenly called upon to pay ten pounds or go to durance vile for a matter of two weeks.

There was only one course before him. His sensitive soul revolted at the thought of languishing in a dungeon for a solid fortnight, so it was imperative that he raise the cash somewhere. And the only way of raising it that he could think of was to apply to his uncle, Lord Blotsam.

So he sent a messenger round to Berkeley Square, explaining that he was in jail and hoping his uncle was the same, and presently a letter was brought back by the butler, containing ten pounds in postal orders, the Curse of the Blotsams, a third-class ticket to Blotsam Regis in Shropshire and instructions that, as soon as they smote the fetters from his wrists, he was to take the first train there and go and stay at Blotsam Castle till further notice.

Because at the castle, his uncle said in a powerful passage, even a blasted pimply pop-eyed good-for-nothing scallywag and nincompoop like his nephew couldn't get into mischief and disgrace the family name.

And in this, Mervyn tells me, there was a good deal of rugged sense. Blotsam Castle, a noble pile, is situated at least half a dozen miles from anywhere, and the only time anybody ever succeeded in disgracing the family name, while in residence, was back in the reign of Edward the Confessor, when the then Earl of Blotsam, having lured a number of neighbouring landowners into the banqueting hall on the specious pretence of standing them mulled sack, had proceeded to murder one and all with a battle-axe – subsequently cutting their heads off and – in rather loud taste – sticking them on spikes along the outer battlements.

So Mervyn went down to Blotsam Regis and started to camp at the castle, and it was not long, he tells me, before he began to find the time hanging a little heavy on his hands. For a couple of days he managed to endure the monotony, occupying himself in carving the girl's initials on the immemorial elms with a heart round them. But on the third morning, having broken his Boy Scout pocket-knife, he was at something of a loose end. And to fill in the time he started on a moody stroll through the messuages and pleasances, feeling a good deal cast down.

After pacing hither and thither for a while, thinking of the girl Clarice, he came to a series of hothouses. And, it being extremely cold, with an east wind that went through his plus-fours like a javelin, he thought it would make an agreeable change if he were to go inside where it was warm and smoke two or perhaps three cigarettes.

And, scarcely had he got past the door, when he found he was almost entirely surrounded by strawberries. There they were, scores of them, all hot and juicy.

For a moment, he tells me, Mervyn had a sort of idea that a miracle had occurred. He seemed to remember a similar thing having happened to the Israelites in the desert – that time, he reminded me, when they were all saying to each other how well a spot of manna would go down and what a dashed shame it was they hadn't any manna and that was the slipshod way the commissariat department ran things and they wouldn't be surprised if it wasn't a case of graft in high places, and then suddenly out of a blue sky all the manna they could do with and enough over for breakfast next day.

Well, to be brief, that was the view which Mervyn took of the matter in the first flush of his astonishment.

Then he remembered that his uncle always opened the castle for the Christmas festivities, and these strawberries were, no doubt, intended for Exhibit A at some forthcoming rout or merry-making.

Well, after that, of course, everything was simple. A child would have known what to do. Hastening back to the house, Mervyn returned with a cardboard box and, keeping a keen eye out for the head-gardener, hurried in, selected about two dozen of the finest specimens, placed them in the box, ran back to the house again, reached for the railway guide, found that there was a train leaving for London in an hour, changed into town clothes, seized his top hat, borrowed the stable-boy's bicycle, pedalled to the station, and about four hours later was mounting the front-door steps of Clarice Mallaby's house in Eaton Square with the box tucked under his arm.

No, that is wrong. The box was not actually tucked under his arm, because he had left it in the train. Except for that, he had carried the thing through without a hitch.

Sturdy common sense is always a quality of the Mulliners, even of the less mentally gifted of the family. It was obvious to Mervyn that no useful end was to be gained by ringing the bell and rushing into the girl's presence, shouting 'See what I've brought you!'

On the other hand, what to do? He was feeling somewhat unequal to the swirl of events.

Once, he tells me, some years ago, he got involved in some amateur theatricals, to play the role of a butler: and his part consisted of the following lines and business:

(*Enter* JORKINS, *carrying telegram on salver.*)
    JORKINS: A telegram, m'lady.
                (*Exit* JORKINS)

and on the night in he came, full of confidence, and, having said: 'A telegram, m'lady,' extended an empty salver towards the heroine, who, having been expecting on the strength of the telegram to clutch at her heart and say: 'My God!' and tear open the envelope and crush it in nervous fingers and fall over in a swoon, was considerably taken aback, not to say perturbed.

He felt now as he had felt then.

Still, he had enough sense left to see the way out. After a couple of turns up and down the south side of Eaton Square, he came – rather shrewdly, I must confess – to the conclusion that the only person who could help him in this emergency was Oofy Prosser.

The way Mervyn sketched out the scenario in the rough, it all looked pretty plain sailing. He would go to Oofy, whom, as I told you, he had been saving up for years, and with one single impressive gesture get into his ribs for about twenty quid.

He would be losing money on the deal, of course, because he had always had Oofy scheduled for at least fifty. But that could not be helped.

Then off to Bellamy's and buy strawberries. He did not exactly relish the prospect of meeting the black satin girl again, but when love is calling these things have to be done.

He found Oofy at home, and plunged into the agenda without delay.

'Hullo, Oofy, old man!' he said. 'How are you, Oofy, old man? I say, Oofy, old man, I do like that tie you're wearing. What I call something like a tie. Quite the snappiest thing I've seen for years and years and years and years. I wish I could get ties like that. But then, of course, I haven't your exquisite taste. What I've always said about you, Oofy, old man, and what I always will say, is that you have the most extraordinary *flair* – it amounts to genius – in the selection of ties. But, then, one must bear in mind that anything would look well on you, because you have such a clean-cut, virile profile. I met a man the other day who said to me: "I didn't know Ronald Colman was in England." And I said: "He isn't." And he said: "But I saw you talking to him outside the Blotto Kitten." And I said: "That wasn't Ronald Colman. That was my old pal – the best pal any man ever had – Oofy Prosser." And he said: "Well, I never saw such a remarkable resemblance." And I said: "Yes, there is a great resemblance, only, of course, Oofy is much the better-looking." And this fellow said: "Oofy Prosser? Is that *the* Oofy Prosser, the man whose name you hear everywhere?" And I said: "Yes, and I'm proud to call him my friend. I don't suppose," I said, "there's another fellow in London in such demand. Duchesses clamour for him, and, if you ask a princess to dinner, you have to add: 'To meet Oofy Prosser,' or she won't come. This," I explained, "is because, in addition to being the handsomest and best-dressed man in Mayfair, he is famous for his sparkling wit and keen – but always kindly – repartee. And yet, in spite of all, he remains simple, unspoilt, unaffected." Will you lend me twenty quid, Oofy, old man?'

'No,' said Oofy Prosser.

Mervyn paled.

'What did you say?'

'I said No.'

'No?'

'N – ruddy – o!' said Oofy firmly.

Mervyn clutched at the mantelpiece.

'But, Oofy, old man, I need the money – need it sorely.'

'I don't care.'

It seemed to Mervyn that the only thing to do was to tell all. Clearing his throat, he started in at the beginning. He sketched the course of his great love in burning words, and brought the story up to the point where the girl had placed her order for strawberries.

'She must be cuckoo,' said Oofy Prosser.

Mervyn was respectful, but firm.

'She isn't cuckoo,' he said. 'I have felt all along that the incident showed what a spiritual nature she has. I mean to say, reaching out yearningly for the unattainable and all that sort of thing, if you know what I mean. Anyway, the broad, basic point is that she wants strawberries, and I've got to collect enough money to get her them.'

'Who is this half-wit?' asked Oofy.

Mervyn told him, and Oofy seemed rather impressed.

'I know her.' He mused awhile. 'Dashed pretty girl.'

'Lovely,' said Mervyn. 'What eyes!'

'Yes.'

'What hair!'

'Yes.'

'What a figure!'

'Yes,' said Oofy. 'I always think she's one of the prettiest girls in London.'

'Absolutely,' said Mervyn. 'Then, on second thoughts, old pal, you will lend me twenty quid to buy her strawberries?'

'No,' said Oofy.

And Mervyn could not shift him. In the end he gave it up.

'Very well,' he said. 'Oh, very well. If you won't, you won't. But, Alexander Prosser,' proceeded Mervyn, with a good deal of dignity, 'just let me tell you this. I wouldn't be seen dead in a tie like that beastly thing you're wearing. I don't like your profile. Your hair is getting thin on the top. And I heard a certain prominent society hostess say the other day that the great drawback to living in London was that a woman couldn't give so much as the simplest luncheon-party without suddenly finding that that appalling man Prosser – I quote her words – had wriggled out of the woodwork and was in her midst. Prosser, I wish you a very good afternoon!'

Brave words, of course, but, when you came right down to it, they could not be said to have got him anywhere. After the first thrill of telling Oofy what he thought of him had died away, Mervyn realized that his quandary was now greater than ever. Where was he to look for aid and comfort? He had friends, of course, but the best of them wasn't good for more than an occasional drink or possibly a couple of quid, and what use was that to a man who needed at least a dozen strawberries at a pound apiece?

Extremely bleak the world looked to my cousin's unfortunate son, and he was in sombre mood as he wandered along Piccadilly. As he surveyed the passing populace, he suddenly realized, he tells me, what these Bolshevist blokes were driving at. They had spotted – as he had spotted now – that what was wrong with the world was that all the cash seemed to be centred in the wrong hands and needed a lot of broad-minded redistribution.

Where money was concerned, he perceived, merit counted for nothing. Money was too apt to be collared by some rotten bounder or bounders, while the good and deserving man was left standing on the outside, looking in. The sight of all those expensive cars rolling along, crammed to the bulwarks with overfed males and females with fur coats and double chins, made him feel, he tells me, that he wanted to buy a red tie and a couple of bombs and start the Social Revolution. If Stalin had come along at that moment, Mervyn would have shaken him by the hand.

Well, there is, of course, only one thing for a young man to do when he feels like that. Mervyn hurried along to the club and in rapid succession drank three Martini cocktails.

The treatment was effective, as it always is. Gradually the stern, censorious mood passed, and he began to feel an optimistic glow. As the revivers slid over the larynx, he saw that all was not lost. He perceived that he had been leaving out of his reckoning that sweet, angelic pity which is such a characteristic of woman.

Take the case of a knight of old, he meant to say. Was anyone going to tell him that if a knight of old had been sent off by a damsel on some fearfully tricky quest and had gone through all sorts of perils and privations for her sake, facing dragons in black satin and risking going to chokey and what not, the girl would have given him the bird when he got back, simply because – looking at the matter from a severely technical standpoint – he had failed to bring home the gravy?

Absolutely not, Mervyn considered. She would have been most awfully braced with him for putting up such a good show and would have comforted and cosseted him.

This girl Clarice, he felt, was bound to do the same, so obviously the move now was to toddle along to Eaton Square again and explain matters to her. So he gave his hat a brush, flicked a spot of dust from his coat-sleeve, and shot off in a taxi.

All during the drive he was rehearsing what he would say to her, and it sounded pretty good to him. In his mind's eye he could see the tears coming into her gentle eyes as he told her about the Arm of the Law gripping his trouser-seat. But, when he arrived, a hitch occurred. There was a stage wait. The butler at Eaton Square told him the girl was dressing.

'Say that Mr Mulliner has called,' said Mervyn.

So the butler went upstairs, and presently from aloft there came the clear penetrating voice of his loved one telling the butler to bung Mr Mulliner into the drawing-room and lock up all the silver.

And Mervyn went into the drawing-room and settled down to wait.

It was one of those drawing-rooms where there is not a great deal to entertain and amuse the visitor. Mervyn tells me that he got a good laugh out of a photograph of the girl's late father on the mantelpiece – a heavily-whiskered old gentleman who reminded him of a burst horsehair sofa – but the rest of the appointments were on the dull side. They consisted of an album of views of Italy and a copy of Indian Love Lyrics bound in limp cloth: and it was not long before he began to feel a touch of ennui.

He polished his shoes with one of the sofa-cushions, and took his hat from the table where he had placed it and gave it another brush: but after that there seemed to be nothing in the way of intellectual occupation offering itself, so he just leaned back in a chair and unhinged his lower jaw and let it droop, and sank into a sort of coma. And it was while he was still in this trance that he was delighted to hear a dog-fight in progress in the street. He went to the window and looked out, but the thing was apparently taking place somewhere near the front door, and the top of the porch hid it from him.

Now, Mervyn hated to miss a dog-fight. Many of his happiest hours had been spent at dog-fights. And this one appeared from the sound of it to be on a more or less major scale. He ran down the stairs and opened the front door.

As his trained senses had told him, the encounter was being staged at the foot of the steps. He stood in the open doorway and drank it in. He had always maintained that you got the best dog-fights down in the Eaton Square neighbourhood, because there tough animals from the King's Road, Chelsea, district, were apt to wander in – dogs who had trained on gin and flat-irons at the local public-houses and could be relied on to give of their best.

The present encounter bore out this view. It was between a sort of *consommé* of mastiff and Irish terrier, on the one hand, and, on the other, a long-haired *macédoine* of about seven breeds of dog who had an indescribable raffish look, as if he had been mixing with the artist colony down by the river. For about five minutes it was as inspiring a contest as you could have wished to see; but at the end of that time it stopped suddenly, both principals simultaneously observing a cat at an area gate down the road and shaking hands hastily and woofing after her.

Mervyn was not a little disappointed at this abrupt conclusion to the entertainment, but it was no use repining. He started to go back into the house and was just closing the front door, when a messenger-boy appeared, carrying a parcel.

'Sign, please,' said the messenger-boy.

The lad's mistake was a natural one. Finding Mervyn standing in the doorway without a hat, he had assumed him to be the butler. He pushed the parcel into his hand, made him sign a yellow paper, and went off, leaving Mervyn with the parcel.

And Mervyn, glancing at it, saw that it was addressed to the girl – Clarice.

But it was not this that made him reel where he stood. What made him reel where he stood was the fact that on the paper outside the thing was a label with 'Bellamy & Co., Bespoke Fruitists' on it. And he was convinced, prodding it, that there was some squashy substance inside which certainly was not apples, oranges, nuts, bananas, or anything of that nature.

Mervyn lowered his shapely nose and gave a good hard sniff at the parcel. And, having done so, he reeled where he stood once more.

A frightful suspicion had shot through him.

It was not that my cousin's son was gifted beyond the ordinary in the qualities that go to make a successful detective. You would not have found him deducing anything much from footprints or cigar-ash. In fact, if this parcel had contained cigar-ash, it would have meant nothing to him. But in the circumstances anybody with his special knowledge would have been suspicious.

For consider the facts. His sniff had told him that beneath the outward wrapping of paper lay strawberries. And the only person beside himself who knew that the girl wanted strawberries was Oofy Prosser. About the only man in London able to buy strawberries at that time of year was Oofy. And Oofy's manner, he recalled, when they were talking about the girl's beauty and physique generally, had been furtive and sinister.

To rip open the paper, therefore, and take a look at the enclosed card was with Mervyn Mulliner the work of a moment.

And, sure enough, it was as he had foreseen. 'Alexander C. Prosser' was the name on the card, and Mervyn tells me he wouldn't be a bit surprised if the C. didn't stand for 'Clarence'.

His first feeling, he tells me, as he stood there staring at that card, was one of righteous indignation at the thought that any such treacherous, double-crossing hound as Oofy Prosser should have been permitted to pollute the air of London, W.1, all these years. To refuse a fellow twenty quid with one hand, and then to go and send his girl strawberries with the other, struck Mervyn as about as low-down a bit of hornswoggling as you could want.

He burned with honest wrath. And he was still burning when the last cocktail he had had at the club, which had been lying low inside him all this while, suddenly came to life and got action. Quite unexpectedly, he tells me, it began to frisk about like a young lamb, until it leaped into his head and gave him the idea of a lifetime.

What, he asked himself, was the matter with suppressing this card, freezing on to the berries, and presenting them to the girl with a modest flourish as coming from M. Mulliner, Esq? And, he answered himself, there was abso-bally-nothing the matter with it. It was a jolly sound scheme and showed what three medium dry Martinis could do.

He quivered all over with joy and elation. Standing there in the hall, he felt that there was a Providence, after all, which kept an eye on good men and saw to it that they came out on top in the end. In fact, he felt so extremely elated that he burst into song. And he had not got much beyond the first high note when he heard Clarice Mallaby giving tongue from upstairs.

'Stop it!'

'What did you say?' said Mervyn.

'I said "Stop it!" The cat's downstairs with a headache, trying to rest.'

'I say,' said Mervyn, 'are you going to be long?'

'How do you mean – long?'

'Long dressing. Because I've something I want to show you.'

'What?'

'Oh, nothing much,' said Mervyn carelessly. 'Nothing particular. Just a few assorted strawberries.'

'Eek!' said the girl. 'You don't mean you've really got them?'

'Got them?' said Mervyn. 'Didn't I say I would?'

'I'll be down in just one minute,' said the girl.

Well, you know what girls are. The minute stretched into five minutes, and the five minutes into a quarter of an hour, and Mervyn made the tour of the drawing-room, and looked at the photograph of her late father, and picked up the album of Views of Italy, and opened Indian Love Lyrics at page forty-three and shut it again, and took up the cushion and gave his shoes another rub, and brushed his hat once more, and still she didn't come.

And so, by way of something else to do, he started brooding on the strawberries for a space.

Considered purely as strawberries, he tells me, they were a pretty rickety collection, not to say spavined. They were an unhealthy whitish-pink in colour and looked as if they had just come through a lingering illness which had involved a good deal of blood-letting by means of leeches.

'They don't look much,' said Mervyn to himself.

Not that it really mattered, of course, because all the girl had told him to do was to get her strawberries, and nobody could deny that these were strawberries. C.3, though they might be, they were genuine strawberries, and from that fact there was no getting away.

Still, he did not want the dear little soul to be disappointed.

'I wonder if they have any flavour at all?' said Mervyn to himself.

Well, the first one had not. Nor had the second. The third was rather better. And the fourth was quite juicy. And the best of all, oddly enough, was the last one in the basket.

He was just finishing it when Clarice Mallaby came running in.

Well, Mervyn tried to pass it off, of course. But his efforts were not rewarded with any great measure of success. In fact, he tells me that he did not get beyond a tentative 'Oh, I say . . .' And the upshot of the whole matter was that the girl threw him out into the winter evening without so much as giving him a chance to take his hat.

Nor had he the courage to go back and fetch it later, for Clarice Mallaby stated specifically that if he dared to show his ugly face at the house again the butler had instructions to knock him down and skin him, and the butler was looking forward to it, as he had never liked Mervyn.

So there the matter rests. The whole thing has been a great blow to my cousin's son, for he considers – and rightly, I suppose – that, if you really come down to it, he failed in his quest. Nevertheless, I think that we must give him credit for the possession of the old knightly spirit to which our friend here was alluding just now.

He meant well. He did his best. And even of a Mulliner more cannot be said than that.

At the ancient and historic public-school which stands a mile or two up the river from the Angler's Rest there had recently been a change of headmasters, and our little group in the bar-parlour, naturally interested, was discussing the new appointment.

A grizzled Tankard of Stout frankly viewed it with concern. 'Benger!' he exclaimed. 'Fancy making Benger a headmaster.'

'He has a fine record.'

'Yes, but, dash it, he was at school with me.'

'One lives these things down in time,' we urged.

The Tankard said we had missed his point, which was that he could remember young Scrubby Benger in an Eton collar with jam on it, getting properly cursed by the Mathematics beak for bringing white mice into the form-room.

'He was a small, fat kid with a pink face,' proceeded the Tankard. 'I met him again only last July, and he looked just the same. I can't see him as a headmaster. I thought they had to be a hundred years old and seven feet high, with eyes of flame, and long white beards. To me, a headmaster has always been a sort of blend of Epstein's Genesis and something out of the Book of Revelations.'

Mr Mulliner smiled tolerantly.

'You left school at an early age, I imagine?'

'Sixteen. I had to go into my uncle's business.'

'Exactly,' said Mr Mulliner, nodding sagely. 'You completed your school career, in other words, before the age at which a boy, coming into personal relationship with the man up top, learns to regard him as a guide, philosopher and friend. The result is that you are suffering from the well-known Headmaster Fixation or Phobia – precisely as my nephew Sacheverell did. A rather delicate youth, he was removed by his parents from Harborough College shortly after his fifteenth birthday and educated at home by a private tutor; and I have frequently heard him assert that the Rev. J. G. Smethurst, the ruling spirit of Harborough, was a man who chewed broken bottles and devoured his young.'

'I strongly suspected my headmaster of conducting human sacrifices behind the fives-courts at the time of the full moon,' said the Tankard.

'Men like yourself and my nephew Sacheverell who leave school early,' said Mr Mulliner, 'never wholly lose these poetic boyish fancies. All their lives, the phobia persists. And sometimes this has curious results – as in the case of my nephew Sacheverell.'

It was to the terror inspired by his old headmaster (said Mr Mulliner) that I always attributed my nephew Sacheverell's extraordinary mildness and timidity. A nervous boy, the years seemed to bring him no store of self-confidence. By the time he arrived at man's estate, he belonged definitely to the class of humanity which never gets a seat on an underground train and is ill at ease in the presence of butlers, traffic policemen, and female assistants in post offices. He was the sort of young fellow at whom people laugh when the waiter speaks to them in French.

And this was particularly unfortunate, as he had recently become secretly affianced to Muriel, only daughter of Lieut.-Colonel Sir Redvers Branksome, one of the old-school type of squire and as tough an egg as ever said 'Yoicks' to a fox-hound. He had met her while she was on a visit to an aunt in London, and had endeared himself to her partly by his modest and diffident demeanour and partly by doing tricks with a bit of string, an art at which he was highly proficient.

Muriel was one of those hearty, breezy girls who abound in the hunting counties of England. Brought up all her life among confident young men who wore gaiters and smacked them with riding-crops, she had always yearned subconsciously for something different: and Sacheverell's shy, mild, shrinking personality seemed to wake the maternal in her. He was so weak, so helpless, that her heart went out to him. Friendship speedily ripened into love, with the result that one afternoon my nephew found himself definitely engaged and faced with the prospect of breaking the news to the old folks at home.

'And if you think you've got a picnic ahead of you,' said Muriel, 'forget it. Father's a gorilla. I remember when I was engaged to my cousin Bernard—'

'When you were what to your what?' gasped Sacheverell.

'Oh, yes,' said the girl. 'Didn't I tell you? I was engaged once to my cousin Bernard, but I broke it off because he tried to boss me. A little too much of the dominant male there was about old B., and I handed him his hat. Though we're still good friends. But what I was saying was that Bernard used to gulp like a seal and stand on one leg when father came along. And he's in the Guards. That just shows you. However, we'll start the thing going. I'll get you down to the Towers for a week-end, and we'll see what happens.'

If Muriel had hoped that a mutual esteem would spring up between her father and her betrothed during this week-end visit, she was doomed to disappointment. The thing was a failure from the start. Sacheverell's host did him extremely well, giving him the star guest-room, the Blue Suite, and bringing out the oldest port for his benefit, but it was plain that he thought little of the young man. The colonel's subjects were sheep (in sickness and in health), manure, wheat, mangold-wurzels, huntin', shootin' and fishin': while Sacheverell was at his best on Proust, the Russian Ballet, Japanese prints, and the Influence of James Joyce on the younger Bloomsbury novelists. There was no fusion between these men's souls. Colonel Branksome did not actually bite Sacheverell in the leg, but when you had said that you had said everything.

Muriel was deeply concerned.

'I'll tell you what it is, Dogface,' she said, as she was seeing her loved one to his train on the Monday, 'we've got off on the wrong foot. The male parent may have loved you at sight, but, if he did, he took another look and changed his mind.'

'I fear we were not exactly *en rapport*,' sighed Sacheverell. 'Apart from the fact that the mere look of him gave me a strange, sinking feeling, my conversation seemed to bore him.'

'You didn't talk about the right things.'

'I couldn't. I know so little of mangold-wurzels. Manure is a sealed book to me.'

'Just what I'm driving at,' said Muriel. 'And all that must be altered. Before you spring the tidings on father, there will have to be a lot of careful preliminary top-dressing of the soil, if you follow what I mean. By the time the bell goes for the second round and old Dangerous Dan McGrew comes out of his corner at you, breathing fire, you must have acquired a good working knowledge of Scientific Agriculture. That'll tickle him pink.'

'But how?'

'I'll tell you how. I was reading a magazine the other day, and there was an advertisement in it of a Correspondence School which teaches practically everything. You put a cross against the course you want to take and clip out the coupon and bung it in, and they do the rest. I suppose they send you pamphlets and things. So the moment you get back to London, look up this advertisement – it was in the *Piccadilly Magazine* – and write to these people and tell them to shoot the works.'

Sacheverell pondered this advice during the railway journey, and the more he pondered it the more clearly did he see how excellent it was. It offered the solution to all his troubles. There was no doubt whatever that the bad impression he had made on Colonel Branksome was due chiefly to his ignorance of the latter's pet subjects. If he were in a position to throw off a good thing from time to time on Guano or the Influence of Dip on the Younger Leicestershire Sheep, Muriel's father would unquestionably view him with a far kindlier eye.

He lost no time in clipping out the coupon and forwarding it with a covering cheque to the address given in the advertisement. And two days later a bulky package arrived, and he settled down to an intensive course of study.

By the time Sacheverell had mastered the first six lessons, a feeling of perplexity had begun to steal over him. He knew nothing, of course, of the methods of Correspondence Schools and was prepared to put his trust blindly in his unseen tutor; but it did strike him as odd that a course on Scientific Agriculture should have absolutely no mention of Scientific Agriculture in it.

Though admittedly a child in these matters, he had supposed that that was one of the first topics on which the thing would have touched.

But such was not the case. The lessons contained a great deal of advice about deep breathing and regular exercise and cold baths and Yogis and the training of the mind, but on the subject of Scientific Agriculture they were vague and elusive. They simply would not come to the point. They said nothing about sheep, nothing about manure, and from the way they avoided mangold-wurzels you might have thought they considered these wholesome vegetables almost improper.

At first, Sacheverell accepted this meekly, as he accepted everything in life. But gradually, as his reading progressed, a strange sensation of annoyance began to grip him. He found himself chafing a good deal, particularly in the mornings. And when the seventh lesson arrived and still there was this absurd coyness on the part of his instructors to come to grips with Scientific Agriculture, he decided to put up with it no longer. He was enraged. These people, he considered, were deliberately hornswoggling him. He resolved to go round and see them and put it to them straight that he was not the sort of man to be trifled with in this fashion.

The headquarters of the Leave-It-To-Us Correspondence School were in a large building off Kingsway. Sacheverell, passing through the front door like an east wind, found himself confronted by a small boy with a cold and super-cilious eye.

'Yes?' said the boy, with deep suspicion. He seemed to be a lad who distrusted his fellow-men and attributed the worst motives to their actions.

Sacheverell pointed curtly to a door on which was the legend 'Jno. B. Philbrick, Mgr'.

'I wish to see Jno. B. Philbrick, Mgr,' he said.

The boy's lip curled contemptuously. He appeared to be on the point of treating the application with silent disdain. Then he vouchsafed a single, scornful word.

'Can'tseeMrPhilbrickwithoutanappointment,' he said.

A few weeks before, a rebuff like this would have sent Sacheverell stumbling blushfully out of the place, tripping over his feet. But now he merely brushed the child aside like a feather, and strode to the inner office.

A bald-headed man with a walrus moustache was seated at the desk.

'Jno. Philbrick?' said Sacheverell brusquely.

'That is my name.'

'Then listen to me, Philbrick,' said Sacheverell. 'I paid fifteen guineas in advance for a course on Scientific Agriculture. I have here the seven lessons which you have sent me to date, and if you can find a single word in them that has anything even remotely to do with Scientific Agriculture, I will eat my hat – and yours, too, Philbrick.'

The manager had produced a pair of spectacles and through them was gazing at the mass of literature which Sacheverell had hurled before him. He raised his eyebrows and clicked his tongue.

'Stop clicking!' said Sacheverell. 'I came here to be explained to, not clicked at.'

'Dear me!' said the manager. 'How very curious.'

Sacheverell banged the desk forcefully.

'Philbrick,' he shouted, 'do not evade the issue. It is not curious. It is scandalous, monstrous, disgraceful, and I intend to take very strong steps. I shall give this outrage the widest and most pitiless publicity, and spare no effort to make a complete *exposé*.'

The manager held up a deprecating hand.

'Please!' he begged. 'I appreciate your indignation, Mr... Mulliner? Thank you...I appreciate your indignation, Mr Mulliner. I sympathize with your concern. But I can assure you that there has been no desire to deceive. Merely an unfortunate blunder on the part of our clerical staff, who shall be severely reprimanded. What has happened is that the wrong course has been sent to you.'

Sacheverell's righteous wrath cooled a little.

'Oh?' he said, somewhat mollified. 'I see. The wrong course, eh?'

'The wrong course,' said Mr Philbrick. 'And,' he went on, with a sly glance at his visitor, 'I think you will agree with me that such immediate results are a striking testimony to the efficacy of our system.'

Sacheverell was puzzled.

'Results?' he said. 'How do you mean, results?'

The manager smiled genially.

'What you have been studying for the past few weeks, Mr Mulliner,' he said, 'is our course on How to Acquire Complete Self-Confidence and an Iron Will.'

A strange elation filled Sacheverell Mulliner's bosom as he left the offices of the Correspondence School. It is always a relief to have a mystery solved which has been vexing one for any considerable time: and what Jno. Philbrick had told him made several puzzling things clear. For quite a little while he had been aware that a change had taken place in his relationship to the world about him. He recalled taxi-cabmen whom he had looked in the eye and made to wilt; intrusive pedestrians to whom he had refused to yield an inch of the pavement, where formerly he would have stepped meekly aside. These episodes had perplexed him at the time, but now everything was explained.

But what principally pleased him was the thought that he was now relieved of the tedious necessity of making a study of Scientific Agriculture, a subject from which his artist soul had always revolted. Obviously, a man with a will as iron as his would be merely wasting time boning up a lot of dull facts simply with the view of pleasing Sir Redvers Branksome. Sir Redvers Branksome, felt Sacheverell, would jolly well take him as he was, and like it.

He anticipated no trouble from that quarter. In his mind's eye he could see himself lolling at the dinner-table at the Towers and informing the Colonel over a glass of port that he proposed, at an early date, to marry his daughter. Possibly, purely out of courtesy, he would make the graceful gesture of affecting to seek the old buster's approval of the match: but at the slightest sign of obduracy he would know what to do about it.

Well pleased, Sacheverell was walking to the Carlton Hotel, where he intended to lunch, when, just as he entered the Haymarket, he stopped abruptly, and a dark frown came into his resolute face.

A cab had passed him, and in that cab was sitting his fiancée, Muriel Branksome. And beside her, with a grin on his beastly face, was a young man in a Brigade of Guards tie. They had the air of a couple on their way to enjoy a spot of lunch somewhere.

That Sacheverell should have deduced immediately that the young man was Muriel's cousin, Bernard, was due to the fact that, like all the Mulliners, he was keenly intuitive. That he should have stood, fists clenched and eyes blazing, staring after the cab, we may set down to the circumstance that the spectacle of these two, squashed together in carefree proximity on the seat of a taxi, had occasioned in him the utmost rancour and jealousy.

Muriel, as she had told him, had once been engaged to her cousin, and the thought that they were still on terms of such sickening intimacy acted like acid on Sacheverell's soul.

Hobnobbing in cabs, by Jove! Revelling *tête-à-tête* at luncheon-tables, forsooth! Just the sort of goings-on that got the Cities of the Plain so disliked. He saw clearly that Muriel was a girl who would have to be handled firmly. There was nothing of the possessive Victorian male about him – he flattered himself that he was essentially modern and broadminded in his outlook – but if Muriel supposed that he was going to stand by like a clam while she went on Babylonian orgies all over the place with pop-eyed, smirking, toothbrush-moustached Guardees, she was due for a rude awakening.

And Sacheverell Mulliner did not mean maybe.

For an instant, he toyed with the idea of hailing another cab and following them. Then he thought better of it. He was enraged, but still master of himself. When he ticked Muriel off, as he intended to do, he wished to tick her off alone. If she was in London, she was, no doubt, staying with her aunt in Ennismore Gardens. He would get a bit of food and go on there at his leisure.

The butler at Ennismore Gardens informed Sacheverell, when he arrived, that Muriel was, as he supposed, visiting the house, though for the moment out to lunch. Sacheverell waited, and presently the door of the drawing-room opened and the girl came in.

She seemed delighted to see him.

'Hullo, old streptococcus,' she said. 'Here you are, eh? I rang you up this morning to ask you to give me a bite of lunch, but you were out, so I roped in Bernard instead and we buzzed off to the Savoy in a taximeter.'

'I saw you,' said Sacheverell coldly.

'Did you? You poor chump, why didn't you yell?'

'I had no desire to meet your Cousin Bernard,' said Sacheverell, still speaking in the same frigid voice. 'And, while we are on this distasteful subject, I must request you not to see him again.'

The girl stared.

'You must do how much?'

'I must request you not to see him again,' repeated Sacheverell. 'I do not wish you to continue your Cousin Bernard's acquaintance. I do not like his looks, nor do I approve of my fiancée lunching alone with young men.'

Muriel seemed bewildered.

'You want me to tie a can to poor old Bernard?' she gasped.

'I insist upon it.'

'But, you poor goop, we were children together.'

Sacheverell shrugged his shoulders.

'If,' he said, 'you survived knowing Bernard as a child, why not be thankful and let it go at that? Why deliberately come up for more punishment by seeking him out now? Well, there it is,' said Sacheverell crisply. 'I have told you my wishes, and you will respect them.'

Muriel appeared to be experiencing a difficulty in finding words. She was bubbling like a saucepan on the point of coming to the boil. Nor could any unprejudiced critic have blamed her for her emotion. The last time she had seen Sacheverell, it must be remembered, he had been the sort of man who made a shrinking violet look like a Chicago gangster. And here he was now, staring her in the eye and shooting off his head for all the world as if he were Mussolini informing the Italian Civil Service of a twelve per cent cut in their weekly salary.

'And now,' said Sacheverell, 'there is another matter of which I wish to speak. I am anxious to see your father as soon as possible, in order to announce our engagement to him. It is quite time that he learned what my plans are. I shall be glad, therefore, if you will make arrangements to put me up at the Towers this coming week-end. Well,' concluded Sacheverell, glancing at his watch, 'I must be going. I have several matters to attend to, and your luncheon with your cousin was so prolonged that the hour is already late. Good-bye. We shall meet on Saturday.'

Sacheverell was feeling at the top of his form when he set out for Branksome Towers on the following Saturday. The eighth lesson of his course on how to develop an iron will had reached him by the morning post, and he studied it on the train. It was a pippin. It showed you exactly how Napoleon had got that way, and there was some technical stuff about narrowing the eyes and fixing them keenly on people which alone was worth the money. He alighted at Market Branksome Station in a glow of self-confidence. The only thing that troubled him was a fear lest Sir Redvers might madly attempt anything in the nature of opposition to his plans. He did not wish to be compelled to scorch the poor old man to a crisp at his own dinner-table.

He was meditating on this and resolving to remember to do his best to let the Colonel down as lightly as possible, when a voice spoke his name.

'Mr Mulliner?'

He turned. He supposed he was obliged to believe his eyes.

And, if he did believe his eyes, the man standing beside him was none other than Muriel's cousin Bernard.

'They sent me down to meet you,' continued Bernard. 'I'm the old boy's nephew. Shall we totter to the car?'

Sacheverell was beyond speech. The thought that, after what he had said, Muriel should have invited her cousin to the Towers had robbed him of utterance. He followed the other to the car in silence.

In the drawing-room of the Towers they found Muriel, already dressed for dinner, brightly shaking up cocktails.

'So you got here?' said Muriel.

At another time her manner might have struck Sacheverell as odd. There was an unwonted hardness in it. Her eye, though he was too preoccupied to notice it, had a dangerous gleam.

'Yes,' he replied shortly. 'I got here.'

'The Bish. arrived yet?' asked Bernard.

'Not yet. Father had a telegram from him. He won't be along till late-ish. The Bishop of Bognor is coming to confirm a bevy of the local yokels,' said Muriel, turning to Sacheverell.

'Oh?' said Sacheverell. He was not interested in Bishops. They left him cold. He was interested in nothing but her explanation of how her repellent cousin came to be here to-night in defiance of his own expressed wishes.

'Well,' said Bernard, 'I suppose I'd better be going up and disguising myself as a waiter.'

'I, too,' said Sacheverell. He turned to Muriel. 'I take it I am in the Blue Suite, as before?'

'No,' said Muriel. 'You're in the Garden Room. You see—'

'I see perfectly,' said Sacheverell curtly.

He turned on his heel and stalked to the door.

* * *

The indignation which Sacheverell had felt on seeing Bernard at the station was as nothing compared with that which seethed within him as he dressed for dinner. That Bernard should be at the Towers at all was monstrous. That he should have been given the star bedroom in preference to himself, Sacheverell Mulliner, was one of those things before which the brain reels.

As you are doubtless aware, the distribution of bedrooms in country houses is as much a matter of rigid precedence as the distribution of dressing-rooms at a theatre. The nibs get the best ones, the small fry squash in where they can. If Sacheverell had been a *prima donna* told off to dress with the second character-woman, he could not have been more mortified.

It was not simply that the Blue Suite was the only one in the house with a bathroom of its own: it was the principle of the thing. The fact that he was pigging it in the Garden Room, while Bernard wallowed in luxury in the Blue Suite was tantamount to a declaration on Muriel's part that she intended to get back at him for the attitude which he had taken over her luncheon-party. It was a slight, a deliberate snub, and Sacheverell came down to dinner coldly resolved to nip all this nonsense in the bud without delay.

Wrapped in his thoughts, he paid no attention to the conversation during the early part of dinner. He sipped a moody spoonful or two of soup and toyed with a morsel of salmon, but spiritually he was apart. It was only when the saddle of lamb had been distributed and the servitors had begun to come round with the vegetables that he was roused from his reverie by a sharp, barking noise from the head of the table, not unlike the note of a man-eating tiger catching sight of a Hindu peasant;

and, glancing up, he perceived that it proceeded from Sir Redvers Branksome. His host was staring in an unpleasant manner at a dish which had just been placed under his nose by the butler.

It was in itself a commonplace enough occurrence – merely the old, old story of the head of the family kicking at the spinach; but for some reason it annoyed Sacheverell intensely. His strained nerves were jangled by the animal cries which had begun to fill the air, and he told himself that Sir Redvers, if he did not switch it off pretty quick, was going to be put through it in no uncertain fashion.

Sir Redvers, meanwhile, unconscious of impending doom, was glaring at the dish.

'What,' he enquired in a hoarse, rasping voice, 'is this dashed, sloppy, disgusting, slithery, gangrened mess?'

The butler did not reply. He had been through all this before. He merely increased in volume the detached expression which good butlers wear on these occasions. He looked like a prominent banker refusing to speak without advice of counsel. It was Muriel who supplied the necessary information.

'It's spinach, father.'

'Then take it away and give it to the cat. You know I hate spinach.'

'But it's so good for you.'

'Who says it's good for me?'

'All the doctors. It bucks you up if you haven't enough hæmoglobins.'

'I have plenty of hæmoglobins,' said the Colonel testily. 'More than I know what to do with.'

'It's full of iron.'

'Iron!' The Colonel's eyebrows had drawn themselves

together into a single, formidable zareba of hair. He snorted
fiercely. 'Iron! Do you take me for a sword-swallower? Are you
under the impression that I am an ostrich, that I should browse
on iron? Perhaps you would like me to tuck away a few door-
knobs and a couple of pairs of roller-skates? Or a small portion
of tin-tacks? Iron, forsooth!'

Just, in short, the ordinary, conventional spinach-row of the
better-class English home; but Sacheverell was in no mood for
it. This bickering and wrangling irritated him, and he decided
that it must stop. He half rose from his chair.

'Branksome,' he said in a quiet, level voice, 'you will eat your
spinach.'

'Eh? What? What's that?'

'You will eat your nice spinach immediately, Branksome,' said
Sacheverell. And at the same time he narrowed his eyes and fixed
them keenly on his host.

And suddenly the rich purple colour began to die out of the
old man's cheeks. Gradually his eyebrows crept back into their
normal position. For a brief while he met Sacheverell's eye; then
he dropped his own and a weak smile came into his face.

'Well, well,' he said, with a pathetic attempt at bluffness, as he
reached over and grabbed the spoon. 'What have we here?
Spinach, eh? Capital, capital! Full of iron, I believe, and highly
recommended by the medical profession.'

And he dug in and scooped up a liberal portion.

A short silence followed, broken only by the sloshing sound
of the Colonel eating spinach. Then Sacheverell spoke.

'I wish to see you in your study immediately after dinner,
Branksome,' he said curtly.

* * *

Muriel was playing the piano when Sacheverell came into the drawing-room some forty minutes after the conclusion of dinner. She was interpreting a work by one of those Russian composers who seem to have been provided by Nature especially with a view to soothing the nervous systems of young girls who are not feeling quite themselves. It was a piece from which the best results are obtained by hauling off and delivering a series of overhand swings which make the instrument wobble like the engine-room of a liner; and Muriel, who was a fine, sturdy girl, was putting a lot of beef into it.

The change in Sacheverell had distressed Muriel Branksome beyond measure. Contemplating him, she felt as she had sometimes felt at a dance when she had told her partner to bring her ice-cream and he had come frisking up with a bowl of mock-turtle soup. Cheated – that is what she felt she had been. She had given her heart to a mild, sweet-natured, lovable lamb; and the moment she had done so he had suddenly flung off his sheep's clothing and said: 'April fool! I'm a wolf!'

Haughty by nature, Muriel Branksome was incapable of bearing anything in the shape of bossiness from the male. Her proud spirit revolted at it. And bossiness had become Sacheverell Mulliner's middle name.

The result was that, when Sacheverell entered the drawing-room, he found his loved one all set for the big explosion.

He suspected nothing. He was pleased with himself, and looked it.

'I put your father in his place all right at dinner, what?' said Sacheverell, buoyantly. 'Put him right where he belonged, I think.'

Muriel gnashed her teeth in a quiet undertone.

'He isn't so hot,' said Sacheverell. 'The way you used to talk about him, one would have thought he was the real ginger. Quite the reverse I found him. As nice a soft-spoken old bird as one could wish to meet. When I told him about our engagement, he just came and rubbed his head against my leg and rolled over with his paws in the air.'

Muriel swallowed softly.

'Our what?' she said.

'Our engagement.'

'Oh?' said Muriel. 'You told him we were engaged, did you?'

'I certainly did.'

'Then you can jolly well go back,' said Muriel, blazing into sudden fury, 'and tell him you were talking through your hat.'

Sacheverell started.

'That last remark once again, if you don't mind.'

'A hundred times, if you wish it,' said Muriel. 'Get this well into your fat head. Memorize it carefully. If necessary, write it on your cuff. I am not going to marry you. I wouldn't marry you to win a substantial bet or to please an old school-friend. I wouldn't marry you if you offered me all the money in the world. So there!'

Sacheverell blinked. He was taken aback.

'This sounds like the bird,' he said.

'It is the bird.'

'You are really giving me the old raspberry?'

'I am.'

'Don't you love your little Sacheverell?'

'No, I don't. I think my little Sacheverell is a mess.'

There was a silence. Sacheverell regarded her with lowered brows. Then he uttered a short, bitter laugh.

'Oh, very well,' he said.

* * *

Sacheverell Mulliner boiled with jealous rage. Of course, he saw what had happened. The girl had fallen once more under the glamorous spell of her cousin Bernard, and proposed to throw a Mulliner's heart aside like a soiled glove. But if she thought he was going to accept the situation meekly and say no more about it, she would soon discover her error.

Sacheverell loved this girl – not with the tepid preference which passes for love in these degenerate days, but with all the medieval fervour of a rich and passionate soul. And he intended to marry her. Yes, if the whole Brigade of Guards stood between, he was resolved to walk up the aisle with her arm in his and help her cut the cake at the subsequent breakfast.

Bernard . . . ! He would soon settle Bernard.

For all his inner ferment, Sacheverell retained undiminished the clearness of mind which characterizes Mulliners in times of crisis. An hour's walk up and down the terrace had shown him what he must do. There was nothing to be gained by acting hastily. He must confront Bernard alone in the silent night, when they would be free from danger of interruption and he could set the full force of his iron personality playing over the fellow like a hose.

And so it came about that the hour of eleven, striking from the clock above the stables, found Sacheverell Mulliner sitting grimly in the Blue Suite, waiting for his victim to arrive.

His brain was like ice. He had matured his plan of campaign. He did not intend to hurt the man – merely to order him to leave the house instantly and never venture to see or speak to Muriel again.

So mused Sacheverell Mulliner, unaware that no Cousin Bernard would come within ten yards of the Blue Suite that night. Bernard had already retired to rest in the Pink Room on the third floor, which had been his roosting-place from the beginning of his visit. The Blue Suite, being the abode of the most honoured guest, had, of course, been earmarked from the start for the Bishop of Bognor.

Carburettor trouble and a series of detours had delayed the Bishop in his journey to Branksome Towers. At first, he had hoped to make it in time for dinner. Then he had anticipated an arrival at about nine-thirty. Finally, he was exceedingly relieved to reach his destination shortly after eleven.

A quick sandwich and a small limejuice and soda were all that the prelate asked of his host at that advanced hour. These consumed, he announced himself ready for bed, and Colonel Branksome conducted him to the door of the Blue Suite.

'I hope you will find everything comfortable, my dear Bishop,' he said.

'I am convinced of it, my dear Branksome,' said the Bishop. 'And to-morrow I trust I shall feel less fatigued and in a position to meet the rest of your guests.'

'There is only one beside my nephew Bernard. A young fellow named Mulliner.'

'Mulligan?'

'Mulliner.'

'Ah, yes,' said the Bishop. 'Mulliner.'

And simultaneously, inside the room, my nephew Sacheverell sprang from his chair, and stood frozen, like a statue.

In narrating this story, I have touched lightly upon Sacheverell's career at Harborough College. I shall not be digressing now if I relate briefly what had always been to him the high spot in it.

One sunny summer day, when a lad of fourteen and a half, my nephew had sought to relieve the tedium of school routine by taking a golf-ball and flinging it against the side of the building, his intention being to catch it as it rebounded. Unfortunately, when it came to the acid test, the ball did not rebound. Instead of going due north, it went nor'-nor'-east, with the result that it passed through the window of the headmaster's library at the precise moment when that high official was about to lean out for a breath of air. And the next moment, a voice, proceeding apparently from heaven, had spoken one word. The voice was like the deeper notes of a great organ, and the word was the single word:

'MULLINER!!!'

And, just as the word Sacheverell now heard was the same word, so was the voice the same voice.

To appreciate my nephew's concern, you must understand that the episode which I have just related had remained green in his memory right through the years. His pet nightmare, and the one which had had so depressing an effect on his *morale*, had always been the one where he found himself standing, quivering and helpless, while a voice uttered the single word 'Mulliner!'

Little wonder, then, that he now remained for an instant paralysed. His only coherent thought was a bitter reflection that somebody might have had the sense to tell him that the Bishop of Bognor was his old headmaster, the Rev. J. G. Smethurst. Naturally, in that case, he would have been out of the place in two strides. But they had simply said the Bishop of Bognor, and it had meant nothing to him.

Now that it was too late, he seemed to recall having heard somebody somewhere say something about the Rev. J. G. Smethurst becoming a bishop; and even in this moment of collapse he was able to feel a thrill of justifiable indignation at the shabbiness of the act. It wasn't fair for headmasters to change their names like this and take people unawares. The Rev. J. G. Smethurst might argue as much as he liked, but he couldn't get away from the fact that he had played a shady trick on the community. The man was practically going about under an *alias*.

But this was no time for abstract meditations on the question of right and wrong. He must hide ... hide.

Yet why, you are asking, should my nephew Sacheverell wish to hide? Had he not in eight easy lessons from the Leave-It-To-Us School of Correspondence acquired complete self-confidence and an iron will? He had, but in this awful moment all that he had learned had passed from him like a dream. The years had rolled back, and he was a fifteen-year-old jelly again, in the full grip of his Headmaster Phobia.

To dive under the bed was with Sacheverell Mulliner the work of a moment. And there, as the door opened, he lay, holding his breath and trying to keep his ears from rustling in the draught.

Smethurst (*alias* Bognor) was a leisurely undresser. He doffed his gaiters, and then for some little time stood, apparently in a reverie, humming one of the song-hits from the psalms. Eventually, he resumed his disrobing, but even then the ordeal was not over. As far as Sacheverell could see, in the constrained position in which he was lying, the Bishop was doing a few setting-up exercises. Then he went into the bathroom and cleaned his teeth. It was only at the end of half an hour that he finally climbed between the sheets and switched off the light.

For a long while after he had done so, Sacheverell remained where he was, motionless. But presently a faint, rhythmical sound from the neighbourhood of the pillows assured him that the other was asleep, and he crawled cautiously from his lair.

Then, stepping with infinite caution, he moved to the door, opened it, and passed through.

The relief which Sacheverell felt as he closed the door behind him would have been less intense, had he realized that through a slight mistake in his bearings he had not, as he supposed, reached the haven of the passage outside but had merely entered the bathroom. This fact was not brought home to him until he had collided with an unexpected chair, upset it, tripped over a bathmat, clutched for support into the darkness and brushed from off the glass shelf above the basin a series of bottles, containing – in the order given – Scalpo ('It Fertilizes the Follicles'), Soothine – for applying to the face after shaving, and Doctor Wilberforce's Golden Gargle in the large or seven-and-sixpenny size. These, crashing to the floor, would have revealed the truth to a far duller man than Sacheverell Mulliner.

He acted swiftly. From the room beyond, there had come to his ears the unmistakable sound of a Bishop sitting up in bed, and he did not delay. Hastily groping for the switch, he turned on the light. He found the bolt and shot it. Only then did he sit down on the edge of the bath and attempt to pass the situation under careful review.

He was not allowed long for quiet thinking. Through the door came the sound of deep breathing. Then a voice spoke.

'Who is they-ah?'

As always in the dear old days of school, it caused Sacheverell to leap six inches. He had just descended again, when another voice spoke in the bedroom. It was that of Colonel Sir Redvers Branksome, who had heard the crashing of glass and had come, in the kindly spirit of a good host, to make enquiries.

'What is the matter, my dear Bishop?' he asked.

'It is a burglar, my dear Colonel,' said the Bishop.

'A burglar?'

'A burglar. He has locked himself in the bathroom.'

'Then how extremely fortunate,' said the Colonel heartily, 'that I should have brought along this battle-axe and shot-gun on the chance.'

Sacheverell felt that it was time to join in the conversation. He went to the door and put his lips against the keyhole.

'It's all right,' he said, quaveringly.

The Colonel uttered a surprised exclamation.

'He says it's all right,' he reported.

'Why does he say it is all right?' asked the Bishop.

'I didn't ask him,' replied the Colonel. 'He just said it was all right.'

The Bishop sniffed peevishly.

'It is not all right,' he said, with a certain heat. 'And I am at a loss to understand why the man should affect to assume that it is. I suggest, my dear Colonel, that our best method of procedure is as follows, you take the shot-gun and stand in readiness, and I will hew down the door with this admirable battle-axe.'

And it was at this undeniably critical point in the proceedings that something soft and clinging brushed against Sacheverell's right ear, causing him to leap again – this time a matter of eight inches and a quarter. And, spinning round, he discovered that what had touched his ear was the curtain of the bathroom window.

There now came a splintering crash, and the door shook on its hinges. The Bishop, with all the blood of a hundred Militant Churchmen ancestors afire within him, had started operations with the axe.

But Sacheverell scarcely heard the noise. The sight of the open window had claimed his entire attention. And now, moving nimbly, he clambered through it, alighting on what seemed to be leads.

For an instant he gazed wildly about him; then, animated, perhaps, by some subconscious memory of the boy who bore 'mid snow and ice the banner with the strange device 'Excelsior!' he leaped quickly upwards and started to climb the roof.

Muriel Branksome, on retiring to her room on the floor above the Blue Suite, had not gone to bed. She was sitting at her open window, thinking, thinking.

Her thoughts were bitter ones. It was not that she felt remorseful. In giving Sacheverell the air at their recent interview, her conscience told her that she had acted rightly. He had behaved like a domineering sheik of the desert: and a dislike for domineering sheiks of the desert had always been an integral part of her spiritual make-up.

But the consciousness of having justice on her side is not always enough to sustain a girl at such a time: and an aching pain gripped Muriel as she thought of the Sacheverell she had loved – the old, mild, sweet-natured Sacheverell who had asked nothing better than to gaze at her with adoring eyes, removing them only when he found it necessary to give his attention to the bit of string with which he was doing tricks. She mourned for this vanished Sacheverell.

Obviously, after what had happened, he would leave the house early in the morning – probably long before she came down, for she was a late riser. She wondered if she would ever see him again.

At this moment, she did. He was climbing up the slope of the roof towards her on his hands and knees – and, for one who was not a cat, doing it extremely well. She had hardly risen to her feet before he was standing at the window, clutching the sill.

Muriel choked. She stared at him with wide, tragic eyes.

'What do you want?' she asked harshly.

'Well, as a matter of fact,' said Sacheverell, 'I was wondering if you would mind if I hid under your bed for a bit.'

And suddenly, in the dim light, the girl saw that his face was contorted with a strange terror. And, at the spectacle, all her animosity seemed to be swept away as if on a tidal wave, and back came the old love and esteem, piping hot and as fresh as ever. An instant before, she had been wanting to beat him over the head with a brick. Now, she ached to comfort and protect him. For here once more was the Sacheverell she had worshipped – the poor, timid, fluttering, helpless pipsqueak whose hair she had always wanted to stroke and to whom she had felt a strange, intermittent urge to offer lumps of sugar.

'Come right in,' she said.

He threw her a hasty word of thanks and shot over the sill. Then abruptly he stiffened, and the wild, hunted look was in his eyes again. From somewhere below there had come the deep baying of a Bishop on the scent. He clutched at Muriel, and she held him to her like a mother soothing a nightmare-ridden child.

'Listen!' he whispered.

'Who are they?' asked Muriel.

'Headmasters,' panted Sacheverell. 'Droves of headmasters. And colonels. Coveys of colonels. With battle-axes and shot-guns. Save me, Muriel!'

'There, there!' said Muriel. 'There, there, there!'

She directed him to the bed, and he disappeared beneath it like a diving duck.

'You will be quite safe there,' said Muriel. 'And now tell me what it is all about.'

Outside, they could hear the noise of the hue-and-cry. The original strength of the company appeared to have been augmented by the butler and a few sporting footmen. Brokenly, Sacheverell told her all.

'But what were you doing in the Blue Suite?' asked the girl, when he had concluded his tale. 'I don't understand.'

'I went to interview your cousin Bernard, to tell him that he should marry you only over my dead body.'

'What an unpleasant idea!' said Muriel, shivering a little. 'And I don't see how it could have been done, anyway.' She paused a moment, listening to the uproar. Somewhere downstairs, footmen seemed to be falling over one another: and once there came the shrill cry of a Hunting Bishop stymied by a hat-stand. 'But what on earth,' she asked, resuming her remarks, 'made you think that I was going to marry Bernard?'

'I thought that that was why you gave me the bird.'

'Of course it wasn't. I gave you the bird because you had suddenly turned into a beastly, barking, bullying, overbearing blighter.'

There was a pause before Sacheverell spoke.

'Had I?' he said at length. 'Yes, I suppose I had. Tell me,' he continued, 'is there a good milk-train in the morning?'

'At three-forty, I believe.'

'I'll catch it.'

'Must you really go?'

'I must, indeed.'

'Oh, well,' said Muriel. 'It won't be long before we meet again. I'll run up to London one of these days, and we'll have a bit of lunch together and get married and . . .'

A gasp came from beneath the bed.

'Married! Do you really mean that you will marry me, Muriel?'

'Of course I will. The past is dead. You are my own precious angel pet again, and I love you madly, passionately. What's been the matter with you these last few weeks I can't imagine, but I can see it's all over now, so don't let's talk any more about it. Hark!' she said, holding up a finger as a sonorous booming noise filled the night, accompanied by a flood of rich oaths in what appeared to be some foreign language, possibly Hindustani. 'I think father has tripped over the dinner-gong.'

Sacheverell did not answer. His heart was too full for words. He was thinking how deeply he loved this girl and how happy those few remarks of hers had made him.

And yet, mingled with his joy, there was something of sorrow. As the old Roman poet has it, *surgit amari aliquid*. He had just remembered that he had paid the Leave-It-To-Us Correspondence School fifteen guineas in advance for a course of twenty lessons. He was abandoning the course after taking eight. And the thought that stabbed him like a knife was that he no longer had enough self-confidence and iron will left to enable him to go to Jno. B. Philbrick, Mgr, and demand a refund.

Mr Mulliner put away the letter he had been reading, and beamed contentedly on the little group in the bar-parlour of the Angler's Rest.

'Most gratifying,' he murmured.

'Good news?' we asked.

'Excellent,' said Mr Mulliner. 'The letter was from my nephew Eustace, who is attached to our Embassy in Switzerland. He has fully justified the family's hopes.'

'Doing well, is he?'

'Capitally,' said Mr Mulliner.

He chuckled reflectively.

'Odd,' he said, 'now that the young fellow has made so signal a success, to think what a business we had getting him to undertake the job. At one time it seemed as if it would be hopeless to try to persuade him. Indeed, if Fate had not taken a hand...'

'Didn't he want to become attached to the Embassy?'

The idea revolted him (said Mr Mulliner). Here was this splendid opening, dangled before his eyes through the influence of his godfather, Lord Knubble of Knopp, and he stoutly refused to avail himself of it. He wanted to stay in London, he said. He liked

London, he insisted, and he jolly well wasn't going to stir from the good old place.

To the rest of his relations this obduracy seemed mere capriciousness. But I, possessing the young fellow's confidence, knew that there were solid reasons behind his decision. In the first place, he knew himself to be the favourite nephew of his Aunt Georgiana, relict of the late Sir Cuthbert Beazley-Beazley, Bart, a woman of advanced years and more than ample means. And, secondly, he had recently fallen in love with a girl of the name of Marcella Tyrrwhitt.

'A nice sort of chump I should be, buzzing off to Switzerland,' he said to me one day when I had been endeavouring to break down his resistance. 'I've got to stay on the spot, haven't I, to give Aunt Georgiana the old oil from time to time? And if you suppose a fellow can woo a girl like Marcella Tyrrwhitt through the medium of the post, you are vastly mistaken. Something occurred this morning which makes me think she's weakening, and that's just the moment when the personal touch is so essential. Come one, come all, this rock shall fly from its firm base as soon as I,' said Eustace, who, like so many of the Mulliners, had a strong vein of the poetic in him.

What had occurred that morning, I learned later, was that Marcella Tyrrwhitt had rung my nephew up on the telephone.

'Hullo!' she said. 'Is that Eustace?'

'Yes,' said Eustace, for it was.

'I say, Eustace,' proceeded the girl, 'I'm leaving for Paris tomorrow.'

'You aren't!' said Eustace.

'Yes, I am, you silly ass,' said the girl, 'and I've got the tickets to prove it. Listen, Eustace. There's something I want you to do for me. You know my canary?'

'William?'

'William is right. And you know my Peke?'

'Reginald?'

'Reginald is correct. Well, I can't take them with me, because William hates travelling and Reginald would have to go into quarantine for six months when I got back, which would make him froth with fury. So will you give them a couple of beds at your flat while I'm away?'

'Absolutely,' said Eustace. 'We keep open house, we Mulliners.'

'You won't find them any trouble. There's nothing of the athlete about Reginald. A brisk walk of twenty minutes in the park sets him up for the day, as regards exercise. And, as for food, give him whatever you're having yourself – raw meat, puppy biscuits and so on. Don't let him have cocktails. They unsettle him.'

'Right-ho,' said Eustace. 'The scenario seems pretty smooth so far. How about William?'

'In *re* William, he's a bit of an eccentric in the food line. Heaven knows why, but he likes bird-seed and groundsel. Couldn't touch the stuff myself. You get bird-seed at a bird-seed shop.'

'And groundsel, no doubt, at the groundseller's?'

'Exactly. And you have to let William out of his cage once or twice a day, so that he can keep his waist-line down by fluttering about the room. He comes back all right as soon as he's had his bath. Do you follow all that?'

'Like a leopard,' said Eustace.

'I bet you don't.'

'Yes, I do. Brisk walk Reginald. Brisk flutter William.'

'You've got it. All right, then. And remember that I set a high value on those two, so guard them with your very life.'

'Absolutely,' said Eustace. 'Rather! You bet. I should say so. Positively.'

Ironical, of course, it seems now, in the light of what occurred subsequently, but my nephew told me that that was the happiest moment of his life.

He loved this girl with every fibre of his being, and it seemed to him that, if she selected him out of all her circle for this intensely important trust, it must mean that she regarded him as a man of solid worth and one she could lean on.

'These others,' she must have said to herself, running over the roster of her friends. 'What are they, after all? Mere butterflies. But Eustace Mulliner – ah, that's different. Good stuff there. A young fellow of character.'

He was delighted, also, for another reason. Much as he would miss Marcella Tyrrwhitt, he was glad that she was leaving London for a while, because his love-life at the moment had got into something of a tangle, and her absence would just give him nice time to do a little adjusting and unscrambling.

Until a week or so before he had been deeply in love with another girl – a certain Beatrice Watterson. And then, one night at a studio-party, he had met Marcella and had instantly discerned in her an infinitely superior object for his passion.

It is this sort of thing that so complicates life for the young man about town. He is too apt to make his choice before walking the whole length of the counter. He bestows a strong man's love on Girl A. and is just congratulating himself when along comes Girl B. whose very existence he had not suspected, and he finds that he has picked the wrong one and has to work like a beaver to make the switch.

What Eustace wanted to do at this point was to taper off with Beatrice, thus clearing the stage and leaving himself free to

concentrate his whole soul on Marcella. And Marcella's departure from London would afford him the necessary leisure for the
process.

So, by the way of tapering off with Beatrice, he took her to tea
the day Marcella left, and at tea Beatrice happened to mention,
as girls will, that it would be her birthday next Sunday, and
Eustace said: 'Oh, I say, really? Come and have a bite of lunch at
my flat,' and Beatrice said that she would love it, and Eustace
said that he must give her something tophole as a present, and
Beatrice said: 'Oh, no, really, you mustn't,' and Eustace said Yes,
dash it, he was resolved. Which started the tapering process
nicely, for Eustace knew that on the Sunday he was due down at
his Aunt Georgiana's at Wittleford-cum-Bagsley-on-Sea for
the week-end, so that when the girl arrived all eager for lunch
and found not only that her host was not there but that there was
not a birthday present in sight of any description, she would be
deeply offended and would become cold and distant and aloof.

Tact, my nephew tells me, is what you need on these occasions. You want to gain the desired end without hurting anybody's feelings. And, no doubt, he is right.

After tea he came back to his flat and took Reginald for a
brisk walk and gave William a flutter, and went to bed that
night, feeling that God was in His heaven and all right with
the world.

The next day was warm and sunny, and it struck Eustace that
William would appreciate it if he put his cage out on the
window-sill, so that he could get the actinic rays into his system.
He did this, accordingly, and, having taken Reginald for his
saunter, returned to the flat, feeling that he had earned the
morning bracer. He instructed Blenkinsop, his man, to bring

the materials, and soon peace was reigning in the home to a noticeable extent. William was trilling lustily on the window-sill, Reginald was resting from his exertions under the sofa, and Eustace had begun to sip his whisky-and-soda without a care in the world, when the door opened and Blenkinsop announced a visitor.

'Mr Orlando Wotherspoon,' said Blenkinsop, and withdrew, to go on with the motion-picture magazine which he had been reading in the pantry.

Eustace placed his glass on the table and rose to extend the courtesies in a somewhat puzzled, not to say befogged, state of mind. The name Wotherspoon had struck no chord, and he could not recollect ever having seen the man before in his life.

And Orlando Wotherspoon was not the sort of person who, once seen, is easily forgotten. He was built on large lines, and seemed to fill the room to overflowing. In physique, indeed, he was not unlike what Primo Carnera would have been, if Carnera had not stunted his growth by smoking cigarettes when a boy. He was preceded by a flowing moustache of the outsize soup-strainer kind, and his eyes were of the piercing type which one associates with owls, sergeant-majors, and Scotland Yard in-spectors.

Eustace found himself not a little perturbed.

'Oh, hullo!' he said.

Orlando Wotherspoon scrutinized him keenly and, it appeared to Eustace, with hostility. If Eustace had been a rather more than ordinarily unpleasant black-beetle this man would have looked at him in much the same fashion. The expression in his eyes was that which comes into the eyes of suburban house-holders when they survey slugs among their lettuces.

'Mr Mulliner?' he said.

'I shouldn't wonder,' said Eustace, feeling that this might well be so.

'My name is Wotherspoon.'

'Yes,' said Eustace. 'So Blenkinsop was saying, and he's a fellow I've found I can usually rely on.'

'I live in the block of flats across the gardens.'

'Yes?' said Eustace, still at a loss. 'Have a pretty good time?'

'In answer to your question, my life is uniformly tranquil. This morning, however, I saw a sight which shattered my peace of mind and sent the blood racing hotly through my veins.'

'Too bad when it's like that,' said Eustace. 'What made your blood carry on in the manner described?'

'I will tell you, Mr Mulliner. I was seated in my window a few minutes ago, drafting out some notes for my forthcoming speech at the annual dinner of Our Dumb Chums' League, of which I am perpetual vice-president, when, to my horror, I observed a fiend torturing a helpless bird. For a while I gazed in appalled stupefaction, while my blood ran cold.'

'Hot, you said.'

'First hot, then cold. I seethed with indignation at this fiend.'

'I don't blame you,' said Eustace. 'If there's one type of chap I bar, it's a fiend. Who was the fellow?'

'Mulliner,' said Orlando Wotherspoon, pointing a finger that looked like a plantain or some unusually enlarged banana, 'thou art the man!'

'What!'

'Yes,' repeated the other, 'you! Mulliner, the Bird-Bullier! Mulliner, the Scourge of Our Feathered Friends! What do you mean, you Torquemada, by placing that canary on the window-sill in the full force of the burning sun? How would you feel if some pop-eyed assassin left *you* out in the sun without a hat, to fry where you stood?' He went to the window and hauled the cage in. 'It is men like you, Mulliner, who block the wheels of the world's progress and render societies like Our Dumb Chums' League necessary.'

'I thought the bally bird enjoyed it,' said Eustace feebly.

'Mulliner, you lie!' said Orlando Wotherspoon.

And he looked at Eustace in a way that convinced the latter, who had suspected it from the first, that he had not made a new friend.

'By the way,' he said, hoping to ease the strain, 'have a spot?'

'I will not have a spot!'

'Right-ho,' said Eustace. 'No spot. But, coming back to the agenda, you wrong me, Wotherspoon. Foolish, mistaken, I may have been, but, as God is my witness, I meant well. Honestly, I thought William would be tickled pink if I put his cage out in the sun.'

'Tchah!' said Orlando Wotherspoon.

And, as he spoke, the dog Reginald, hearing voices, crawled out from under the sofa in the hope that something was going on which might possibly culminate in coffee-sugar.

At the sight of Reginald's honest face, Eustace brightened. A cordial friendship had sprung up between these two based on mutual respect. He extended a hand and chirruped.

Unfortunately, Reginald, suddenly getting a close-up of that moustache and being convinced by the sight of it that plots against his person were toward, uttered a piercing scream and dived back under the sofa, where he remained, calling urgently for assistance.

Orlando Wotherspoon put the worst construction on the incident.

'Ha, Mulliner!' he said. 'This is vastly well! Not content with inflicting fiendish torments on canaries, it would seem that you also slake your inhuman fury on this innocent dog, so that he runs, howling, at the mere sight of you.'

Eustace tried to put the thing right.

'I don't think it's the mere sight of me he objects to,' he said. 'In fact, I've frequently seen him take quite a long, steady look at me without wincing.'

'Then to what, pray, do you attribute the animal's visible emotion?'

'Well, the fact is,' said Eustace, 'I fancy the root of the trouble is that he doesn't much care for that moustache of yours.'

His visitor began to roll up his left coat-sleeve in a meditative way.

'Are you venturing, Mulliner, to criticize my moustache?'

'No, no,' said Eustace. 'I admire it.'

'I would be sorry,' said Orlando Wotherspoon, 'to think that you were aspersing my moustache, Mulliner. My grandmother has often described it as the handsomest in the West End of London. "Leonine" is the adjective she applies to it. But perhaps you regard my grandmother as prejudiced? Possibly you consider her a foolish old woman whose judgments may be lightly set aside?'

'Absolutely not,' said Eustace.

'I am glad,' said Wotherspoon. 'You would have been the third man I have thrashed within an inch of his life for insulting my grandmother. Or is it,' he mused, 'the fourth? I could consult my books and let you know.'

'Don't bother,' said Eustace.

There was a lull in the conversation.

'Well, Mulliner,' said Orlando Wotherspoon at length, 'I will leave you. But let me tell you this. You have not heard the last of me. You see this?' He produced a note-book. 'I keep here a black list of fiends who must be closely watched. Your Christian name, if you please?'

'Eustace.'

'Age?'

'Twenty-four.'

'Height?'

'Five foot ten.'

'Weight?'

'Well,' said Eustace, 'I was around ten stone eleven when you came in. I think I'm a bit lighter now.'

'Let us say ten stone seven. Thank you, Mr Mulliner. Everything is now in order. You have been entered on the list of suspects on whom I make a practice of paying surprise visits. From now on, you will never know when I may or may not knock upon your door.'

'Any time you're passing,' said Eustace.

'Our Dumb Chums' League,' said Orlando Wotherspoon, putting away his note-book, 'is not unreasonable in these matters. We of the organization have instructions to proceed in the matter of fiends with restraint and deliberation. For the first offence, we are content to warn. After that... I must remember, when I return home, to post you a copy of our latest booklet. It sets forth in detail what happened to J. B. Stokes, of 9 Manglesbury Mansions, West Kensington, on his ignoring our warning to him to refrain from throwing vegetables at his cat. Good morning, Mr Mulliner. Do not trouble to see me to the door.'

Young men of my nephew Eustace's type are essentially resili-
ent. This interview had taken place on the Thursday. By Friday,
at about one o'clock, he had practically forgotten the entire
episode. And by noon on Saturday he was his own merry self
once more.

It was on this Saturday, as you may remember, that Eustace
was to go down to Wittleford-cum-Bagsley-on-Sea to spend
the week-end with his Aunt Georgiana.

Wittleford-cum-Bagsley-on-Sea, so I am informed by those
who have visited it, is not a Paris or a pre-War Vienna. In fact,
once the visitor has strolled along the pier and put pennies in
the slot machines, he has shot his bolt as far as the hectic whirl
of pleasure, for which the younger generation is so avid, is
concerned.

Nevertheless, Eustace found himself quite looking forward to
the trip. Apart from the fact that he would be getting himself in
solid with a woman who combined the possession of a hundred
thousand pounds in Home Rails with a hereditary tendency to
rheumatic trouble of the heart, it was pleasant to reflect that in
about twenty-four hours from the time he started the girl
Beatrice would have called at the empty flat and gone away in
a piqued and raised-eyebrow condition, leaving him free to
express his individuality in the matter of the girl Marcella.

He whistled gaily as he watched Blenkinsop pack.

'You have thoroughly grasped the programme outlined for
the period of my absence, Blenkinsop?' he said.

'Yes, sir.'

'Take Master Reginald for the daily stroll.'

'Yes, sir.'

'See that Master William does his fluttering.'

'Yes, sir.'

'And don't get them mixed. I mean, don't let Reginald flutter and take William for a walk.'

'No, sir.'

'Right!' said Eustace. 'And on Sunday, Blenkinsop – to-morrow, that is to say – a young lady will be turning up for lunch. Explain to her that I'm not here, and give her anything she wants.'

'Very good, sir.'

Eustace set out upon his journey with a light heart. Arrived at Wittleford-cum-Bagsley-on-Sea, he passed a restful week-end playing double patience with his aunt, tickling her cat under the left ear from time to time, and walking along the esplanade. On the Monday he caught the one-forty train back to London, his aunt cordial to the last.

'I shall be passing through London on my way to Harrogate next Friday,' she said, as he was leaving. 'Perhaps you will give me tea?'

'I shall be more than delighted, Aunt Georgiana,' said Eustace. 'It has often been a great grief to me that you allow me so few opportunities of entertaining you in my little home. At four-thirty next Friday. Right!'

Everything seemed to him to be shaping so satisfactorily that his spirits were at their highest. He sang in the train to quite a considerable extent.

'What ho, Blenkinsop!' he said, entering the flat in a very nearly rollicking manner. 'Everything all right?'

'Yes, sir,' said Blenkinsop. 'I trust that you have enjoyed an agreeable week-end, sir?'

'Topping,' said Eustace. 'How are the dumb chums?'

'Master William is in robust health, sir.'

'Splendid! And Reginald?'

'Of Master Reginald I cannot speak with the authority of first-hand knowledge, sir, as the young lady removed him yesterday.'

Eustace clutched at a chair.

'Removed him?'

'Yes, sir. Took him away. If you recall your parting instructions, sir, you enjoined upon me that I should give the young lady anything she wanted. She selected Master Reginald. She desired me to inform you that she was sorry to have missed you but quite understood that you could not disappoint your aunt, and that, as you insisted on giving her a birthday present, she had taken Master Reginald.'

Eustace pulled himself together with a strong effort. He saw that nothing was to be gained by upbraiding the man. Blenkinsop, he realized, had acted according to his lights. He told himself that he should have remembered that his valet was of a literal turn of mind, who always carried out instructions to the letter.

'Get her on the 'phone, quick,' he said.

'Impossible, I fear, sir. The young lady informed me that she was leaving for Paris by the two o'clock train this afternoon.'

'Then, Blenkinsop,' said Eustace, 'give me a quick one.'

'Very good, sir.'

The restorative seemed to clear the young man's head.

'Blenkinsop,' he said, 'give me your attention. Don't let your mind wander. We've got to do some close thinking – some very close thinking.'

'Yes, sir.'

In simple words Eustace explained the position of affairs. Blenkinsop clicked his tongue. Eustace held up a restraining hand.

'Don't do that, Blenkinsop.'

'No, sir.'

'At any other moment I should be delighted to listen to you giving your imitation of a man drawing corks out of champagne bottles. But not now. Reserve it for the next party you attend.'

'Very good, sir.'

Eustace returned to the matter in hand.

'You see the position I am in? We must put our heads together, Blenkinsop. How can I account satisfactorily to Miss Tyrrwhitt for the loss of her dog?'

'Would it not be feasible to inform the young lady that you took the animal for a walk in the park and that it slipped its collar and ran away?'

'Very nearly right, Blenkinsop,' said Eustace, 'but not quite. What actually happened was that *you* took it for a walk and, like a perfect chump, went and lost it.'

'Well, really, sir—'

'Blenkinsop,' said Eustace, 'if there is one drop of the old feudal spirit in your system, now is the time to show it. Stand by me in this crisis, and you will not be the loser.'

'Very good, sir.'

'You realize, of course, that when Miss Tyrrwhitt returns it will be necessary for me to curse you pretty freely in her presence, but you must read between the lines and take it all in a spirit of pure badinage.'

'Very good, sir.'

'Right-ho, then, Blenkinsop. Oh, by the way, my aunt will be coming to tea on Friday.'

'Very good, sir.'

These preliminaries settled, Eustace proceeded to pave the way. He wrote a long and well-phrased letter to Marcella, telling her that, as he was unfortunately confined to the house with one of his bronchial colds, he had been compelled to depute the walk-in-the-park-taking of Reginald to his man Blenkinsop, in whom he had every confidence. He went on to say that Reginald, thanks to his assiduous love and care, was in the enjoyment of excellent health and that he would always look back with wistful pleasure to the memory of their long, cosy evenings together. He drew a picture of Reginald and himself sitting side by side in silent communion – he deep in some good book, Reginald meditating on this and that – which almost brought the tears to his eyes.

Nevertheless, he was far from feeling easy in his mind. Women, he knew, in moments of mental stress, are always apt to spray the blame a good deal. And, while Blenkinsop would presumably get the main stream, there might well be a few drops left over which would come in his direction.

For, if this girl Marcella Tynwhitt had a defect, it was that the generous warmth of her womanly nature led her now and then to go off the deep end somewhat heartily. She was one of those tall, dark girls with flashing eyes who tend to a certain extent, in times of stress, to draw themselves to their full height and let their male *vis-à-vis* have it squarely in the neck. Time had done much to heal the wound, but he could still recall some of the things she had said to him the night when they had arrived late at the theatre, to discover that he had left the tickets on his sitting-room mantelpiece. In two minutes any competent biographer would have been able to gather material for a complete character-sketch. He had found out more about himself in that one brief interview than in all the rest of his life.

Naturally, therefore, he brooded a good deal during the next few days. His friends were annoyed at this period by his absent-mindedness. He developed a habit of saying 'What?' with a glazed look in his eyes and then sinking back and draining his glass, all of which made him something of a dead weight in general conversation.

You would see him sitting hunched up in a corner with his jaw drooping, and a very unpleasant spectacle it was. His fellow-members began to complain about it. They said the taxidermist had no right to leave him lying about the club after removing his insides, but ought to buckle to and finish stuffing him and make a job of it.

He was sitting like this one afternoon, when suddenly, as he raised his eyes to see if there was a waiter handy, he caught sight of the card on the wall which bore upon it the date and the day of the week. And the next moment a couple of fellow-members who had thought he was dead and were just going to ring to have him swept away were stunned to observe him leap to his feet and run swiftly from the room.

He had just discovered that it was Friday, the day his Aunt Georgiana was coming to tea at his flat. And he only had about three and a half minutes before the kick-off.

A speedy cab took him quickly home, and he was relieved, on entering the flat, to find that his aunt was not there. The tea-table had been set out, but the room was empty except for William, who was trying over a song in his cage. Greatly relieved, Eustace went to the cage and unhooked the door, and William, after jumping up and down for a few moments in the eccentric way canaries do, hopped out and started to flutter to and fro.

It was at this moment that Blenkinsop came in with a well-laden plate.

'Cucumber sandwiches, sir,' said Blenkinsop. 'Ladies are usually strongly addicted to them.'

Eustace nodded. The man's instinct had not led him astray. His aunt was passionately addicted to cucumber sandwiches. Many a time he had seen her fling herself on them like a starving wolf.

'Her ladyship not arrived?' he said.

'Yes, sir. She stepped down the street to dispatch a telegram. Would you desire me to serve cream, sir, or will the ordinary milk suffice?'

'Cream? Milk?'

'I have laid out an extra saucer.'

'Blenkinsop,' said Eustace, passing a rather feverish hand across his brow, for he had much to disturb him these days. 'You appear to be talking of something, but it does not penetrate. What is all this babble of milk and cream? Why do you speak in riddles of extra saucers?'

'For the cat, sir.'

'What cat?'

'Her ladyship was accompanied by her cat, Francis.'

The strained look passed from Eustace's face.

'Oh? Her cat?'

'Yes, sir.'

'Well, in regard to nourishment, it gets milk – the same as the rest of us – and likes it. But serve it in the kitchen, because of the canary.'

'Master Francis is not in the kitchen, sir.'

'Well, in the pantry or my bedroom or wherever he is.'

'When last I saw Master Francis, sir, he was enjoying a cooling stroll on the window-sill.'

And at this juncture there silhouetted itself against the evening sky a lissom form.

'Here! Hi! My gosh! I say! Dash it!' exclaimed Eustace, eyeing it with unconcealed apprehension.

'Yes, sir,' said Blenkinsop. 'Excuse me, sir. I fancy I heard the front door-bell.'

And he withdrew, leaving Eustace a prey to the liveliest agitation.

Eustace, you see, was still hoping, in spite of having been so remiss in the matter of the dog, to save his stake, if I may use the expression, on the canary. In other words, when Marcella Tyrrwhitt returned and began to be incisive on the subject of the vanished Reginald, he wished to be in a position to say: 'True! True! In the matter of Reginald, I grant that I have failed you. But pause before you speak and take a look at that canary – fit as a fiddle and bursting with health. And why? Because of my unremitting care.'

A most unpleasant position he would be in if, in addition to having to admit that he was one Peke down on the general score, he also had to reveal that William, his sheet-anchor, was inextricably mixed up with the gastric juices of a cat which the girl did not even know by sight.

And that this tragedy was imminent he was sickeningly aware from the expression on the animal's face. It was a sort of devout, ecstatic look. He had observed much the same kind of look on the face of his Aunt Georgiana when about to sail into the cucumber sandwiches. Francis was inside the room now, and was gazing up at the canary with a steady, purposeful eye. His tail was twitching at the tip.

The next moment, to the accompaniment of a moan of horror from Eustace, he had launched himself into the air in the bird's direction.

Well, William was no fool. Where many a canary would have blenched, he retained his *sang froid* unimpaired. He moved a little to the left, causing the cat to miss by a foot. And his beak, as he did so, was curved in a derisive smile. In fact, thinking it over later, Eustace realized that right from the beginning William had the situation absolutely under control and wanted nothing but to be left alone to enjoy a good laugh.

At the moment, however, this did not occur to Eustace. Shaken to the core, he supposed the bird to be in the gravest peril. He imagined it to stand in need of all the aid and comfort he could supply. And, springing quickly to the tea-table, he rummaged among its contents for something that would serve him as ammunition in the fray.

The first thing he put his hand on was the plate of cucumber sandwiches. These, with all the rapidity at his command, he discharged, one after the other. But, though a few found their mark, there was nothing in the way of substantial results. The very nature of a cucumber sandwich makes it poor throwing. He could have obtained direct hits on Francis all day without slowing him up. In fact, the very moment after the last sandwich had struck him in the ribs, he was up in the air again, clawing hopefully.

William side-stepped once more, and Francis returned to earth. And Eustace, emotion ruining his aim, missed him by inches with a sultana cake, three muffins, and a lump of sugar.

Then, desperate, he did what he should, of course, have done at the very outset. Grabbing the table-cloth, he edged round with extraordinary stealth till he was in the cat's immediate rear, and dropped it over him just as he was tensing his muscles for another leap. Then, flinging himself on the mixture of cat and table-cloth, he wound them up into a single convenient parcel.

Exceedingly pleased with himself Eustace felt at this point. It seemed to him that he had shown resource, intelligence, and an agility highly creditable in one who had not played Rugby football for years. A good deal of bitter criticism was filtering through the cloth, but he overlooked it. Francis, he knew, when he came to think the thing over calmly, would realize that he deserved all he was getting. He had always found Francis a fair-minded cat, when the cold sobriety of his judgment was not warped by the sight of canaries.

He was about to murmur a word or two to this effect, in the hope of inducing the animal to behave less like a gyroscope, when, looking round, he perceived that he was not alone.

Standing grouped about the doorway were his Aunt Georgiana, the girl, Marcella Tyrrwhitt, and the well-remembered figure of Orlando Wotherspoon.

'Lady Beazley-Beazley, Miss Tyrrwhitt, Mr Orlando Wotherspoon,' announced Blenkinsop. 'Tea is served, sir.'

A wordless cry broke from Eustace's lips. The table-cloth fell from his nerveless fingers. And the cat, Francis, falling on his head on the carpet, shot straight up the side of the wall and entrenched himself on top of the curtains.

There was a pause. Eustace did not know quite what to say. He felt embarrassed.

It was Orlando Wotherspoon who broke the silence.

'So!' said Orlando Wotherspoon. 'At your old games, Mulliner, I perceive.'

Eustace's Aunt Georgiana was pointing dramatically.

'He threw cucumber sandwiches at my cat!'

'So I observe,' said Wotherspoon. He spoke in an unpleasant, quiet voice, and he was looking not unlike a high priest of one of the rougher religions who runs his eye over the human sacrifice preparatory to asking his caddy for the niblick. 'Also, if I mistake not, sultana cake and muffins.'

'Would you require fresh muffins, sir?' asked Blenkinsop.

'The case, in short, would appear to be on all fours,' proceeded Wotherspoon, 'with that of J. B. Stokes, of 9, Manglesbury Mansions, West Kensington.'

'Listen!' said Eustace, backing towards the window. 'I can explain everything.'

'There is no need of explanations, Mulliner,' said Orlando Wotherspoon. He had rolled up the left sleeve of his coat and was beginning to roll up the right. He twitched his biceps to limber it up. 'The matter explains itself.'

Eustace's Aunt Georgiana, who had been standing under the curtain making chirruping noises, came back to the group in no agreeable frame of mind. Overwrought by what had occurred, Francis had cut her dead, and she was feeling it a good deal.

'If I may use your telephone, Eustace,' she said quietly, 'I would like to ring up my lawyer and disinherit you. But first,' she added to Wotherspoon, who was now inhaling and expelling the breath from his nostrils in rather a disturbing manner, 'would you oblige me by thrashing him within an inch of his life?'

'I was about to do so, madam,' replied Wotherspoon courteously. 'If this young lady will kindly stand a little to one side—'

'Shall I prepare some more cucumber sandwiches, sir?' asked Blenkinsop.

'Wait!' cried Marcella Tyrrwhitt, who hitherto had not spoken.

Orlando Wotherspoon shook his head gently.

'If, deprecating scenes of violence, it is your intention, Miss Tyrrwhitt—Any relation of my old friend, Major-General George Tyrrwhitt of the Buffs, by the way?'

'My uncle.'

'Well, well! I was dining with him only last night.'

'It's a small world, after all,' said Lady Beazley-Beazley.

'It is, indeed,' said Orlando Wotherspoon. 'So small that I feel there is scarcely room in it for both Mulliner the cat-slosher and myself. I shall, therefore, do my humble best to eliminate him. And, as I was about to say, if, deprecating scenes of violence, you were about to plead for the young man, it will, I fear, be useless. I can listen to no intercession. The regulations of Our Dumb Chums' League are very strict.'

Marcella Tyrrwhitt uttered a hard, rasping laugh.

'Intercession?' she said. 'What do you mean – intercession? I wasn't going to intercede for this wambling misfit. I was going to ask if I could have first whack.'

'Indeed? Might I enquire why?'

Marcella's eyes flashed. Eustace became convinced, he tells me, that she had Spanish blood in her.

'Would you desire another sultana cake, sir?' asked Blenkinsop.

'I'll tell you why,' cried Marcella. 'Do you know what this man has done? I left my dog, Reginald, in his care, and he swore to guard and cherish him. And what occurred? My back was hardly turned when he went and gave him away as a birthday present to some foul female of the name of Beatrice Something.'

Eustace uttered a strangled cry.

'Let me explain!'

'I was in Paris,' proceeded Marcella, 'walking along the Champs-Elysées, and I saw a girl coming towards me with a Peke, and I said to myself: "Hullo, that Peke looks extraordinarily like my Reginald," and then she came up and it was Reginald, and I said: "Here! Hey! What are you doing with my Peke Reginald?" and this girl said: "What do you mean, your Peke Reginald? It's my Peke Percival, and it was given to me as a

birthday present by a friend of mine named Eustace Mulliner."
And I bounded on to the next aeroplane and came over here to
tear him into little shreds. And what I say is, it's a shame if I'm
not to be allowed a go at him after all the trouble and expense
I've been put to.'

And, burying her lovely face in her hands, she broke into
uncontrollable sobs.

Orlando Wotherspoon looked at Lady Beazley-Beazley.
Lady Beazley-Beazley looked at Orlando Wotherspoon. There
was pity in their eyes.

'There, there!' said Lady Beazley-Beazley. 'There, there,
there, my dear!'

'Believe me, Miss Tyrrwhitt,' said Orlando Wotherspoon,
patting her shoulder paternally, 'there are few things I would
not do for the niece of my old friend, Major-General George
Tyrrwhitt of the Buffs, but this is an occasion when, much as it
may distress me, I must be firm. I shall have to make my report at
the annual committee-meeting of Our Dumb Chums' League,
and how would I look, explaining that I had stepped aside and
allowed a delicately nurtured girl to act for me in a matter so
important as the one now on the agenda? Consider, Miss Tyrrwhitt! Reflect!'

'That's all very well,' sobbed Marcella, 'but all the way over,
all during those long, weary hours in the aeroplane, I was
buoying myself up with the thought of what I was going to do
to Eustace Mulliner when we met. See! I picked out my heaviest
parasol.'

Orlando Wotherspoon eyed the dainty weapon with an
indulgent smile.

'I fear that would hardly meet such a case as this,' he said. 'You
had far better leave the conduct of this affair to me.'

'Did you say more muffins, sir?' asked Blenkinsop.

'I do not wish to boast,' said Wotherspoon, 'but I have had considerable experience. I have been formally thanked by my committee on several occasions.'

'So you see, dear,' said Lady Beazley-Beazley soothingly, 'it will be ever so much better to—'

'Any buttered toast, fancy cakes, or macaroons?' asked Blenkinsop.

' – leave the matter entirely in Mr Wotherspoon's hands. I know just how you feel. I am feeling the same myself. But even in these modern days, my dear, it is the woman's part to efface herself and—'

'Oh, well!' said Marcella moodily.

Lady Beazley-Beazley folded her in her arms and over her shoulder nodded brightly at Orlando Wotherspoon.

'Please go on, Mr Wotherspoon,' she said.

Wotherspoon bowed, with a formal word of thanks. And, turning, was just in time to see Eustace disappearing through the window.

The fact is, as this dialogue progressed, Eustace had found himself more and more attracted by that open window. It had seemed to beckon to him. And at this juncture, dodging lightly round Blenkinsop, who had now lost his grip entirely and was suggesting things like watercress and fruit-salad, he precipitated himself into the depths and, making a good landing, raced for the open spaces at an excellent rate of speed.

That night, heavily cloaked and disguised in a false moustache, he called at my address, clamouring for tickets to Switzerland. He arrived there some few days later, and ever since has stuck to his duties with unremitting energy.

So much so that, in that letter which you saw me reading, he informs me that he has just been awarded the Order of the Crimson Edelweiss, Third Class, with crossed cuckoo-clocks, carrying with it the right to yodel in the presence of the Vice-President. A great honour for so young a man.

A sharp snort, plainly emanating from a soul in anguish, broke the serene silence that brooded over the bar-parlour of the Angler's Rest. And, looking up, we perceived Miss Postlethwaite, our sensitive barmaid, dabbing at her eyes with a dishcloth.

'Sorry you were troubled,' said Miss Postlethwaite, in answer to our concerned gaze, 'but he's just gone off to India, leaving her standing tight-lipped and dry-eyed in the moonlight outside the old Manor. And her little dog has crawled up and licked her hand, as if he understood and sympathized.'

We stared at one another blankly. It was Mr Mulliner who, with his usual clear insight, penetrated to the heart of the mystery.

'Ah,' said Mr Mulliner, 'you have been reading "Rue for Remembrance", I see. How did you like it?'

''Slovely,' said Miss Postlethwaite. 'It lays the soul of Woman bare as with a scalpel.'

'You do not consider that there is any falling off from the standard of its predecessors? You find it as good as "Parted Ways"?'

'Better.'

'Oh!' said a Stout and Bitter, enlightened. 'You're reading a novel?'

'The latest work,' said Mr Mulliner, 'from the pen of the authoress of "Parted Ways", which, as no doubt you remember, made so profound a sensation some years ago. I have a particular interest in this writer's work, as she is my niece.'

'Your niece?'

'By marriage. In private life she is Mrs Egbert Mulliner.' He sipped his hot Scotch and lemon, and mused a while.

'I wonder,' he said, 'if you would care to hear the story of my nephew Egbert and his bride? It is a simple little story, just one of those poignant dramas of human interest which are going on in our midst every day. If Miss Postlethwaite is not too racked by emotion to replenish my glass, I shall be delighted to tell it to you.'

I will ask you (said Mr Mulliner) to picture my nephew Egbert standing at the end of the pier at the picturesque little resort of Burwash Bay one night in June, trying to nerve himself to ask Evangeline Pembury the question that was so near his heart. A hundred times he had tried to ask it, and a hundred times he had lacked the courage. But to-night he was feeling in particularly good form, and he cleared his throat and spoke.

'There is something,' he said in a low, husky voice, 'that I want to ask you.'

He paused. He felt strangely breathless. The girl was looking out across the moonlit water. The night was very still. From far away in the distance came the faint strains of the town band, as it picked its way through the Star of Eve song from *Tannhäuser* – somewhat impeded by the second trombone, who had got his music-sheets mixed and was playing 'The Wedding of the Painted Doll'.

'Something,' said Egbert, 'that I want to ask you.'

'Go on,' she whispered.

Again he paused. He was afraid. Her answer meant so much to him.

Egbert Mulliner had come to this quiet seaside village for a rest cure. By profession he was an assistant editor, attached to the staff of *The Weekly Booklover*; and, as every statistician knows, assistant editors of literary weeklies are ranked high up among the Dangerous Trades. The strain of interviewing female novelists takes toll of the physique of all but the very hardiest.

For six months, week in and week out, Egbert Mulliner had been listening to female novelists talking about Art and their Ideals. He had seen them in cosy corners in their boudoirs, had watched them being kind to dogs and happiest when among their flowers. And one morning the proprietor of *The Booklover*, finding the young man sitting at his desk with little flecks of foam about his mouth and muttering over and over again in a dull, toneless voice the words, 'Aurelia McGoggin, she draws her inspiration from the scent of white lilies!' had taken him straight off to a specialist.

'Yes,' the specialist had said, after listening at Egbert's chest for a while through a sort of telephone, 'we are a little run down, are we not? We see floating spots, do we not, and are inclined occasionally to bark like a seal from pure depression of spirit? Precisely. What we need is to augment the red corpuscles in our bloodstream.'

And this augmentation of red corpuscles had been effected by his first sight of Evangeline Pembury. They had met at a picnic. As Egbert rested for a moment from the task of trying to dredge the sand from a plateful of chicken salad, his eyes had fallen on a divine girl squashing a wasp with a teaspoon. And for the first time since he had tottered out of the offices of *The Weekly*

Booklover he had ceased to feel like something which a cat, having dragged from an ash-can, has inspected and rejected with a shake of the head as unfit for feline consumption. In an instant his interior had become a sort of Jamboree of red corpuscles. Millions of them were splashing about and calling gaily to other millions, still hesitating on the bank: 'Come on in! The blood's fine!'

Ten minutes later he had reached the conclusion that life without Evangeline Pembury would be a blank.

And yet he had hesitated before laying his heart at her feet. She looked all right. She seemed all right. Quite possibly she *was* all right. But before proposing he had to be sure. He had to make certain that there was no danger of her suddenly producing a manuscript fastened in the top left corner with pink silk and asking his candid opinion of it. Everyone has his pet aversion. Some dislike slugs, others cockroaches. Egbert Mulliner disliked female novelists.

And so now, as they stood together in the moonlight, he said:
'Tell me, have you ever written a novel?'

She seemed surprised.

'A novel? No.'

'Short stories, perhaps?'

'No.'

Egbert lowered his voice.

'Poems?' he whispered, hoarsely.

'No.'

Egbert hesitated no longer. He produced his soul like a conjurer extracting a rabbit from a hat and slapped it down before her. He told her of his love, stressing its depth, purity, and lasting qualities. He begged, pleaded, rolled his eyes, and clasped her little hand in his. And when, pausing for a reply, he found that she had been doing a lot of thinking along the same lines and felt much the same about him as he did about her, he nearly fell over backwards. It seemed to him that his cup of joy was full.

It is odd how love will affect different people. It caused Egbert next morning to go out on the links and do the first nine in one over bogey. Whereas Evangeline, finding herself filled with a strange ferment which demanded immediate outlet, sat down at a little near-Chippendale table, ate five marsh-mallows, and began to write a novel.

Three weeks of the sunshine and ozone of Burwash Bay had toned up Egbert's system to the point where his medical adviser felt that it would be safe for him to go back to London and resume his fearful trade. Evangeline followed him a month later. She arrived home at four-fifteen on a sunny afternoon, and at four-sixteen-and-a-half Egbert shot through the door with the love-light in his eyes.

'Evangeline!'

'Egbert!'

But we will not dwell on the ecstasies of the reunited lovers. We will proceed to the point where Evangeline raised her head from Egbert's shoulder and uttered a little giggle. One would prefer to say that she gave a light laugh. But it was not a light laugh. It was a giggle – a furtive, sinister, shamefaced giggle, which froze Egbert's blood with a nameless fear. He stared at her, and she giggled again.

'Egbert,' she said, 'I want to tell you something.'

'Yes?' said Egbert.

Evangeline giggled once more.

'I know it sounds too silly for words,' she said, 'but—'

'Yes? Yes?'

'I've written a novel, Egbert.'

In the old Greek tragedies it was a recognized rule that any episode likely to excite the pity and terror of the audience to too great an extent must be enacted behind the scenes. Strictly speaking, therefore, this scene should be omitted. But the modern public can stand more than the ancient Greeks, so it had better remain on the records.

The room stopped swimming before Egbert Mulliner's tortured eyes. Gradually the piano, the chairs, the pictures, and the case of stuffed birds on the mantelpiece resumed their normal positions. He found speech.

'You've written a novel?' he said, dully.

'Well, I've got to chapter twenty-four.'

'You've got to chapter twenty-four?'

'And the rest will be easy.'

'The rest will be easy?'

Silence fell for a space – a silence broken only by Egbert's laboured breathing. Then Evangeline spoke impulsively.

'Oh, Egbert!' she cried. 'I really do think some of it is rather good. I'll read it to you now.'

How strange it is, when some great tragedy has come upon us, to look back at the comparatively mild beginnings of our misfortunes and remember how we thought then that Fate had done its worst. Egbert, that afternoon, fancied that he had plumbed the lowest depths of misery and anguish. Evangeline, he told himself, had fallen from the pedestal on which he had set her. She had revealed herself as a secret novel-writer. It was the limit, he felt, the extreme edge. It put the tin hat on things.

It was, alas! nothing of the kind. It bore the same resemblance to the limit that the first drop of rain bears to the thunderstorm.

The mistake was a pardonable one. The acute agony which he suffered that afternoon was more than sufficient excuse for Egbert Mulliner's blunder in supposing that he had drained the bitter cup to the dregs. He writhed, as he listened to this thing which she had entitled 'Parted Ways', unceasingly. It tied his very soul in knots.

Evangeline's novel was a horrible, an indecent production. Not in the sense that it would be likely to bring a blush to any cheek but his, but because she had put on paper in bald words every detail of the only romance that had ever come under her notice – her own. There it was, his entire courtship, including the first holy kiss and not omitting the quarrel which they had had within two days of the engagement. In the novel she had elaborated this quarrel, which in fact had lasted twenty-three minutes, into a ten years' estrangement – thus justifying the title and preventing the story finishing in the first five thousand words. As for his proposal, that was inserted *verbatim*; and, as he listened, Egbert shuddered to think that he could have polluted the air with such frightful horse-radish.

He marvelled, as many a man has done before and will again, how women can do these things. Listening to 'Parted Ways' made him, personally, feel as if he had suddenly lost his trousers while strolling along Piccadilly.

Something of these feelings he would have liked to put into words, but the Mulliners are famous for their chivalry. He would, he imagined, feel a certain shame if he ever hit Evangeline or walked on her face in thick shoes; but that shame would be as nothing to the shame he would feel if he spoke one millimetre of what he thought about 'Parted Ways'.

'Great!' he croaked.

Her eyes were shining.

'Do you really think so?'

'Fine!'

He found it easier to talk in monosyllables.

'I don't suppose any publisher would buy it,' said Evangeline.

Egbert began to feel a little better. Nothing, of course, could alter the fact that she had written a novel; but it might be possible to hush it up.

'So what I am going to do is to pay the expenses of publication.'

Egbert did not reply. He was staring into the middle distance and trying to light a fountain-pen with an unlighted match.

And Fate chuckled grimly, knowing that it had only just begun having fun with Egbert.

Once in every few publishing seasons there is an Event. For no apparent reason, the great heart of the Public gives a startled jump, and the public's great purse is emptied to secure copies of some novel which has stolen into the world without advance advertising and whose only claim to recognition is that *The Licensed Victuallers' Gazette* has stated in a two-line review that it is 'readable'.

The rising firm of Mainprice and Peabody published a first edition of three hundred copies of 'Parted Ways'. And when they found, to their chagrin, that Evangeline was only going to buy twenty of these – somehow Mainprice, who was an optimist, had got the idea that she was good for a hundred ('You can sell them to your friends') their only interest in the matter was to keep an eye on the current quotations for waste paper. The book they were going to make their money on was Stultitia Bodwin's 'Offal', in connection with which they had arranged in advance for a newspaper discussion on 'The Growing Menace of the Sex Motive in Fiction: Is There to be no Limit?'

Within a month 'Offal' was off the map. The newspaper discussion raged before an utterly indifferent public, which had made one of its quick changes and discovered that it had had enough of sex, and that what it wanted now was good, sweet, wholesome, tender tales of the pure love of a man for a maid, which you could leave lying about and didn't have to shove under the cushions of the chesterfield every time you heard your growing boys coming along. And the particular tale which it selected for its favour was Evangeline's 'Parted Ways'.

It is these swift, unheralded changes of the public mind which make publishers stick straws in their hair and powerful young novelists rush round to the wholesale grocery firms to ask if the berth of junior clerk is still open. Up to the very moment of the Great Switch, sex had been the one safe card. Publishers' lists were congested with scarlet tales of Men Who Did and Women Who Shouldn't Have Done but Who Took a Pop at It. And now the bottom had dropped out of the market without a word of warning, and practically the only way in which readers could gratify their new-born taste for the pure and simple was by fighting for copics of 'Parted Ways'.

They fought like tigers. The offices of Mainprice and Peabody hummed like a hive. Printing machines worked day and night. From the Butes of Kyle to the rock-bound coasts of Cornwall, a great cry went up for 'Parted Ways'. In every home in Ealing West 'Parted Ways' was found on the whatnot, next to the aspidistra and the family album. Clergymen preached about it, parodists parodied it, stockbrokers stayed away from Cochran's Revue to sit at home and cry over it.

Numerous paragraphs appeared in the Press concerning its probable adaptation into a play, a musical comedy, and a talking picture. Nigel Playfair was stated to have bought it for Sybil Thorndike, Sir Alfred Butt for Nellie Wallace. Laddie Cliff was reported to be planning a musical play based on it, starring Stanley Lupino and Leslie Henson. It was rumoured that Carnera was considering the part of 'Percy', the hero.

And on the crest of this wave, breathless but happy, rode Evangeline.

And Egbert? Oh, that's Egbert, spluttering down in the trough there. We can't be bothered about Egbert now.

Egbert, however, found ample time to be bothered about himself. He passed the days in a frame of mind which it would be ridiculous to call bewilderment. He was stunned, over-whelmed, sandbagged. Dimly he realized that considerably more than a hundred thousand perfect strangers were gloating over the most sacred secrecies of his private life, and that the exact words of his proposal of marriage were engraven on considerably over a hundred thousand minds. But, except that it made him feel as if he were being tarred and feathered in front of a large and interested audience, he did not mind that so much. What really troubled him was the alteration in Evangeline.

The human mind adjusts itself readily to prosperity. Evangeline's first phase, when celebrity was new and bewildering, soon passed. The stammering reception of the first reporter became a memory. At the end of two weeks she was talking to the Press with the easy nonchalance of a prominent politician, and coming back at note-book-bearing young men with words which they had to look up in the office Webster. Her art, she told them, was rhythmical rather than architectural, and she inclined, if anything, to the school of the surrealists.

She had soared above Egbert's low-browed enthusiasms. When he suggested motoring out to Addington and putting in a few holes of golf, she excused herself. She had letters to answer. People would keep writing to her, saying how much 'Parted Ways' had helped them, and one had to be civil to one's public. Autographs, too. She really could not spare a moment.

He asked her to come with him to the Amateur Championship. She shook her head. The date, she said, clashed with her lecture to the East Dulwich Daughters of Minerva Literary and Progress Club on 'Some Tendencies of Modern Fiction'.

All these things Egbert might have endured, for, despite the fact that she could speak so lightly of the Amateur Championship, he still loved her dearly. But at this point there suddenly floated into his life like a cloud of poison-gas the sinister figure of Jno. Henderson Banks.

'Who,' he asked, suspiciously, one day, as she was giving him ten minutes before hurrying off to address the Amalgamated Mothers of Manchester on 'The Novel: Should It Teach?' – 'was that man I saw you coming down the street with?'

'That wasn't a man,' replied Evangeline. 'That was my literary agent.'

And so it proved. Jno. Henderson Banks was now in control of Evangeline's affairs. This outstanding blot on the public weal was a sort of human *charlotte russe* with tortoiseshell-rimmed eye-glasses and a cooing, reverential manner towards his female clients. He had a dark, romantic face, a lissom figure, one of those beastly cravat things that go twice round the neck, and a habit of beginning his remarks with the words 'Dear lady'. The last man, in short, whom a fiancé would wish to have hanging about his betrothed. If Evangeline had to have a literary agent, the sort of literary agent Egbert would have selected for her would have been one of those stout, pie-faced literary agents who chew half-smoked cigars and wheeze as they enter the editorial sanctum.

A jealous frown flitted across his face.

'Looked a bit of a Gawd-help-us to me,' he said, critically.

'Mr Banks,' retorted Evangeline, 'is a superb man of business.'

'Oh, yeah?' said Egbert, sneering visibly.

And there for a time the matter rested.

But not for long. On the following Monday morning Egbert called Evangeline up on the telephone and asked her to lunch.

'I am sorry,' said Evangeline. 'I am engaged to lunch with Mr Banks.'

'Oh?' said Egbert.

'Yes,' said Evangeline.

'Ah!' said Egbert.

Two days later Egbert called Evangeline up on the telephone and invited her to dinner.

'I am sorry,' said Evangeline. 'I am dining with Mr Banks.'

'Ah?' said Egbert.

'Yes,' said Evangeline.

'Oh!' said Egbert.

Three days after that Egbert arrived at Evangeline's flat with tickets for the theatre.

'I am sorry—' began Evangeline.

'Don't say it,' said Egbert. 'Let me guess. You are going to the theatre with Mr Banks?'

'Yes, I am. He has seats for the first night of Tchekov's "Six Corpses in Search of an Undertaker".'

'He has, has he?'
'Yes, he has.'
'He *has*, eh?'
'Yes, he has.'

Egbert took a couple of turns about the room, and for a space there was silence except for the sharp grinding of his teeth. Then he spoke.

'Touching lightly on this gumboil Banks,' said Egbert, 'I am the last man to stand in the way of your having a literary agent. If you must write novels, that is a matter between you and your God. And, if you do see fit to write novels, I suppose you must have a literary agent. But – and this is where I want you to follow me very closely – I cannot see the necessity of employing a literary agent who looks like Lord Byron; a literary agent who coos in your left ear, a literary agent who not only addresses you as "Dear lady", but appears to find it essential to the conduct of his business to lunch, dine, and go to the theatre with you daily.'

'I—'

Egbert held up a compelling hand.

'I have not finished,' he said. 'Nobody,' he proceeded, 'could call me a narrow-minded man. If Jno. Henderson Banks looked a shade less like one of the great lovers of history, I would have nothing to say. If, when he talked business to a client, Jno. Henderson Banks's mode of vocal delivery were even slightly less reminiscent of a nightingale trilling to its mate, I would remain silent. But he doesn't, and it isn't. And such being the case, and taking into consideration the fact that you are engaged to me, I feel it my duty to instruct you to see this drooping flower far more infrequently. In fact, I would advocate expunging him altogether. If he wishes to discuss business with you, let him do it over the telephone. And I hope he gets the wrong number.'

Evangeline had risen, and was facing him with flashing eyes.

'Is that so?' she said.

'That,' said Egbert, 'is so.'

'Am I a serf?' demanded Evangeline.

'A what?' said Egbert.

'A serf. A slave. A peon. A creature subservient to your lightest whim.'

Egbert considered the point.

'No,' he said. 'I shouldn't think so.'

'No,' said Evangeline, 'I am not. And I refuse to allow you to dictate to me in the choice of my friends.'

Egbert stared blankly.

'You mean, after all I have said, that you intend to let this blighted chrysanthemum continue to frisk round?'

'I do.'

'You seriously propose to continue chummy with this revolting piece of cheese?'

'I do.'

'You absolutely and literally decline to give this mistake of Nature the push?'

'I do.'

'Well!' said Egbert.

A pleading note came into his voice.

'But, Evangeline, it is your Egbert who speaks.'

The haughty girl laughed a hard, bitter laugh.

'Is it?' she said. She laughed again. 'Do you imagine that we are still engaged?'

'Aren't we?'

'We certainly aren't. You have insulted me, outraged my finest feelings, given an exhibition of malignant tyranny which makes me thankful that I have realized in time the sort of man you are. Good-bye, Mr Mulliner!'

'But listen—' began Egbert.

'Go!' said Evangeline. 'Here is your hat.'

She pointed imperiously to the door. A moment later she had banged it behind him.

It was a grim-faced Egbert Mulliner who entered the elevator, and a grimmer-faced Egbert Mulliner who strode down Sloane Street. His dream, he realized, was over. He laughed harshly as he contemplated the fallen ruins of the castle which he had built in the air.

Well, he still had his work.

In the offices of *The Weekly Booklover* it was whispered that a strange change had come over Egbert Mulliner. He seemed a stronger, tougher man. His editor, who since Egbert's illness had behaved towards him with a touching humanity, allowing him to remain in the office and write paragraphs about Forthcoming Books while others, more robust, were sent off to interview the female novelists, now saw in him a right-hand man on whom he could lean.

When a column on 'Myrtle Bootle Among Her Books' was required, it was Egbert whom he sent out into the No Man's Land of Bloomsbury. When young Eustace Johnson, a novice who ought never to have been entrusted with such a dangerous commission, was found walking round in circles and bumping his head against the railings of Regent's Park after twenty minutes with Laura La Motte Grindlay, the great sex novelist, it was Egbert who was flung into the breach. And Egbert came through, wan but unscathed.

It was during this period that he interviewed Mabelle Grangerson and Mrs Goole-Plank on the same afternoon – a fcat which is still spoken of with bated breath in the offices of *The Weekly Booklover*. And not only in *The Booklover* offices. To this day 'Remember Mulliner!' is the slogan with which every literary editor encourages the faint-hearted who are wincing and hanging back.

'Was Mulliner afraid?' they say. 'Did Mulliner quail?'

And so it came about that when a 'Chat with Evangeline Pembury' was needed for the big Christmas Special Number, it was of Egbert that his editor thought first. He sent for him.

'Ah, Mulliner!'

'Well, chief?'

'Stop me if you've heard this one before,' said the editor, 'but it seems there was once an Irishman, a Scotsman, and a Jew—'

Then, the formalities inseparable from an interview between editor and assistant concluded, he came down to business.

'Mulliner,' he said, in that kind, fatherly way of his which endeared him to all his staff, 'I am going to begin by saying that it is in your power to do a big thing for the dear old paper. But after that I must tell you that, if you wish, you can refuse to do it. You have been through a hard time lately, and if you feel yourself unequal to this task, I shall understand. But the fact is, we have got to have a "Chat with Evangeline Pembury" for our Christmas Special.'

He saw the young man wince, and nodded sympathetically.

'You think it would be too much for you? I feared as much. They say she is the worst of the lot. Rather haughty and talks about uplift. Well, never mind. I must see what I can do with young Johnson. I hear he has quite recovered now, and is anxious to re-establish himself. Quite. I will send Johnson.'

Egbert Mulliner was himself again now.

'No, chief,' he said. 'I will go.'

'You will?'

'I will.'

'We shall need a column and a half.'

'You shall have a column and a half.'

The editor turned away, to hide a not unmanly emotion.

'Do it now, Mulliner,' he said, 'and get it over.'

A strange riot of emotion seethed in Egbert Mulliner's soul as he pressed the familiar bell which he had thought never to press again. Since their estrangement he had seen Evangeline once or twice, but only in the distance. Now he was to meet her face to face. Was he glad or sorry? He could not say. He only knew he loved her still.

He was in the sitting-room. How cosy it looked, how impregnated with her presence. There was the sofa on which he had so often sat, his arm about her waist—

A footstep behind him warned him that the time had come to don the mask. Forcing his features into an interviewer's hard smile, he turned.

'Good afternoon,' he said.

She was thinner. Either she had found success wearing, or she had been on the eighteen-day diet. Her beautiful face seemed drawn, and, unless he was mistaken, care-worn.

He fancied that for an instant her eyes had lit up at the sight of him, but he preserved the formal detachment of a stranger.

'Good afternoon, Miss Pembury,' he said. 'I represent *The Weekly Booklover*. I understand that my editor has been in communication with you and that you have kindly consented to tell us a few things which may interest our readers regarding your art and aims.'

She bit her lip.

'Will you take a seat, Mr—?'

'Mulliner,' said Egbert.

'Mr Mulliner,' said Evangeline. 'Do sit down. Yes, I shall be glad to tell you anything you wish.'

Egbert sat down.

'Are you fond of dogs, Miss Pembury?' he asked.

'I adore them,' said Evangeline.

'I should like, a little later, if I may,' said Egbert, 'to secure a snapshot of you being kind to a dog. Our readers appreciate these human touches, you understand.'

'Oh, quite,' said Evangeline. 'I will send out for a dog. I love dogs – and flowers.'

'You are happiest among your flowers, no doubt?'

'On the whole, yes.'

'You sometimes think they are the souls of little children who have died in their innocence?'

'Frequently.'

'And now,' said Egbert, licking the tip of his pencil, 'perhaps you would tell me something about your ideals. How are the ideals?'

Evangeline hesitated.

'Oh, they're fine,' she said.

'The novel,' said Egbert, 'has been described as among this age's greatest instruments for uplift? How do you check up on *that*?'

'Oh, yes.'

'Of course, there are novels and novels.'

'Oh, yes.'

'Are you contemplating a successor to "Parted Ways"?'

'Oh, yes.'

'Would it be indiscreet, Miss Pembury, to inquire to what extent it has progressed?'

'Oh, Egbert!' said Evangeline.

There are some speeches before which dignity melts like ice in August, resentment takes the full count, and the milk of human kindness surges back into the aching heart as if the dam had burst. Of these, 'Oh, Egbert!', especially when accompanied by tears, is one of the most notable.

Evangeline's 'Oh, Egbert!' had been accompanied by a Niagara of tears. She had flung herself on the sofa and was now chewing the cushion in an ecstasy of grief. She gulped like a bull-pup swallowing a chunk of steak. And, on the instant, Egbert Mulliner's adamantine reserve collapsed as if its legs had been knocked from under it. He dived for the sofa. He clasped her hand. He stroked her hair. He squeezed her waist. He patted her shoulder. He massaged her spine.

'Evangeline!'

'Oh, Egbert!'

The only flaw in Egbert Mulliner's happiness, as he knelt beside her, babbling comforting words, was the gloomy conviction that Evangeline would certainly lift the entire scene, dialogue and all, and use it in her next novel. And it was for this reason that, when he could manage it, he censored his remarks to some extent.

But, as he warmed to his work, he forgot caution altogether. She was clinging to him, whispering his name piteously. By the time he had finished, he had committed himself to about two thousand words of a nature calculated to send Mainprice and Peabody screaming with joy about their office.

He refused to allow himself to worry about it. What of it? He had done his stuff, and if it sold a hundred thousand copies – well, let it sell a hundred thousand copies. Holding Evangeline in his arms, he did not care if he was copyrighted in every language, including the Scandinavian.

'Oh, Egbert!' said Evangeline.

'My darling!'

'Oh, Egbert, I'm in such trouble.'

'My angel! What is it?'

Evangeline sat up and tried to dry her eyes.

'It's Mr Banks.'

A savage frown darkened Egbert Mulliner's face. He told himself that he might have foreseen this. A man who wore a tie that went twice round the neck was sure, sooner or later, to inflict some hideous insult on helpless womanhood. Add tortoiseshell-rimmed glasses, and you had what practically amounted to a fiend in human shape.

'I'll murder him,' he said. 'I ought to have done it long ago, but one keeps putting these things off. What has he done? Did he force his loathsome attentions on you? Has that tortoiseshell-rimmed satyr been trying to kiss you, or something?'

'He has been fixing me up solid.'

Egbert blinked.

'Doing what?'

'Fixing me up solid. With the magazines. He has arranged for me to write three serials and I don't know how many short stories.'

'Getting you contracts, you mean?'

Evangeline nodded tearfully.

'Yes. He seems to have fixed me up solid with almost everybody. And they've been sending me cheques in advance – hundreds of them. What am I to do? Oh, what am I to do?'

'Cash them,' said Egbert.

'But afterwards?'

'Spend the money.'

'But after that?'

Egbert reflected.

'Well, it's a nuisance, of course,' he said, 'but after that I suppose you'll have to write the stuff.'

Evangeline sobbed like a lost soul.

'But I can't! I've been trying for weeks, and I can't write anything. And I never shall be able to write anything. I don't want to write anything. I hate writing. I don't know what to write about. I wish I were dead.'

She clung to him.

'I got a letter from him this morning. He has just fixed me up solid with two more magazines.'

Egbert kissed her tenderly. Before he had become an assistant editor, he, too, had been an author, and he understood. It is not the being paid money in advance that jars the sensitive artist: it is the having to work.

'What shall I do?' cried Evangeline.

'Drop the whole thing,' said Egbert. 'Evangeline, do you remember your first drive at golf? I wasn't there, but I bet it travelled about five hundred yards and you wondered what people meant when they talked about golf being a difficult game. After that, for ages, you couldn't do anything right. And then, gradually, after years of frightful toil, you began to get the knack of it. It is just the same with writing. You've had your first drive, and it has been some smite. Now, if you're going to stick to it, you've got to do the frightful toil. What's the use? Drop it.'

'And return the money?'

Egbert shook his head.

'No,' he said, firmly. 'There you go too far. Stick to the money like glue. Clutch it with both hands. Bury it in the garden and mark the spot with a cross.'

'But what about the stories? Who is going to write them?'

Egbert smiled a tender smile.

'I am,' he said. 'Before I saw the light, I, too, used to write stearine bilge just like "Parted Ways". When we are married, I shall say to you, if I remember the book of words correctly, "With all my worldly goods I thee endow." They will include three novels I was never able to kid a publisher into printing, and at least twenty short stories no editor would accept. I give them to you freely. You can have the first of the novels to-night, and we will sit back and watch Mainprice and Peabody sell half a million copies.'

'Oh, Egbert!' said Evangeline.

'Evangeline!' said Egbert.

From the moment the Draught Stout entered the bar-parlour of the Angler's Rest, it had been obvious that he was not his usual cheery self. His face was drawn and twisted, and he sat with bowed head in a distant corner by the window, contributing nothing to the conversation which, with Mr Mulliner as its centre, was in progress around the fire. From time to time he heaved a hollow sigh.

A sympathetic Lemonade and Angostura, putting down his glass, went across and laid a kindly hand on the sufferer's shoulder.

'What is it, old man?' he asked. 'Lost a friend?'

'Worse,' said the Draught Stout. 'A mystery novel. Got half-way through it on the journey down here, and left it in the train.'

'My nephew Cyril, the interior decorator,' said Mr Mulliner, 'once did the very same thing. These mental lapses are not infrequent.'

'And now,' proceeded the Draught Stout, 'I'm going to have a sleepless night, wondering who poisoned Sir Geoffrey Tuttle, Bart.'

'The Bart was poisoned, was he?'

'You never said a truer word. Personally, I think it was the Vicar who did him in. He was known to be interested in strange poisons.'

Mr Mulliner smiled indulgently.

'It was not the Vicar,' he said. 'I happen to have read "The Murglow Manor Mystery". The guilty man was the plumber.'

'What plumber?'

'The one who comes in chapter two to mend the shower-bath. Sir Geoffrey had wronged his aunt in the year '96, so he fastened a snake in the nozzle of the shower-bath with glue; and when Sir Geoffrey turned on the stream the hot water melted the glue. This released the snake, which dropped through one of the holes, bit the Baronet in the leg, and disappeared down the waste-pipe.'

'But that can't be right,' said the Draught Stout. 'Between chapter two and the murder there was an interval of several days.'

'The plumber forgot his snake and had to go back for it,' explained Mr Mulliner. 'I trust that this revelation will prove sedative.'

'I feel a new man,' said the Draught Stout. 'I'd have lain awake worrying about that murder all night.'

'I suppose you would. My nephew Cyril was just the same. Nothing in this modern life of ours,' said Mr Mulliner, taking a sip of his hot Scotch and lemon, 'is more remarkable than the way in which the mystery novel has gripped the public. Your true enthusiast, deprived of his favourite reading, will stop at nothing in order to get it. He is like a victim of the drug habit when withheld from cocaine. My nephew Cyril—'

'Amazing the things people will leave in trains,' said a Small Lager. 'Bags...umbrellas...even stuffed chimpanzees, occasionally, I've been told. I heard a story the other day—'

* * *

My nephew Cyril (said Mr Mulliner) had a greater passion for mystery stories than anyone I have ever met. I attribute this to the fact that, like so many interior decorators, he was a fragile, delicate young fellow, extraordinarily vulnerable to any ailment that happened to be going the rounds. Every time he caught mumps or influenza or German measles or the like, he occupied the period of convalescence in reading mystery stories. And, as the appetite grows by what it feeds on, he had become, at the time at which this narrative opens, a confirmed addict. Not only did he devour every volume of this type on which he could lay his hands, but he was also to be found at any theatre which was offering the kind of drama where skinny arms come unexpectedly out of the chiffonier and the audience feels a mild surprise if the lights stay on for ten consecutive minutes.

And it was during a performance of 'The Grey Vampire' at the St James's that he found himself sitting next to Amelia Bassett, the girl whom he was to love with all the stored-up fervour of a man who hitherto had been inclined rather to edge away when in the presence of the other sex.

He did not know her name was Amelia Bassett. He had never seen her before. All he knew was that at last he had met his fate, and for the whole of the first act he was pondering the problem of how he was to make her acquaintance.

It was as the lights went up for the first intermission that he was aroused from his thoughts by a sharp pain in the right leg. He was just wondering whether it was gout or sciatica when, glancing down, he perceived that what had happened was that his neighbour, absorbed by the drama, had absent-mindedly collected a handful of his flesh and was twisting it in an ecstasy of excitement.

It seemed to Cyril a good *point d'appui*.

'Excuse me,' he said.

The girl turned. Her eyes were glowing, and the tip of her nose still quivered.

'I beg your pardon?'

'My leg,' said Cyril. 'Might I have it back, if you've finished with it?'

The girl looked down. She started visibly.

'I'm awfully sorry,' she gasped.

'Not at all,' said Cyril. 'Only too glad to have been of assistance.'

'I got carried away.'

'You are evidently fond of mystery plays.'

'I love them.'

'So do I. And mystery novels?'

'Oh, yes!'

'Have you read "Blood on the Banisters"?'

'Oh, *yes*! I thought it was better than "Severed Throats".'

'So did I,' said Cyril. 'Much better. Brighter murders, subtler detectives, crisper clues . . . better in every way.'

The two twin souls gazed into each other's eyes. There is no surer foundation for a beautiful friendship than a mutual taste in literature.

'My name is Amelia Bassett,' said the girl.

'Mine is Cyril Mulliner. Bassett?' He frowned thoughtfully. 'The name seems familiar.'

'Perhaps you have heard of my mother. Lady Bassett. She's rather a well-known big-game hunter and explorer. She tramps through jungles and things. She's gone out to the lobby for a smoke. By the way' – she hesitated – 'if she finds us talking, will you remember that we met at the Polterwoods'?'

'I quite understand.'

'You see, mother doesn't like people who talk to me without a formal introduction. And, when mother doesn't like anyone, she is so apt to hit them over the head with some hard instrument.'

'I see,' said Cyril. 'Like the Human Ape in "Gore by the Gallon".'

'Exactly. Tell me,' said the girl, changing the subject, 'if you were a millionaire, would you rather be stabbed in the back with a paper-knife or found dead without a mark on you, staring with blank eyes at some appalling sight?'

Cyril was about to reply when, looking past her, he found himself virtually in the latter position. A woman of extraordinary formidableness had lowered herself into the seat beyond and was scrutinizing him keenly through a tortoiseshell lorgnette. She reminded Cyril of Wallace Beery.

'Friend of yours, Amelia?' she said.

'This is Mr Mulliner, mother. We met at the Polterwoods'.'

'Ah?' said Lady Bassett.

She inspected Cyril through her lorgnette.

'Mr Mulliner,' she said, 'is a little like the chief of the Lower Isisi – though, of course, he was darker and had a ring through his nose. A dear, good fellow,' she continued reminiscently, 'but inclined to become familiar under the influence of trade gin. I shot him in the leg.'

'Er – why?' asked Cyril.

'He was not behaving like a gentleman,' said Lady Bassett primly.

'After taking your treatment,' said Cyril, awed, 'I'll bet he could have written a Book of Etiquette.'

'I believe he did,' said Lady Bassett carelessly. 'You must come and call on us some afternoon, Mr Mulliner. I am in the telephone book. If you are interested in man-eating pumas, I can show you some nice heads.'

The curtain rose on act two, and Cyril returned to his thoughts. Love, he felt joyously, had come into his life at last. But then so, he had to admit, had Lady Bassett. There is, he reflected, always something.

I will pass lightly over the period of Cyril's wooing. Suffice it to say that his progress was rapid. From the moment he told Amelia that he had once met Dorothy Sayers, he never looked back. And one afternoon, calling and finding that Lady Bassett was away in the country, he took the girl's hand in his and told his love.

For a while all was well. Amelia's reactions proved satisfactory to a degree. She checked up enthusiastically on his proposition. Falling into his arms, she admitted specifically that he was her Dream Man.

Then came the jarring note.

'But it's no use,' she said, her lovely eyes filling with tears. 'Mother will never give her consent.'

'Why not?' said Cyril, stunned. 'What is it she objects to about me?'

'I don't know. But she generally alludes to you as "that pipsqueak".'

'Pipsqueak?' said Cyril. 'What *is* a pipsqueak?'

'I'm not quite sure, but it's something mother doesn't like very much. It's a pity she ever found out that you are an interior decorator.'

'An honourable profession,' said Cyril, a little stiffly.

'I know; but what she admires are men who have to do with the great open spaces.'

'Well, I also design ornamental gardens.'

'Yes,' said the girl doubtfully, 'but still—'

'And, dash it,' said Cyril indignantly, 'this isn't the Victorian age. All that business of Mother's Consent went out twenty years ago.'

'Yes, but no one told mother.'

'It's preposterous!' cried Cyril. 'I never heard such rot. Let's just slip off and get married quietly and send her a picture postcard from Venice or somewhere, with a cross and a "This is our room. Wish you were with us" on it.'

The girl shuddered.

'She would be with us,' she said. 'You don't know mother. The moment she got that picture postcard, she would come over to wherever we were and put you across her knee and spank you with a hair-brush. I don't think I could ever feel the same towards you if I saw you lying across mother's knee, being spanked with a hair-brush. It would spoil the honeymoon.'

Cyril frowned. But a man who has spent most of his life trying out a series of patent medicines is always an optimist.

'There is only one thing to be done,' he said. 'I shall see your mother and try to make her listen to reason. Where is she now?'

'She left this morning for a visit to the Winghams in Sussex.'

'Excellent! I know the Winghams. In fact, I have a standing invitation to go and stay with them whenever I like. I'll send them a wire and push down this evening. I will oil up to your mother sedulously and try to correct her present unfavourable impression of me. Then, choosing my moment, I will shoot her the news. It may work. It may not work. But at any rate I consider it a fair sporting venture.'

'But you are so diffident, Cyril. So shrinking. So retiring and shy. How can you carry through such a task?'

'Love will nerve me.'

'Enough, do you think? Remember what mother is. Wouldn't a good, strong drink be more help?'

Cyril looked doubtful.

'My doctor has always forbidden me alcoholic stimulants. He says they increase the blood pressure.'

'Well, when you meet mother, you will need all the blood pressure you can get. I really do advise you to fuel up a little before you see her.'

'Yes,' agreed Cyril, nodding thoughtfully. 'I think you're right. It shall be as you say. Good-bye, my angel one.'

'Good-bye, Cyril, darling. You will think of me every minute while you're gone?'

'Every single minute. Well, practically every single minute. You see, I have just got Horatio Slingsby's latest book, "Strychnine in the Soup", and I shall be dipping into that from time to time. But all the rest of the while... Have you read it, by the way?'

'Not yet. I had a copy, but mother took it with her.'

'Ah? Well, if I am to catch a train that will get me to Barkley for dinner, I must be going. Good-bye, sweetheart, and never forget that Gilbert Glendale in "The Missing Toe" won the girl he loved in spite of being up against two mysterious stranglers and the entire Black Moustache gang.'

He kissed her fondly, and went off to pack.

* * *

Barkley Towers, the country seat of Sir Mortimer and Lady Wingham, was two hours from London by rail. Thinking of Amelia and reading the opening chapters of Horatio Slingsby's powerful story, Cyril found the journey pass rapidly. In fact, so preoccupied was he that it was only as the train started to draw out of Barkley Regis station that he realized where he was. He managed to hurl himself on to the platform just in time.

As he had taken the five-seven express, stopping only at Gluebury Peveril, he arrived at Barkley Towers at an hour which enabled him not only to be on hand for dinner but also to take part in the life-giving distribution of cocktails which preceded the meal.

The house-party, he perceived on entering the drawing-room, was a small one. Besides Lady Bassett and himself, the only visitors were a nondescript couple of the name of Simpson, and a tall, bronzed, handsome man with flashing eyes who, his hostess informed him in a whispered aside, was Lester Mapledurham (pronounced Mum), the explorer and big-game hunter.

Perhaps it was the oppressive sensation of being in the same room with two explorers and big-game hunters that brought home to Cyril the need for following Amelia's advice as quickly as possible. But probably the mere sight of Lady Bassett alone would have been enough to make him break a lifelong abstinence. To her normal resemblance to Wallace Beery she appeared now to have added a distinct suggestion of Victor McLaglen, and the spectacle was sufficient to send Cyril leaping toward the cocktail tray.

After three rapid glasses he felt a better and a braver man. And so lavishly did he irrigate the ensuing dinner with hock, sherry, champagne, old brandy and port, that at the conclusion of the meal he was pleased to find that his diffidence had completely vanished. He rose from the table feeling equal to asking a dozen Lady Bassetts for their consent to marry a dozen daughters.

In fact, as he confided to the butler, prodding him genially in the ribs as the spoke, if Lady Bassett attempted to put on any dog with *him*, he would know what to do about it. He made no threats, he explained to the butler, he simply stated that he would know what to do about it. The butler said 'Very good, sir. Thank you, sir,' and the incident closed.

It had been Cyril's intention – feeling, as he did, in this singularly uplifted and dominant frame of mind – to get hold of Amelia's mother and start oiling up to her immediately after dinner. But, what with falling into a doze in the smoking-room and then getting into an argument on theology with one of the under-footmen whom he met in the hall, he did not reach the drawing-room until nearly half-past ten. And he was annoyed, on walking in with a merry cry of 'Lady Bassett! Call for Lady Bassett!' on his lips, to discover that she had retired to her room.

Had Cyril's mood been even slightly less elevated, this news might have acted as a check on his enthusiasm. So generous, however, had been Sir Mortimer's hospitality that he merely nodded eleven times, to indicate comprehension, and then, having ascertained that his quarry was roosting in the Blue Room, sped thither with a brief 'Tally-ho!'

Arriving at the Blue Room, he banged heartily on the door and breezed in. He found Lady Bassett propped up with pillows. She was smoking a cigar and reading a book. And that book, Cyril saw with intense surprise and resentment, was none other than Horatio Slingsby's 'Strychnine in the Soup'.

The spectacle brought him to an abrupt halt.

'Well, I'm dashed!' he cried. 'Well, I'm blowed! What do you mean by pinching my book?'

Lady Bassett had lowered her cigar. She now raised her eyebrows.

'What are you doing in my room, Mr Mulliner?'

'It's a little hard,' said Cyril, trembling with self-pity. 'I go to enormous expense to buy detective stories, and no sooner is my back turned than people rush about the place sneaking them.'

'This book belongs to my daughter Amelia.'

'Good old Amelia!' said Cyril cordially. 'One of the best.'

'I borrowed it to read in the train. Now will you kindly tell me what you are doing in my room, Mr Mulliner?'

Cyril smote his forehead.

'Of course. I remember now. It all comes back to me. She told me you had taken it. And, what's more, I've suddenly recollected something which clears you completely. I was hustled and bustled at the end of the journey. I sprang to my feet, hurled bags on to the platform – in a word, lost my head. And, like a chump, I went and left my copy of "Strychnine in the Soup" in the train. Well, I can only apologize.'

'You can not only apologize. You can also tell me what you are doing in my room?'

'What I am doing in your room?'

'Exactly.'

'Ah!' said Cyril, sitting down on the bed. 'You may well ask.'

'I *have* asked. Three times.'

Cyril closed his eyes. For some reason, his mind seemed cloudy and not at its best.

'If you are proposing to go to sleep here, Mr Mulliner,' said Lady Bassett, 'tell me, and I shall know what to do about it.'

The phrase touched a chord in Cyril's memory. He recollected now his reasons for being where he was. Opening his eyes, he fixed them on her.

'Lady Bassett,' he said, 'you are, I believe, an explorer?'

'I am.'

'In the course of your explorations, you have wandered through many a jungle in many a distant land?'

'I have.'

'Tell me, Lady Bassett,' said Cyril keenly, 'while making a pest of yourself to the denizens of those jungles, did you notice one thing? I allude to the fact that Love is everywhere – aye, even in the jungle. Love, independent of bounds and frontiers, of nationality and species, works its spell on every living thing. So that, no matter whether an individual be a Congo native, an American song-writer, a jaguar, an armadillo, a bespoke tailor, or a tsetse-tsetse fly, he will infallibly seek his mate. So why shouldn't an interior decorator and designer of ornamental gardens? I put this to you, Lady Bassett.'

'Mr Mulliner,' said his room-mate, 'you are blotto!'

Cyril waved his hand in a spacious gesture, and fell off the bed.

'Blotto I may be,' he said, resuming his seat, 'but, none the less, argue as you will, you can't get away from the fact that I love your daughter Amelia.'

There was a tense pause.

'What did you say?' cried Lady Bassett.

'When?' said Cyril absently, for he had fallen into a daydream and, as far as the intervening blankets would permit, was playing 'This little pig went to market' with his companion's toes.

'Did I hear you say... my daughter Amelia?'

'Grey-eyed girl, medium height, sort of browny-red hair,' said Cyril, to assist her memory. 'Dash it, you *must* know Amelia. She goes everywhere. And let me tell you something, Mrs – I've forgotten your name. We're going to be married, if I can obtain her foul mother's consent. Speaking as an old friend, what would you say the chances were?'

'Extremely slight.'

'Eh?'

'Seeing that I *am* Amelia's mother. ...'

Cyril blinked, genuinely surprised.

'Why, so you are! I didn't recognize you. Have you been there all the time?'

'I have.'

Suddenly Cyril's gaze hardened. He drew himself up stiffly.

'What are you doing in my bed?' he demanded.

'This is not your bed.'

'Then whose is it?'

'Mine.'

Cyril shrugged his shoulders helplessly.

'Well, it all looks very funny to me,' he said. 'I suppose I must believe your story, but, I repeat, I consider the whole thing odd, and I propose to institute very strict enquiries. I may tell you that I happen to know the ringleaders. I wish you a very hearty good night.'

It was perhaps an hour later that Cyril, who had been walking on the terrace in deep thought, repaired once more to the Blue Room in quest of information. Running over the details of the recent interview in his head, he had suddenly discovered that there was a point which had not been satisfactorily cleared up.

'I say,' he said.

Lady Bassett looked up from her book, plainly annoyed.

'Have you no bedroom of your own, Mr Mulliner?'

'Oh, yes,' said Cyril. 'They've bedded me out in the Moat Room. But there was something I wanted you to tell me.'

'Well?'

'Did you say I might or mightn't?'

'Might or mightn't what?'

'Marry Amelia?'

'No. You may not.'

'No?'

'No!'

'Oh!' said Cyril. 'Well, pip-pip once more.'

It was a moody Cyril Mulliner who withdrew to the Moat Room. He now realized the position of affairs. The mother of the girl he loved refused to accept him as an eligible suitor. A dickens of a situation to be in, felt Cyril, sombrely unshoeing himself.

Then he brightened a little. His life, he reflected, might be wrecked, but he still had two-thirds of 'Strychnine in the Soup' to read.

At the moment when the train reached Barkley Regis station, Cyril had just got to the bit where Detective Inspector Mould looks through the half-open cellar door and, drawing in his breath with a sharp, hissing sound, recoils in horror. It was obviously going to be good. He was just about to proceed to the dressing-table where, he presumed, the footman had placed the book on unpacking his bag, when an icy stream seemed to flow down the centre of his spine and the room and its contents danced before him.

Once more he had remembered that he had left the volume in the train.

He uttered an animal cry and tottered to a chair.

The subject of bereavement is one that has often been treated powerfully by poets, who have run the whole gamut of the emotions while laying bare for us the agony of those who have lost parents, wives, children, gazelles, money, fame, dogs, cats, doves, sweethearts, horses, and even collar-studs. But no poet has yet treated of the most poignant bereavement of all – that of the man half-way through a detective story who finds himself at bedtime without the book.

Cyril did not care to think of the night that lay before him. Already his brain was lashing itself from side to side like a wounded snake as it sought for some explanation of Inspector Mould's strange behaviour. Horatio Slingsby was an author who could be relied on to keep faith with his public. He was not the sort of man to fob the reader off in the next chapter with the statement that what had made Inspector Mould look horrified was the fact that he had suddenly remembered that he had forgotten all about the letter his wife had given him to post. If looking through cellar doors disturbed a Slingsby detective, it was because a dismembered corpse lay there, or at least a severed hand.

A soft moan, as of some thing in torment, escaped Cyril. What to do? What to do? Even a makeshift substitute for 'Strychnine in the Soup' was beyond his reach. He knew so well what he would find if he went to the library in search of something to read. Sir Mortimer Wingham was heavy and country-squire-ish. His wife affected strange religions. Their literature was in keeping with their tastes. In the library there would be books on Ba-ha-ism, volumes in old leather of the Rural Encyclopædia, 'My Two Years in Sunny Ceylon', by the Rev. Orlo Waterbury... but of anything that would interest Scotland Yard, of anything with a bit of blood in it and a corpse or two into which a fellow could get his teeth, not a trace.

What, then, coming right back to it, to do?

And suddenly, as if in answer to the question, came the solution. Electrified, he saw the way out.

The hour was now well advanced. By this time Lady Bassett must surely be asleep. 'Strychnine in the Soup' would be lying on the table beside her bed. All he had to do was to creep in and grab it.

The more he considered the idea, the better it looked. It was not as if he did not know the way to Lady Bassett's room or the topography of it when he got there. It seemed to him as if most of his later life had been spent in Lady Bassett's room. He could find his way about it with his eyes shut.

He hesitated no longer. Donning a dressing-gown, he left his room and hurried along the passage.

Pushing open the door of the Blue Room and closing it softly behind him, Cyril stood for a moment full of all those emotions which come to man revisiting some long-familiar spot. There the dear old room was, just the same as ever. How it all came back to him! The place was in darkness, but that did not deter him. He knew where the bed-table was, and he made for it with stealthy steps.

In the manner in which Cyril Mulliner advanced towards the bed-table there was much which would have reminded Lady Bassett, had she been an eye-witness, of the furtive prowl of the Lesser Iguanodon tracking its prey. In only one respect did Cyril and this creature of the wild differ in their technique.

Iguanodons – and this applies not only to the Lesser but to the Larger Iguanodon – seldom, if ever, trip over cords on the floor and bring the lamps to which they are attached crashing to the ground like a ton of bricks.

Cyril did. Scarcely had he snatched up the book and placed it in the pocket of his dressing-gown, when his foot became entangled in the trailing cord and the lamp on the table leaped nimbly into the air and, to the accompaniment of a sound not unlike that made by a hundred plates coming apart simultaneously in the hands of a hundred scullery-maids, nose-dived to the floor and became a total loss.

At the same moment, Lady Bassett, who had been chasing a bat out of the window, stepped in from the balcony and switched on the lights.

To say that Cyril Mulliner was taken aback would be to understate the facts. Nothing like his recent misadventure had happened to him since his eleventh year, when, going surreptitiously to his mother's cupboard for jam, he had jerked three shelves down on his head, containing milk, butter, home-made preserves, pickles, cheese, eggs, cakes, and potted-meat. His feelings on the present occasion closely paralleled that boyhood thrill.

Lady Bassett also appeared somewhat discomposed.

'You!' she said.

Cyril nodded, endeavouring the while to smile in a reassuring manner.

'Hullo!' he said.

His hostess's manner was now one of unmistakable displeasure.

'Am I not to have a moment of privacy, Mr Mulliner?' she asked severely. 'I am, I trust, a broad-minded woman, but I cannot approve of this idea of communal bedrooms.'

Cyril made an effort to be conciliatory.

'I do keep coming in, don't I?' he said.

'You do,' agreed Lady Bassett. 'Sir Mortimer informed me, on learning that I had been given this room, that it was supposed to be haunted. Had I known that it was haunted by you, Mr Mulliner, I should have packed up and gone to the local inn.'

Cyril bowed his head. The censure, he could not but feel, was deserved.

'I admit,' he said, 'that my conduct has been open to criticism. In extenuation, I can but plead my great love. This is no idle social call, Lady Bassett. I looked in because I wished to take up again this matter of my marrying your daughter Amelia. You say I can't. Why can't I? Answer me that, Lady Bassett.'

'I have other views for Amelia,' said Lady Bassett stiffly. 'When my daughter gets married it will not be to a spineless, invertebrate product of our modern hot-house civilization, but to a strong, upstanding, keen-eyed, two-fisted he-man of the open spaces. I have no wish to hurt your feelings, Mr Mulliner,' she continued, more kindly, 'but you must admit that you are, when all is said and done, a pipsqueak.'

'I deny it,' cried Cyril warmly. 'I don't even know what a pipsqueak is.'

'A pipsqueak is a man who has never seen the sun rise beyond the reaches of the Lower Zambezi; who would not know what to do if faced by a charging rhinoceros. What, pray, would you do if faced by a charging rhinoceros, Mr Mulliner?'

'I am not likely,' said Cyril, 'to move in the same social circles as charging rhinoceri.'

'Or take another simple case, such as happens every day. Suppose you are crossing a rude bridge over a stream in Equatorial Africa. You have been thinking of a hundred trifles and are in a reverie. From this you wake to discover that in the branches overhead a python is extending its fangs towards you. At the same time, you observe that at one end of the bridge is a crouching puma; at the other are two head hunters – call them Pat and Mike – with poisoned blow-pipes to their lips. Below, half hidden in the stream, is an alligator. What would you do in such a case, Mr Mulliner?'

Cyril weighed the point.

'I should feel embarrassed,' he had to admit. 'I shouldn't know where to look.'

Lady Bassett laughed an amused, scornful little laugh.

'Precisely. Such a situation would not, however, disturb Lester Mapledurham.'

'Lester Mapledurham!'

'The man who is to marry my daughter Amelia. He asked me for her hand shortly after dinner.'

Cyril reeled. The blow, falling so suddenly and unexpectedly, had made him feel boneless. And yet, he felt, he might have expected this. These explorers and big-game hunters stick together.

'In a situation such as I have outlined, Lester Mapledurham would simply drop from the bridge, wait till the alligator made its rush, insert a stout stick between its jaws, and then hit it in the eye with a spear, being careful to avoid its lashing tail. He would then drift down-stream and land at some safer spot. That is the type of man I wish for as a son-in-law.'

Cyril left the room without a word. Not even the fact that he now had 'Strychnine in the Soup' in his possession could cheer his mood of unrelieved blackness. Back in his room, he tossed the book moodily on to the bed and began to pace the floor. And he had scarcely completed two laps when the door opened.

For an instant, when he heard the click of the latch, Cyril supposed that his visitor must be Lady Bassett, who, having put two and two together on discovering her loss, had come to demand her property back. And he cursed the rashness which had led him to fling it so carelessly upon the bed, in full view.

But it was not Lady Bassett. The intruder was Lester Mapledurham. Clad in a suit of pyjamas which in their general colour scheme reminded Cyril of a boudoir he had recently decorated for a Society poetess, he stood with folded arms, his keen eyes fixed menacingly on the young man.

'Give me those jewels!' said Lester Mapledurham.

Cyril was at a loss.

'Jewels?'

'Jewels!'

'What jewels?'

Lester Mapledurham tossed his head impatiently.

'I don't know what jewels. They may be the Wingham Pearls or the Bassett Diamonds or the Simpson Sapphires. I'm not sure which room it was I saw you coming out of.'

Cyril began to understand.

'Oh, did you see me coming out of a room?'

'I did. I heard a crash and, when I looked out, you were hurrying along the corridor.'

'I can explain everything,' said Cyril. 'I had just been having a chat with Lady Bassett on a personal matter. Nothing to do with diamonds.'

'You're sure?' said Mapledurham.

'Oh, rather,' said Cyril. 'We talked about rhinoceri and pythons and her daughter Amelia and alligators and all that sort of thing, and then I came away.'

Lester Mapledurham seemed only half convinced.

'H'm!' he said. 'Well, if anything is missing in the morning, I shall know what to do about it.' His eye fell on the bed. 'Hullo!' he went on, with sudden animation. 'Slingsby's latest? Well, well! I've been wanting to get hold of this. I hear it's good. The *Leeds Mercury* says: "These gripping pages...".'

He turned to the door, and with a hideous pang of agony Cyril perceived that it was plainly his intention to take the book with him. It was swinging lightly from a bronzed hand about the size of a medium ham.

'Here!' he cried, vehemently.

Lester Mapledurham turned.

'Well?'

'Oh, nothing,' said Cyril. 'Just good night.'

He flung himself face downwards on the bed as the door closed, cursing himself for the craven cowardice which had kept him from snatching the book from the explorer. There had been a moment when he had almost nerved himself to the deed, but it was followed by another moment in which he had caught the other's eye. And it was as if he had found himself exchanging glances with Lady Bassett's charging rhinoceros.

And now, thanks to this pusillanimity, he was once more 'Strychnine in the Soup'-less.

How long Cyril lay there, a prey to the gloomiest thoughts, he could not have said. He was aroused from his meditations by the sound of the door opening again.

Lady Bassett stood before him. It was plain that she was deeply moved. In addition to resembling Wallace Beery and Victor McLaglen, she now had a distinct look of George Bancroft.

She pointed a quivering finger at Cyril.

'You hound!' she cried. 'Give me that book!'

Cyril maintained his poise with a strong effort.

'What book?'

'The book you sneaked out of my room?'

'Has someone sneaked a book out of your room?' Cyril struck his forehead. 'Great heavens!' he cried.

'Mr Mulliner,' said Lady Bassett coldly, 'more book and less gibbering!'

Cyril raised a hand.

'I know who's got your book. Lester Mapledurham!'

'Don't be absurd.'

'He has, I tell you. As I was on my way to your room just now, I saw him coming out, carrying something in a furtive manner. I remember wondering a bit at the time. He's in the Clock Room. If we pop along there now, we shall just catch him red-handed.'

Lady Bassett reflected.

'It is impossible,' she said at length. 'He is incapable of such an act. Lester Mapledurham is a man who once killed a lion with a sardine-opener.'

'The very worst sort,' said Cyril. 'Ask anyone.'

'And he is engaged to my daughter.' Lady Bassett paused. 'Well, he won't be long, if I find that what you say is true. Come, Mr Mulliner!'

Together the two passed down the silent passage. At the door of the Clock Room they paused. A light streamed from beneath it. Cyril pointed silently to this sinister evidence of reading in bed, and noted that his companion stiffened and said something to herself in an undertone in what appeared to be some sort of native dialect.

The next moment she had flung the door open and, with a spring like that of a crouching zebu, had leaped to the bed and wrenched the book from Lester Mapledurham's hands.

'So!' said Lady Bassett.

'So!' said Cyril, feeling that he could not do better than follow the lead of such a woman.

'Hullo!' said Lester Mapledurham, surprised. 'Something the matter?'

'So it was you who stole my book!'

'Your book?' said Lester Mapledurham. 'I borrowed this from Mr Mulliner there.'

'A likely story!' said Cyril. 'Lady Bassett is aware that I left my copy of "Strychnine in the Soup" in the train.'

'Certainly,' said Lady Bassett. 'It's no use talking, young man, I have caught you with the goods. And let me tell you one thing that may be of interest. If you think that, after a dastardly act like this, you are going to marry Amelia, forget it!'

'Wipe it right out of your mind,' said Cyril.

'But listen—!'

'I will not listen. Come, Mr Mulliner.'

She left the room, followed by Cyril. For some moments they walked in silence.

'A merciful escape,' said Cyril.

'For whom?'

'For Amelia. My gosh, think of her tied to a man like that. Must be a relief to you to feel that she's going to marry a respectable interior decorator.'

Lady Bassett halted. They were standing outside the Moat Room now. She looked at Cyril, her eyebrows raised.

'Are you under the impression, Mr Mulliner,' she said, 'that, on the strength of what has happened, I intend to accept you as a son-in-law?'

Cyril reeled.

'Don't you?'

'Certainly not.'

Something inside Cyril seemed to snap. Recklessness descended upon him. He became for a space a thing of courage and fire, like the African leopard in the mating season.

'Oh!' he said.

And, deftly whisking 'Strychnine in the Soup' from his companion's hand, he darted into his room, banged the door, and bolted it.

'Mr Mulliner!'

It was Lady Bassett's voice, coming pleadingly through the woodwork. It was plain that she was shaken to the core, and Cyril smiled sardonically. He was in a position to dictate terms.

'Give me that book, Mr Mulliner!'

'Certainly not,' said Cyril. 'I intend to read it myself. I hear good reports of it on every side. The *Peebles Intelligencer* says: "Vigorous and absorbing".'

A low wail from the other side of the door answered him.

'Of course,' said Cyril, suggestively, 'if it were my future mother-in-law who was speaking, her word would naturally be law.'

There was a silence outside.

'Very well,' said Lady Bassett.

'I may marry Amelia?'

'You may.'

Cyril unbolted the door.

'Come – Mother,' he said, in a soft, kindly voice. 'We will read it together, down in the library.'

Lady Bassett was still shaken.

'I hope I have acted for the best,' she said.

'You have,' said Cyril.

'You will make Amelia a good husband?'

'Grade A,' Cyril assured her.

'Well, even if you don't,' said Lady Bassett resignedly, 'I can't go to bed without that book. I had just got to the bit where Inspector Mould is trapped in the underground den of the Faceless Fiend.'

Cyril quivered.

'*Is* there a Faceless Fiend?' he cried.

'There are two Faceless Fiends,' said Lady Bassett.

'My gosh!' said Cyril. 'Let's hurry.'

The bar-parlour of the Angler's Rest was fuller than usual. Our local race meeting had been held during the afternoon, and this always means a rush of custom. In addition to the *habitués*, that faithful little band of listeners which sits nightly at the feet of Mr Mulliner, there were present some half a dozen strangers. One of these, a fair-haired young Stout and Mild, wore the unmistakable air of a man who has not been fortunate in his selections. He sat staring before him with dull eyes and a drooping jaw, and nothing that his companions could do seemed able to cheer him up.

A genial Sherry and Bitters, one of the regular patrons, eyed the sufferer with bluff sympathy.

'What your friend appears to need, gentlemen,' he said, 'is a dose of Mulliner's Buck-U-Uppo.'

'What's Mulliner's Buck-U-Uppo?' asked one of the strangers, a Whisky Sour, interested. 'Never heard of it myself.'

Mr Mulliner smiled indulgently.

'He is referring,' he explained, 'to a tonic invented by my brother Wilfred, the well-known analytical chemist. It is not often administered to human beings, having been designed primarily to encourage elephants in India to conduct themselves with an easy nonchalance during the tiger-hunts which are so popular in that country. But occasionally human beings do partake of it, with impressive results. I was telling the company here not long ago of the remarkable effect it had on my nephew Augustine, the curate.'

'It bucked him up?'

'It bucked him up very considerably. It acted on his bishop, too, when he tried it, in a similar manner. It is undoubtedly a most efficient tonic, strong and invigorating.'

'How is Augustine, by the way?' asked the Sherry and Bitters.

'Extremely well. I received a letter from him only this morning. I am not sure if I told you, but he is a vicar now, at Walsingford-below-Chiveney-on-Thames. A delightful resort, mostly honeysuckle and apple-cheeked villagers.'

'Anything been happening to him lately?'

'It is strange that you should ask that,' said Mr Mulliner, finishing his hot Scotch and lemon and rapping gently on the table. 'In this letter to which I allude he has quite an interesting story to relate. It deals with the loves of Ronald Bracy-Gascoigne and Hypatia Wace. Hypatia is a school-friend of my nephew's wife. She has been staying at the vicarage, nursing her through a sharp attack of mumps. She is also the niece and ward of Augustine's superior of the Cloth, the Bishop of Stortford.'

'Was that the bishop who took the Buck-U-Uppo?'

'The same,' said Mr Mulliner. 'As for Ronald Bracy-Gascoigne, he is a young man of independent means who resides in the neighbourhood. He is, of course, one of the Berkshire Bracy-Gascoignes.'

'Ronald,' said a Lemonade and Angostura thoughtfully. 'Now, there's a name I never cared for.'

'In that respect,' said Mr Mulliner, 'you differ from Hypatia Wace. She thought it swell. She loved Ronald Bracy-Gascoigne with all the fervour of a young girl's heart, and they were provisionally engaged to be married. Provisionally, I say, because, before the firing-squad could actually be assembled, it was necessary for the young couple to obtain the consent of the Bishop of Stortford. Mark that, gentlemen. Their engagement was subject to the Bishop of Stortford's consent. This was the snag that protruded jaggedly from the middle of the primrose path of their happiness, and for quite a while it seemed as if Cupid must inevitably stub his toe on it.'

I will select as the point at which to begin my tale (said Mr Mulliner), a lovely evening in June, when all Nature seemed to smile and the rays of the setting sun fell like molten gold upon the picturesque garden of the vicarage at Walsingford-below-Chiveney-on-Thames. On a rustic bench beneath a spreading elm, Hypatia Wace and Ronald Bracy-Gascoigne watched the shadows lengthening across the smooth lawn: and to the girl there appeared something symbolical and ominous about this creeping blackness. She shivered. To her, it was as if the sun-bathed lawn represented her happiness and the shadows the doom that was creeping upon it.

'Are you doing anything at the moment, Ronnie?' she asked.

'Eh?' said Ronald Bracy-Gascoigne. 'What? Doing anything? Oh, you mean doing anything? No, I'm not doing anything.'

'Then kiss me,' cried Hypatia.

'Right-ho,' said the young man. 'I see what you mean. Rather a scheme. I will.'

He did so: and for some moments they clung together in a close embrace. Then Ronald, releasing her gently, began to slap himself between the shoulder-blades.

'Beetle or something down my back,' he explained. 'Probably fell off the tree.'

'Kiss me again,' whispered Hypatia.

'In one second, old girl,' said Ronald. 'The instant I've dealt with this beetle or something. Would you mind just fetching me a whack on about the fourth knob of the spine, reading from the top downwards. I fancy that would make it think a bit.'

Hypatia uttered a sharp exclamation.

'Is this a time,' she cried passionately, 'to talk of beetles?'

'Well, you know, don't you know,' said Ronald, with a touch of apology in his voice, 'they seem rather to force themselves on your attention when they get down your back. I daresay you've had the same experience yourself. I don't suppose in the ordinary way I mention beetles half a dozen times a year, but ... I should say the fifth knob would be about the spot now. A good, sharp slosh with plenty of follow-through ought to do the trick.'

Hypatia clenched her hands. She was seething with that febrile exasperation which, since the days of Eve, has come upon women who find themselves linked to a cloth-head.

'You poor sap,' she said tensely. 'You keep babbling about beetles, and you don't appear to realize that, if you want to kiss me, you'd better cram in all the kissing you can now, while the going is good. It doesn't seem to have occurred to you that after to-night you're going to fade out of the picture.'

'Oh, I say, no! Why?'

'My Uncle Percy arrives this evening.'

'The Bishop?'

'Yes. And my Aunt Priscilla.'

'And you think they won't be any too frightfully keen on me?'

'I know they won't. I wrote and told them we were engaged, and I had a letter this afternoon saying you wouldn't do.'

'No, I say, really? Oh, I say, dash it!'

'"Out of the question", my uncle said. And underlined it.'

'Not really? Not absolutely underlined it?'

'Yes. Twice. In very black ink.'

A cloud darkened the young man's face. The beetle had begun to try out a few tentative dance-steps on the small of his back, but he ignored it. A Tiller troupe of beetles could not have engaged his attention now.

'But what's he got against me?'

'Well, for one thing he has heard that you were sent down from Oxford.'

'But all the best men are. Look at What's-his-name. Chap who wrote poems. Shellac, or some such name.'

'And then he knows that you dance a lot.'

'What's wrong with dancing? I'm not very well up in these things, but didn't David dance before Saul? Or am I thinking of a couple of other fellows? Anyway, I know that somebody danced before somebody and was extremely highly thought of in consequence.'

'David...'

'I'm not saying it *was* David, mind you. It may quite easily have been Samuel.'

'David...'

'Or even Nimshi, the son of Bimshi, or somebody like that.'

'David, or Samuel, or Nimshi the son of Bimshi,' said Hypatia, 'did not dance at the Home from Home.'

Her allusion was to the latest of those frivolous night-clubs which spring up from time to time on the reaches of the Thames which are within a comfortable distance from London. This one stood some half a mile from the vicarage gates.

'Is *that* what the Bish is beefing about?' demanded Ronald, genuinely astonished. 'You don't mean to tell me he really objects to the Home from Home? Why, a cathedral couldn't be more rigidly respectable. Does he realize that the place has only been raided five times in the whole course of its existence? A few simple words of explanation will put all this right. I'll have a talk with the old boy.'

Hypatia shook her head.

'No,' she said. 'It's no use talking. He has made his mind up. One of the things he said in his letter was that, rather than countenance my union to a worthless worldling like you, he would gladly see me turned into a pillar of salt like Lot's wife, Genesis 19, 26. And nothing could be fairer than that, could it? So what I would suggest is that you start in immediately to fold me in your arms and cover my face with kisses. It's the last chance you'll get.'

The young man was about to follow her advice, for he could see that there was much in what she said: but at this moment there came from the direction of the house the sound of a manly voice trolling the Psalm for the Second Sunday after Septuagesima. And an instant later their host, the Rev. Augustine Mulliner, appeared in sight. He saw them and came hurrying across the garden, leaping over the flower-beds with extraordinary lissomness.

'Amazing elasticity that bird has, both physical and mental,' said Ronald Bracy-Gascoigne, eyeing Augustine, as he approached, with a gloomy envy. 'How does he get that way?'

'He was telling me last night,' said Hypatia. 'He has a tonic which he takes regularly. It is called Mulliner's Buck-U-Uppo, and acts directly upon the red corpuscles.'

'I wish he would give the Bish a swig of it,' said Ronald moodily. A sudden light of hope came into his eyes. 'I say, Hyp, old girl,' he exclaimed. 'That's rather a notion. Don't you think it's rather a notion? It looks to me like something of an idea. If the Bish were to dip his beak into the stuff, it might make him take a brighter view of me.'

Hypatia, like all girls who intend to be good wives, made it a practice to look on any suggestions thrown out by her future lord and master as fatuous and futile.

'I never heard anything so silly,' she said.

'Well, I wish you would try it. No harm in trying it, what?'

'Of course I shall do nothing of the kind.'

'Well, I do think you might try it,' said Ronald. 'I mean, try it, don't you know.'

He could speak no further on the matter, for now they were no longer alone. Augustine had come up. His kindly face looked grave.

'I say, Ronnie, old bloke,' said Augustine, 'I don't want to hurry you, but I think I ought to inform you that the Bishes, male and female, are even now on their way up from the station. I should be popping, if I were you. The prudent man looketh well to his going. Proverbs, 14, 15.'

'All right,' said Ronald sombrely. 'I suppose,' he added, turning to the girl, 'you wouldn't care to sneak out to-night and come and have one final spot of shoe-slithering at the Home from Home? It's a Gala Night. Might be fun, what? Give us a chance of saying good-bye properly, and all that.'

'I never heard anything so silly,' said Hypatia, mechanically. 'Of course I'll come.'

'Right-ho. Meet you down the road about twelve then,' said Ronald Bracy-Gascoigne.

He walked swiftly away, and presently was lost to sight behind the shrubbery. Hypatia turned with a choking sob, and Augustine took her hand and squeezed it gently.

'Cheer up, old onion,' he urged. 'Don't lose hope. Remember, many waters cannot quench love. Song of Solomon, 8, 7.'

'I don't see what quenching love has got to do with it,' said Hypatia peevishly. 'Our trouble is that I've got an uncle complete with gaiters and a hat with bootlaces on it who can't see Ronnie with a telescope.'

'I know.' Augustine nodded sympathetically. 'And my heart bleeds for you. I've been through all this sort of thing myself. When I was trying to marry Jane, I was stymied by a father-in-law-to-be who had to be seen to be believed. A chap, I assure you, who combined chronic shortness of temper with the ability to bend pokers round his biceps. Tact was what won him over, and tact is what I propose to employ in your case. I have an idea at the back of my mind. I won't tell you what it is, but you may take it from me it's the real tabasco.'

'How kind you are, Augustine!' sighed the girl.

'It comes from mixing with Boy Scouts. You may have noticed that the village is stiff with them. But don't you worry, old girl. I owe you a lot for the way you've looked after Jane these last weeks, and I'm going to see you through. If I can't fix up your little affair, I'll eat my Hymns Ancient and Modern. And uncooked at that.'

And with these brave words Augustine Mulliner turned two hand-springs, vaulted over the rustic bench, and went about his duties in the parish.

Augustine was rather relieved, when he came down to dinner that night, to find that Hypatia was not to be among those present. The girl was taking her meal on a tray with Jane, his wife, in the invalid's bedroom, and he was consequently able to embark with freedom on the discussion of her affairs. As soon as the servants had left the room, accordingly he addressed himself to the task.

'Now listen, you two dear good souls,' he said. 'What I want to talk to you about, now that we are alone, is this business of Hypatia and Ronald Bracy-Gascoigne.'

The Lady Bishopess pursed her lips, displeased. She was a woman of ample and majestic build. A friend of Augustine's, who had been attached to the Tank Corps during the War, had once said that he knew nothing that brought the old days back more vividly than the sight of her. All she needed, he maintained, was a steering-wheel and a couple of machine-guns, and you could have moved her up into any Front Line and no questions asked.

'Please, Mr Mulliner!' she said coldly.

Augustine was not to be deterred. Like all the Mulliners, he was at heart a man of reckless courage.

'They tell me you are thinking of bunging a spanner into the works,' he said. 'Not true, I hope?'

'Quite true, Mr Mulliner. Am I not right, Percy?'

'Quite,' said the Bishop.

'We have made careful enquiries about the young man, and are satisfied that he is entirely unsuitable.'

'Would you say that?' said Augustine. 'A pretty good egg, I've always found him. What's your main objection to the poor lizard?'

The Lady Bishopess shivered.

'We learn that he is frequently to be seen dancing at an advanced hour, not only in gilded London night-clubs but even in what should be the purer atmosphere of Walsingford-below-Chiveney-on-Thames. There is a resort in this neighbourhood known, I believe, as the Home from Home.'

'Yes, just down the road,' said Augustine. 'It's a Gala Night to-night, if you cared to look in. Fancy dress optional.'

'I understand that he is to be seen there almost nightly. Now, against dancing *qua* dancing,' proceeded the Lady Bishopess, 'I have nothing to say. Properly conducted, it is a pleasing and innocuous pastime. In my own younger days I myself was no mean exponent of the polka, the schottische and the Roger de Coverley. Indeed, it was at a Dance in Aid of the Distressed Daughters of Clergymen of the Church of England Relief Fund that I first met my husband.'

'Really?' said Augustine. 'Well, cheerio!' he said, draining his glass of port.

'But dancing, as the term is understood nowadays, is another matter. I have no doubt that what you call a Gala Night would prove, on inspection, to be little less than one of those orgies where perfect strangers of both sexes unblushingly throw coloured celluloid balls at one another and in other ways behave in a manner more suitable to the Cities of the Plain than to our dear England. No, Mr Mulliner, if this young man Ronald Bracy-Gascoigne is in the habit of frequenting places of the type of the Home from Home, he is not a fit mate for a pure young girl like my niece Hypatia. Am I not correct, Percy?'

'Perfectly correct, my dear.'

'Oh, right-ho, then,' said Augustine philosophically, and turned the conversation to the forthcoming Pan-Anglican synod.

Living in the country had given Augustine Mulliner the excellent habit of going early to bed. He had a sermon to compose on the morrow, and in order to be fresh and at his best in the morning he retired shortly before eleven. And, as he had anticipated an unbroken eight hours of refreshing sleep, it was with no little annoyance that he became aware, towards midnight, of a hand on his shoulder, shaking him. Opening his eyes, he found that the light had been switched on and that the Bishop of Stortford was standing at his bedside.

'Hullo!' said Augustine. 'Anything wrong?'

The Bishop smiled genially, and hummed a bar or two of the hymn for those of riper years at sea. He was plainly in excellent spirits.

'Nothing, my dear fellow,' he replied. 'In fact, very much the reverse. How are you, Mulliner?'

'I feel fine, Bish.'

'I'll bet you two chasubles to a hassock you don't feel as fine as I do,' said the Bishop. 'It must be something in the air of this place. I haven't felt like this since Boat Race Night of the year 1893. Wow!' he continued. 'Whoopee! How goodly are thy tents, O Jacob, and thy tabernacles, O Israel! Numbers, 44, 5.' And, gripping the rail of the bed, he endeavoured to balance himself on his hands with his feet in the air.

Augustine looked at him with growing concern. He could not rid himself of a curious feeling that there was something sinister behind this ebullience. Often before, he had seen his guest in a mood of dignified animation, for the robust cheerfulness of the other's outlook was famous in ecclesiastical circles. But here, surely, was something more than dignified animation.

'Yes,' proceeded the Bishop, completing his gymnastics and sitting down on the bed, 'I feel like a fighting-cock, Mulliner. I am full of beans. And the idea of wasting the golden hours of the night in bed seemed so silly that I had to get up and look in on you for a chat. Now, this is what I want to speak to you about, my dear fellow. I wonder if you recollect writing to me – round about Epiphany, it would have been – to tell me of the hit you made in the Boy Scouts pantomime here? You played Sindbad the Sailor, if I am not mistaken?'

'That's right.'

'Well, what I came here to ask, my dear Mulliner, was this. Can you, by any chance, lay your hand on that Sindbad costume? I want to borrow it, if I may.'

'What for?'

'Never mind what for, Mulliner. Sufficient for you to know that motives of the soundest churchmanship render it essential for me to have that suit.'

'Very well, Bish. I'll find it for you tomorrow.'

'To-morrow will not do. This dilatory spirit of putting things off, this sluggish attitude of *laissez-faire* and procrastination,' said the Bishop, frowning, 'are scarcely what I expected to find in you, Mulliner. But there,' he added, more kindly, 'let us say no more. Just dig up that Sindbad costume and look slippy about it, and we will forget the whole matter. What does it look like?'

'Just an ordinary sailor-suit, Bish.'

'Excellent. Some species of head-gear goes with it, no doubt?'

'A cap with H.M.S. *Blotto* on the band.'

'Admirable. Then, my dear fellow,' said the Bishop, beaming, 'if you will just let me have it, I will trouble you no further to-night. Your day's toil in the vineyard has earned repose. The sleep of the labouring man is sweet. Ecclesiastes, 5, 12.'

As the door closed behind his guest, Augustine was conscious of a definite uneasiness. Only once before had he seen his spiritual superior in quite this exalted condition. That had been two years ago, when they had gone down to Harchester College to unveil the statue of Lord Hemel of Hempstead. On that occasion, he recollected, the Bishop, under the influence of an overdose of Buck-U-Uppo, had not been content with unveiling the statue. He had gone out in the small hours of the night and painted it pink. Augustine could still recall the surge of emotion which had come upon him when, leaning out of the window, he had observed the prelate climbing up the waterspout on his way back to his room. And he still remembered the sorrowful pity with which he had listened to the other's lame explanation that he was a cat belonging to the cook.

Sleep, in the present circumstances, was out of the question. With a pensive sigh, Augustine slipped on a dressing-gown and went downstairs to his study. It would ease his mind, he thought, to do a little work on that sermon of his.

Augustine's study was on the ground floor, looking on to the garden. It was a lovely night, and he opened the French windows, the better to enjoy the soothing scents of the flowers beyond. Then, seating himself at his desk, he began to work.

The task of composing a sermon which should practically make sense and yet not be above the heads of his rustic flock was always one that caused Augustine Mulliner to concentrate tensely. Soon he was lost in his labour and oblivious to everything but the problem of how to find a word of one syllable that meant Supralapsarianism. A glaze of preoccupation had come over his eyes, and the tip of his tongue, protruding from the left corner of his mouth, revolved in slow circles.

From this waking trance he emerged slowly to the realization that somebody was speaking his name and that he was no longer alone in the room.

Seated in his arm-chair, her lithe young body wrapped in a green dressing-gown, was Hypatia Wace.

'Hullo!' said Augustine, staring. 'You here?'

'Hullo,' said Hypatia. 'Yes, I'm here.'

'I thought you had gone to the Home from Home to meet Ronald.'

Hypatia shook her head.

'We never made it,' she said. 'Ronnie rang up to say that he had had a private tip that the place was to be raided to-night. So we thought it wasn't safe to start anything.'

'Quite right,' said Augustine approvingly. 'Prudence first. Whatsoever thou takest in hand, remember the end and thou shalt never do amiss. Ecclesiastes, 7, 36.'

Hypatia dabbed at her eyes with her handkerchief.

'I couldn't sleep, and I saw the light, so I came down. I'm so miserable, Augustine.'

'About this Ronnie business?'

'Yes.'

'There, there. Everything's going to be hotsy-totsy.'

'I don't see how you make that out. Have you heard Uncle Percy and Aunt Priscilla talk about Ronnie? They couldn't be more off the poor, unfortunate fish if he were the Scarlet Woman of Babylon.'

'I know. I know. But, as I hinted this afternoon, I have a little plan. I have been giving your case a good deal of thought, and I think you will agree with me that it is your Aunt Priscilla who is the real trouble. Sweeten her, and the Bish will follow her lead. What she thinks to-day, he always thinks to-morrow. In other words, if we can win her over, he will give his consent in a minute. Am I wrong or am I right?'

Hypatia nodded.

'Yes,' she said. 'That's right, as far as it goes. Uncle Percy always does what Aunt Priscilla tells him to. But how are you going to sweeten her?'

'With Mulliner's Buck-U-Uppo. You remember how often I have spoken to you of the properties of that admirable tonic. It changes the whole mental outlook like magic. We have only to slip a few drops into your Aunt Priscilla's hot milk to-morrow night, and you will be amazed at the results.'

'You really guarantee that?'

'Absolutely.'

'Then that's fine,' said the girl, brightening visibly, 'because that's exactly what I did this evening. Ronnie was suggesting it when you came up this afternoon, and I thought I might as well try it. I found the bottle in the cupboard in here, and I put some in Aunt Priscilla's hot milk and, in order to make a good job of it, some in Uncle Percy's toddy, too.'

An icy hand seemed to clutch at Augustine's heart. He began to understand the inwardness of the recent scene in his bedroom.

'How much?' he gasped.

'Oh, not much,' said Hypatia. 'I didn't want to poison the dear old things. About a tablespoonful apiece.'

A shuddering groan came raspingly from Augustine's lips.

'Are you aware,' he said in a low, toneless voice, 'that the medium dose for an adult elephant is one teaspoonful?'

'No!'

'Yes. The most fearful consequences result from anything in the nature of an overdose.' He groaned. 'No wonder the Bishop seemed a little strange in his manner just now.'

'Did he seem strange in his manner?'

Augustine nodded dully.

'He came into my room and did hand-springs on the end of the bed and went away in my Sindbad the Sailor suit.'

'What did he want that for?'

Augustine shuddered.

'I scarcely dare to face the thought,' he said, 'but can he have been contemplating a visit to the Home from Home? It is Gala Night, remember.'

'Why, of course,' said Hypatia. 'And that must have been why Aunt Priscilla came to me about an hour ago and asked me if I could lend her my Columbine costume.'

'She did!' cried Augustine.

'Certainly she did. I couldn't think what she wanted it for. But now, of course, I see.'

Augustine uttered a moan that seemed to come from the depths of his soul.

'Run up to her room and see if she is still there,' he said. 'If I'm not very much mistaken, we have sown the wind and we shall reap the whirlwind. Hosea, 8, 7.'

The girl hurried away, and Augustine began to pace the floor feverishly. He had completed five laps and was beginning a sixth, when there was a noise outside the French windows and a sailorly form shot through and fell panting into the arm-chair.

'Bish!' cried Augustine.

The Bishop waved a hand, to indicate that he would be with him as soon as he had attended to this matter of taking in a fresh supply of breath, and continued to pant. Augustine watched him, deeply concerned. There was a shop-soiled look about his guest. Part of the Sindbad costume had been torn away as if by some irresistible force, and the hat was missing. His worst fears appeared to have been realized.

'Bish!' he cried. 'What has been happening?'

The Bishop sat up. He was breathing more easily now, and a pleased, almost complacent, look had come into his face.

'Woof!' he said. 'Some binge!'

'Tell me what happened,' pleaded Augustine, agitated.

The Bishop reflected, arranging his facts in chronological order.

'Well,' he said, 'when I got to the Home from Home, everybody was dancing. Nice orchestra. Nice tune. Nice floor. So I danced, too.'

'You danced?'

'Certainly I danced, Mulliner,' replied the Bishop with a dignity that sat well upon him. 'A hornpipe. I consider it the duty of the higher clergy on these occasions to set an example. You didn't suppose I would go to a place like the Home from Home to play solitaire? Harmless relaxation is not forbidden, I believe?'

'But can you dance?'

'*Can* I dance?' said the Bishop. 'Can I *dance*, Mulliner? Have you ever heard of Nijinsky?'

'Yes.'

'My stage name,' said the Bishop.

Augustine swallowed tensely.

'Who did you dance with?' he asked.

'At first,' said the Bishop, 'I danced alone. But then, most fortunately, my dear wife arrived, looking perfectly charming in some sort of filmy material, and we danced together.'

'But wasn't she surprised to see you there?'

'Not in the least. Why should she be?'

'Oh, I don't know.'

'Then why did you put the question?'

'I wasn't thinking.'

'Always think before you speak, Mulliner,' said the Bishop reprovingly.

The door opened, and Hypatia hurried in.

'She's not—' She stopped. 'Uncle!' she cried.

'Ah, my dear,' said the Bishop. 'But I was telling you, Mulliner. After we had been dancing for some time, a most annoying thing occurred. Just as we were enjoying ourselves – everybody cutting up and having a good time – who should come in but a lot of interfering policemen. A most brusque and unpleasant body of men. Inquisitive, too. One of them kept asking me my name and address. But I soon put a stop to all that sort of nonsense. I plugged him in the eye.'

'You plugged him in the eye?'

'I plugged him in the eye, Mulliner. That's when I got this suit torn. The fellow was annoying me intensely. He ignored my repeated statement that I gave my name and address only to my oldest and closest friends, and had the audacity to clutch me by what I suppose a costumier would describe as the slack of my garment. Well, naturally I plugged him in the eye. I come of a fighting line, Mulliner. My ancestor, Bishop Odo, was famous in William the Conqueror's day for his work with the battle-axe. So I biffed this bird. And did he take a toss? Ask me!' said the Bishop, chuckling contentedly.

Augustine and Hypatia exchanged glances.

'But, uncle—' began Hypatia.

'Don't interrupt, my child,' said the Bishop. 'I cannot marshal my thoughts if you persist in interrupting. Where was I? Ah, yes. Well, then the already existing state of confusion grew intensified. The whole *tempo* of the proceedings became, as it were, quickened. Somebody turned out the lights, and somebody else upset a table and I decided to come away.' A pensive look flitted over his face. 'I trust,' he said, 'that my dear wife also contrived to leave without undue inconvenience. The last I saw of her, she was diving through one of the windows in a manner which, I thought, showed considerable lissomness and resource. Ah, here she is, and looking none the worse for her adventures. Come in, my dear. I was just telling Hypatia and our good host here of our little evening from home.'

The Lady Bishopess stood breathing heavily. She was not in the best of training. She had the appearance of a Tank which is missing on one cylinder.

'Save me, Percy,' she gasped.

'Certainly, my dear,' said the Bishop cordially. 'From what?'

In silence the Lady Bishopess pointed at the window. Through it, like some figure of doom, was striding a policeman. He, too, was breathing in a laboured manner, like one touched in the wind.

The Bishop drew himself up.

'And what, pray,' he asked coldly, 'is the meaning of this intrusion?'

'Ah!' said the policeman.

He closed the windows and stood with his back against them.

It seemed to Augustine that the moment had arrived for a man of tact to take the situation in hand.

'Good evening, constable,' he said genially. 'You appear to have been taking exercise. I have no doubt that you would enjoy a little refreshment.'

The policeman licked his lips, but did not speak.

'I have an excellent tonic here in my cupboard,' proceeded Augustine, 'and I think you will find it most restorative. I will mix it with a little seltzer.'

The policeman took the glass, but in a preoccupied manner. His attention was still riveted on the Bishop and his consort.

'Caught you, have I?' he said.

'I fail to understand you, officer,' said the Bishop frigidly.

'I've been chasing her,' said the policeman, pointing to the Lady Bishopess, 'a good mile it must have been.'

'Then you acted,' said the Bishop severely, 'in a most offensive and uncalled-for way. On her physician's recommendation, my dear wife takes a short cross-country run each night before retiring to rest. Things have come to a sorry pass if she cannot follow her doctor's orders without being pursued – I will use a stronger word – chivvied – by the constabulary.'

'And it was by her doctor's orders that she went to the Home from Home, eh?' said the policeman keenly.

'I shall be vastly surprised to learn,' said the Bishop, 'that my dear wife has been anywhere near the resort you mention.'

'And you were there, too. I saw you.'

'Absurd!'

'I saw you punch Constable Booker in the eye.'

'Ridiculous!'

'If you weren't there,' said the policeman, 'what are you doing wearing that sailor-suit?'

The Bishop raised his eyebrows.

'I cannot permit my choice of costume,' he said, 'arrived at – I need scarcely say – only after much reflection and meditation, to be criticized by a man who habitually goes about in public in a blue uniform and a helmet. What, may I enquire, is it that you object to in this sailor-suit? There is nothing wrong, I venture to believe, nothing degrading in a sailor-suit. Many of England's greatest men have worn sailor-suits. Nelson ...Admiral Beatty—'

'And Arthur Prince,' said Hypatia.

'And, as you say, Arthur Prince.'

The policeman was scowling darkly. As a dialectician, he seemed to be feeling he was outmatched. And yet, he appeared to be telling himself, there must be some answer even to the apparently unanswerable logic to which he had just been listening. To assist thought, he raised the glass of Buck-U-Uppo and seltzer in his hand, and drained it at a draught.

And, as he did so, suddenly, abruptly, as breath fades from steel, the scowl passed from his face, and in its stead there appeared a smile of infinite kindliness and goodwill. He wiped his moustache, and began to chuckle to himself, as at some diverting memory.

'Made me laugh, that did,' he said. 'When old Booker went head over heels that time. Don't know when I've seen a nicer punch. Clean, crisp.... Don't suppose it travelled more than six inches, did it? I reckon you've done a bit of boxing in your time, sir.'

At the sight of the constable's smiling face, the Bishop had relaxed the austerity of his demeanour. He no longer looked like Savonarola rebuking the sins of the people. He was his old genial self once more.

'Quite true, officer,' he said, beaming. 'When I was a some-what younger man than I am at present, I won the Curates' Open Heavyweight Championship two years in succession. Some of the ancient skill still lingers, it would seem.'

The policeman chuckled again.

'I should say it does, sir. But,' he continued, a look of annoy-ance coming into his face, 'what all the fuss was about is more than I can say. Our fat-headed Inspector says, "You go and raid that Home from Home, chaps, see?" he says, and so we went and done it. But my heart wasn't in it, no more was any of the other fellers' hearts in it. What's wrong with a little rational enjoy-ment? That's what I say. What's wrong with it?'

'Precisely, officer.'

'That's what I say. What's wrong with it? Let people enjoy themselves how they like is what I say. And if the police come interfering – well, punch them in the eye, I say, same as you did Constable Booker. That's what I say.'

'Exactly,' said the Bishop. He turned to his wife. 'A fellow of considerable intelligence, this, my dear.'

'I liked his face right from the beginning,' said the Lady Bishopess. 'What is your name, officer?'

'Smith, lady. But call me Cyril.'

'Certainly,' said the Lady Bishopess. 'It will be a pleasure to do so. I used to know some Smiths in Lincolnshire years ago, Cyril. I wonder if they were any relation.'

'Maybe, lady. It's a small world.'

'Though, now I come to think of it, their name was Robinson.'

'Well, that's life, lady, isn't it?' said the policeman.

'That's just about what it is, Cyril,' agreed the Bishop. 'You never spoke a truer word.'

Into this love-feast, which threatened to become more glutinous every moment, there cut the cold voice of Hypatia Wace.

'Well, I must say,' said Hypatia, 'that you're a nice lot!'

'Who's a nice lot, lady?' asked the policeman.

'These two,' said Hypatia. 'Are you married, officer?'

'No, lady. I'm just a solitary chip drifting on the river of life.'

'Well, anyway, I expect you know what it feels like to be in love.'

'Too true, lady.'

'Well, I'm in love with Mr Bracy-Gascoigne. You've met him, probably. Wouldn't you say he was a person of the highest character?'

'The whitest man I know, lady.'

'Well, I want to marry him, and my uncle and aunt here won't let me, because they say he's worldly. Just because he goes out dancing. And all the while they are dancing the soles of their shoes through. I don't call it fair.'

She buried her face in her hands with a stifled sob. The Bishop and his wife looked at each other in blank astonishment.

'I don't understand,' said the Bishop.

'Nor I,' said the Lady Bishopess. 'My dear child, what is all this about our not consenting to your marriage with Mr Bracy-Gascoigne? However did you get that idea into your head? Certainly, as far as I am concerned, you may marry Mr Bracy-Gascoigne. And I think I speak for my dear husband?'

'Quite,' said the Bishop. 'Most decidedly.'

Hypatia uttered a cry of joy.

'Good egg! May I really?'

'Certainly you may. You have no objection, Cyril?'

'None whatever, lady.'

Hypatia's face fell.

'Oh, dear!' she said.

'What's the matter?'

'It just struck me that I've got to wait hours and hours before I can tell him. Just think of having to wait hours and hours!'

The Bishop laughed his jolly laugh.

'Why wait hours and hours, my dear? No time like the present.'

'But he's gone to bed.'

'Well, rout him out,' said the Bishop heartily. 'Here is what I suggest that we should do. You and I and Priscilla – and you, Cyril? – will all go down to his house and stand under his window and shout.'

'Or throw gravel at the window,' suggested the Lady Bishopess.

'Certainly, my dear, if you prefer it.'

'And when he sticks his head out,' said the policeman, 'how would it be to have the garden hose handy and squirt him? Cause a lot of fun and laughter, that would.'

'My dear Cyril,' said the Bishop, 'you think of everything. I shall certainly use any influence I may possess with the authorities to have you promoted to a rank where your remarkable talents will enjoy greater scope. Come, let us be going. You will accompany us, my dear Mulliner?'

Augustine shook his head.

'Sermon to write, Bish.'

'Just as you say, Mulliner. Then if you will be so good as to leave the window open, my dear fellow, we shall be able to return to our beds at the conclusion of our little errand of goodwill without disturbing the domestic staff.'

'Right-ho, Bish.'

'Then, for the present, pip-pip, Mulliner.'

'Toodle-oo, Bish,' said Augustine.

He took up his pen, and resumed his composition. Out in the sweet-scented night he could hear the four voices dying away in the distance. They seemed to be singing an old English part-song. He smiled benevolently.

'A merry heart doeth good like a medicine. Proverbs 17, 22,' murmured Augustine.

P. G. Wodehouse

IN ARROW BOOKS

If you have enjoyed Mr Mulliner, you'll love Jeeves and Wooster

FROM

Jeeves in the Offing

JEEVES placed the sizzling eggs and b. on the breakfast table, and Reginald ('Kipper') Herring and I, licking the lips, squared our elbows and got down to it. A lifelong buddy of mine, this Herring, linked to me by what are called imperishable memories. Years ago, when striplings, he and I had done a stretch together at Malvern House, Bramley-on-Sea, the preparatory school conducted by that prince of stinkers, Aubrey Upjohn M.A., and had frequently stood side by side in the Upjohn study awaiting the receipt of six of the juiciest from a cane of the type that biteth like a serpent and stingeth like an adder, as the fellow said. So we were, you might say, rather like a couple of old sweats who had fought shoulder to shoulder on Crispin's day, if I've got the name right.

The *plat du jour* having gone down the hatch, accompanied by some fluid ounces of strengthening coffee, I was about to reach for the marmalade, when I heard the telephone tootling out in the hall and rose to attend to it.

'Bertram Wooster's residence,' I said, having connected with the instrument. 'Wooster in person at this end. Oh hullo,' I added, for the voice that boomed over the wire was that of Mrs Thomas Portarlington Travers of Brinkley Court, Market Snodsbury, near Droitwich – or, putting it another way, my good and deserving Aunt Dahlia. 'A very hearty pip-pip to you, old ancestor,' I said, well pleased, for she is a woman with whom it is always a privilege to chew the fat.

'And a rousing toodle-oo to you, you young blot on the landscape,' she replied cordially. 'I'm surprised to find you up as early as this. Or have you just got in from a night on the tiles?'

I hastened to rebut this slur.

'Certainly not. Nothing of that description whatsoever. I've been upping with the lark this last week, to keep Kipper Herring company. He's staying with me till he can get into his new flat. You remember old Kipper? I brought him down to Brinkley one summer. Chap with a cauliflower ear.'

'I know who you mean. Looks like Jack Dempsey.'

'That's right. Far more, indeed, than Jack Dempsey does. He's on the staff of the *Thursday Review*, a periodical of which you may or may not be a reader, and has to clock in at the office at daybreak. No doubt, when I apprise him of your call, he will send you his love, for I know he holds you in high esteem. The perfect hostess, he often describes you as. Well, it's nice to hear your voice again, old flesh and blood. How's everything down Market Snodsbury way?'

'Oh, we're jogging along. But I'm not speaking from Brinkley. I'm in London.'

'Till when?'

'Driving back this afternoon.'

'I'll give you lunch.'

'Sorry, can't manage it. I'm putting on the nosebag with Sir Roderick Glossop.'

This surprised me. The eminent brain specialist to whom she alluded was a man I would not have cared to lunch with myself, our relations having been on the stiff side since the night at Lady

Wickham's place in Hertfordshire when, acting on the advice of my hostess's daughter Roberta, I had punctured his hot-water bottle with a darning needle in the small hours of the morning. Quite unintentional, of course. I had planned to puncture the h-w-b of his nephew Tuppy Glossop, with whom I had a feud on, and unknown to me they had changed rooms. Just one of those unfortunate misunderstandings.

'What on earth are you doing that for?'

'Why shouldn't I? He's paying.'

I saw her point – a penny saved is a penny earned and all that sort of thing – but I continued surprised. It amazed me that Aunt Dahlia, presumably a free agent, should have selected this very formidable loony-doctor to chew the mid-day chop with. However, one of the first lessons life teaches us is that aunts will be aunts, so I merely shrugged a couple of shoulders.

'Well, it's up to you, of course, but it seems a rash act. Did you come to London just to revel with Glossop?'

'No, I'm here to collect my new butler and take him home with me.'

'New butler? What's become of Seppings?'

'He's gone.'

I clicked the tongue. I was very fond of the major-domo in question, having enjoyed many a port in his pantry, and this news saddened me.

'No, really?' I said. 'Too bad. I thought he looked a little frail when I last saw him. Well, that's how it goes. All flesh is grass, I often say.'

'To Bognor Regis, for his holiday.'

I unclicked the tongue.

'Oh, I see. That puts a different complexion on the matter. Odd how all these pillars of the home seem to be dashing away on toots these days. It's like what Jeeves was telling me about the great race movements of the middle ages. Jeeves starts his holiday this morning. He's off to Herne Bay for the shrimping, and I'm feeling like that bird in the poem who lost his pet gazelle or whatever the animal was. I don't know what I'm going to do without him.'

'I'll tell you what you're going to do. Have you a clean shirt?'

'Several.'

'And a toothbrush?'

'Two, both of the finest quality.'

'Then pack them. You're coming to Brinkley tomorrow.'

The gloom which always envelops Bertram Wooster like a fog when Jeeves is about to take his annual vacation lightened perceptibly. There are few things I find more agreeable than a sojourn at Aunt Dahlia's rural lair. Picturesque scenery, gravel soil, main drainage, company's own water and, above all, the superb French cheffing of her French chef Anatole, God's gift to the gastric juices. A full hand, as you might put it.

'What an admirable suggestion,' I said. 'You solve all my problems and bring the blue bird out of a hat. Rely on me. You will observe me bowling up in the Wooster sports model tomorrow afternoon with my hair in a braid and a song on my lips. My presence will, I feel sure, stimulate Anatole to new heights of endeavour. Got anybody else staying at the old snake pit?'

'Five inmates in all.'

'Five?' I resumed my tongue-clicking. 'Golly! Uncle Tom must be frothing at the mouth a bit,' I said, for I knew the old buster's distaste for guests in the home. Even a single weekender is sometimes enough to make him drain the bitter cup.

'Tom's not there. He's gone to Harrogate with Cream.'

'You mean lumbago.'

'I don't mean lumbago. I mean Cream. Homer Cream. Big American tycoon, who is visiting these shores. He suffers from ulcers, and his medicine man has ordered him to take the waters at Harrogate. Tom has gone with him to hold his hand and listen to him of an evening while he tells him how filthy the stuff tastes.'

'Antagonistic.'

'What?'

'I mean altruistic. You are probably not familiar with the word, but it's one I've heard Jeeves use. It's what you say of a fellow who gives selfless service, not counting the cost.'

'Selfless service, my foot! Tom's in the middle of a very important business deal with Cream. If it goes through, he'll make a packet free of income tax. So he's sucking up to him like a Hollywood Yes-man.'

I gave an intelligent nod, though this of course was wasted on her because she couldn't see me. I could readily understand my uncle-by-marriage's mental processes. T. Portarlington Travers is a man who has accumulated the pieces of eight in sackfuls, but he is always more than willing to shove a bit extra away behind the brick in the fireplace, feeling — and rightly — that every little bit added to what you've got makes just a little bit more. And if there's one thing that's right up his street, it is not paying income tax. He grudges every penny the Government nicks him for.

'That is why, when kissing me goodbye, he urged me with tears in his eyes to lush Mrs Cream and her son Willie up and treat them like royalty. So they're at Brinkley, dug into the woodwork.'

'Willie, did you say?'

'Short for Wilbert.'

I mused. Willie Cream. The name seemed familiar somehow. I seemed to have heard it or seen it in the papers somewhere. But it eluded me.

'Adela Cream writes mystery stories. Are you a fan of hers? No? Well, start boning up on them directly you arrive, because every little helps. I've brought a complete set. They're very good.'

'I shall be delighted to run an eye over her material,' I said, for I am what they call an a-something of novels of suspense. Aficionado, would that be it? 'I can always do with another corpse or two. We have established, then, that among the inmates are this Mrs Cream and her son Wilbert. Who are the other three?'

'Well, there's Lady Wickham's daughter Roberta.'

I started violently, as if some unseen hand had goosed me.

'What! Bobbie Wickham? Oh, my gosh!'

'Why the agitation? Do you know her?'

'You bet I know her.'

'I begin to see. Is she one of the gaggle of girls you've been engaged to?'

'Not actually, no. We were never engaged. But that was merely because she wouldn't meet me half way.'

'Turned you down, did she?'

'Yes, thank goodness.'

'Why thank goodness? She's a one-girl beauty chorus.'

'She doesn't try the eyes, I agree.'

'A pippin, if ever there was one.'

'Very true, but is being a pippin everything? What price the soul?'

'Isn't her soul like mother makes?'

'Far from it. Much below par. What I could tell you . . . But no, let it go. Painful subj.'

I had been about to mention fifty-seven or so of the reasons why the prudent operator, if he valued his peace of mind, deemed it best to stay well away from the red-headed menace under advisement, but realized that at a moment when I was wanting to get back to the marmalade it would occupy too much time. It will be enough to say that I had long since come out of the ether and was fully cognisant of the fact that in declining to fall in with my suggestion that we should start rounding up clergymen and bridesmaids, the beasel had rendered me a signal service, and I'll tell you why.

Aunt Dahlia, describing this young blister as a one-girl beauty chorus, had called her shots perfectly correctly. Her outer crust was indeed of a nature to cause those beholding it to rock back on their heels with a startled whistle. But while equipped with eyes like twin stars, hair ruddier than the cherry, oomph, *espièglerie* and all the fixings, B. Wickham had also the disposition and general outlook on life of a ticking bomb. In her society you always had the uneasy feeling that something was likely to go off at any moment with a pop. You never knew what she was going to do next or into what murky depths of soup she would carelessly plunge you.

'Miss Wickham, sir,' Jeeves had once said to me warningly at the time when the fever was at its height, 'lacks seriousness. She is volatile and frivolous. I would always hesitate to recommend as a life partner a young lady with quite such a vivid shade of red hair.'

His judgment was sound. I have already mentioned how with her subtle wiles this girl had induced me to sneak into Sir Roderick Glossop's sleeping apartment and apply the darning needle to his hot-water bottle, and that was comparatively mild going for her. In a word, Roberta, daughter of the late Sir Cuthbert and Lady Wickham of Skeldings Hall, Herts, was pure dynamite and better kept at a distance by all those who aimed at leading the peaceful life. The prospect of being immured with her in the same house, with all the facilities a country house affords an enterprising girl for landing her nearest and dearest in the mulligatawny, made me singularly dubious about the shape of things to come.

And I was tottering under this blow when the old relative administered another, and it was a haymaker.

'And there's Aubrey Upjohn and his stepdaughter Phyllis Mills,' she said. 'That's the lot. What's the matter with you? Got asthma?'

I took her to be alluding to the sharp gasp which had escaped my lips, and I must confess that it had come out not unlike the last words of a dying duck. But I felt perfectly justified in gasping. A weaker man would have howled like a banshee. There floated into my mind something Kipper Herring had once said to me. 'You know, Bertie,' he had said, in philosophical mood, 'we have much to be thankful for in this life of ours, you and I. However rough the going, there is one sustaining thought to which we can hold. The storm clouds may lower and the horizon grow dark, we may get a nail in our shoe and be caught in the rain without an umbrella, we may come down to breakfast and find that someone else has taken the brown egg, but at least we have the consolation of knowing that we shall never see Aubrey Gawd-help-us Upjohn again. Always remember this in times of despondency,' he said, and I always had. And now here the bounder was, bobbing up right in my midst. Enough to make the stoutest-hearted go into his dying-duck routine.

'Aubrey Upjohn?' I quavered. 'You mean *my* Aubrey Upjohn?'

'That's the one. Soon after you made your escape from his chain gang he married Jane Mills, a friend of mine with a colossal amount of money. She died, leaving a daughter. I'm the daughter's godmother. Upjohn's retired now and going in for politics. The hot tip is that the boys in the back room are going to run him as the Conservative candidate in the Market Snodsbury division at the next by-election. What a thrill it'll be for you, meeting him again. Or does the prospect scare you?'

'Certainly not. We Woosters are intrepid. But what on earth did you invite him to Brinkley for?'

'I didn't. I only wanted Phyllis, but he came along, too.'

'You should have bunged him out.'

'I hadn't the heart to.'

'Weak, very weak.'

'Besides, I needed him in my business. He's going to present the prizes at Market Snodsbury Grammar School. We've been caught short as usual, and somebody has got to make a speech on ideals and the great world outside to those blasted boys, so he fits in nicely. I believe he's a very fine speaker. His only trouble is that he's stymied unless he has his speech with him and can read it. Calls it referring to his notes. Phyllis told me that. She types the stuff for him.'

'A thoroughly low trick,' I said severely. 'Even I, who have never soared above the Yeoman's Wedding Song at a village concert, wouldn't have the crust to face my public unless I'd taken the trouble to memorize the words, though actually with the Yeoman's Wedding Song it is possible to get by quite comfortably by keeping singing "Ding dong, ding dong, ding dong, I hurry along". In short . . .'

I would have spoken further, but at this point, after urging me to put a sock in it, and giving me a kindly word of warning not to step on any banana skins, she rang off.

Also available in Arrow

Mr Mulliner Speaking

P.G. Wodehouse

A Mulliner collection

In the bar-parlour of the Angler's Rest, Mr Mulliner tells his
amazing tales, which hold the assembled company of Pints of
Stout and Whiskies and Splash in the palm of his expressive
hand. Here you can discover what happened to The Man Who
Gave Up Smoking, share a frisson when the butler delivers
Something Squishy on a silver salver ('your serpent, Sir,' said the
voice of Simmons) – and experience the dreadful Unpleasantness
at Bludleigh Court. Throughout the Mulliner clan remains
resourcefully in command in the most outlandish situations.

arrow books

Also available in Arrow

A Pelican at Blandings

P.G. Wodehouse

A Blandings novel

Unwelcome guests are descending on Blandings Castle –
particularly the overbearing Duke of Dunstable, who settles in
the Garden Suite with no intention of leaving, and Lady
Constance, Lord Emsworth's sister and a lady of firm
disposition, who arrives unexpectedly from New York.
Skulduggery is also afoot involving the sale of a modern nude
painting (mistaken by Lord Emsworth for a pig). It's enough to
take the noble earl on the short journey to the end of his wits.

Luckily Clarence's brother Galahad Threepwood, cheery
survivor of the raffish Pelican Club, is on hand to set things
right, restore sundered lovers and even solve all the mysteries.

arrow books

Also available in Arrow

Service with a Smile

P.G. Wodehouse

A Blandings novel

As a peer of the realm, Clarence, Ninth Earl of Emsworth, has an occasional duty to leave the Empress of Blandings, surely the most considerable pig in the whole world, and travel to London for the opening of parliament. It comes hard to him, for he has a proper sense of the priorities in life, which rate pigs and flowerbeds higher than politicians.

But no sooner has he returned to Blandings than his real problems begin: the dastardly Duke of Dunstable is out to steal the Empress. His sister Lady Constance has inflicted on him a particularly nasty new secretary. And the Church Lads' Brigade are camped all over his lawns.

Thank God for the Earl of Ickenham, better known as Uncle Fred, whose own particularly devious brand of sweetness and light aims to banish blackmailers and pig-stealers and restore true love all over the castle grounds.

arrow books

Also available in Arrow

Much Obliged, Jeeves

P.G. Wodehouse

A Jeeves and Wooster novel

Just as Bertie Wooster is a member of the Drones Club, Jeeves
has a club of his own, the Junior Ganymede, exclusively for
butlers and gentlemen's gentlemen. In its inner sanctum is kept
the Book of Revelations, where the less than perfect habits of
their employers are lovingly recorded. The book is, of course,
pure dynamite. So what happens when it disappears into
potentially hostile hands?

Tossed about in the resulting whirlwind you'll find lots of
Wodehouse's favourite characters – and a welcome return to
Market Snodsbury, in the middle of one of the most chaotic
elections of modern times.

arrow books

Also available in Arrow

Jeeves and the Feudal Spirit

P.G. Wodehouse

A Jeeves and Wooster novel

The beefy 'Stilton' Cheesewright has drawn Bertie Wooster as
red-hot favourite in the Drones club annual darts tournament —
which is lucky for Bertie because otherwise Stilton would have
beaten him to a pulp and buttered the lawn with him. Stilton
does not like men who he thinks are trifling with his
fiancée's affections.

Meanwhile Bertie has committed a more heinous offence by
growing a moustache, and Jeeves strongly disapproves — which
is unfortunate, because Jeeves's feudal spirit is desperately
needed. Bertie's Aunt Dahlia is trying to sell her magazine
Milady's Boudoir to the Trotter Empire and still keep her
amazing chef Anatole out of Lady Trotter's clutches. And
Bertie? Bertie simply has to try to keep his moustache and
survive to the end of the novel.

arrow books

The P G Wodehouse Society (UK)

The P G Wodehouse Society (UK) was formed in 1997 to promote the enjoyment of the writings of the twentieth century's greatest humorist. The Society publishes a quarterly magazine, *Wooster Sauce*, which includes articles, features, reviews, and current Society news. Occasional special papers are also published. Society events include regular meetings in central London, cricket matches and a formal biennial dinner, along with other activities. The Society actively supports the preservation of the Berkshire pig, a rare breed, in honour of the incomparable Empress of Blandings.

MEMBERSHIP ENQUIRIES

Membership of the Society is open to applicants from all parts of the world. The cost of a year's membership in 2008 is £15. Enquiries and requests for membership forms should be made to the Membership Secretary, The P G Wodehouse Society (UK), 26 Radcliffe Rd, Croydon, Surrey, CR0 5QE, or alternatively from info@pgwodehousesociety.org.uk

The Society's website can be viewed at
www.pgwodehousesociety.org.uk

Visit our special P.G. Wodehouse website
www.wodehouse.co.uk

Find out about P.G. Wodehouse's books now
reissued with appealing new covers

Read extracts from all your favourite titles

Read the exclusive extra content and immerse
yourself in Wodehouse's world

Sign up for news of future publications
and upcoming events

arrow books